THE DEVIL
AND HIS
LEGACY

ALSO BY MIMA

The Fire series
Fire
A Spark Before the Fire

The Vampire series
The Rock Star of Vampires
Her Name is Mariah

Different Shades of the Same Color

The Hernandez series
We're All Animals
Always be a Wolf
The Devil is Smooth Like Honey
A Devil Named Hernandez
And the Devil Will Laugh
The Devil May Lie

Learn more at www.mimaonfire.com
Also find Mima on Twitter, Facebook and Instagram @mimaonfire

THE DEVIL
AND HIS
LEGACY

MIMA

iUniverse®

THE DEVIL AND HIS LEGACY

iUniverse books may be ordered through booksellers or by contacting:

iUniverse
1663 Liberty Drive
Bloomington, IN 47403
www.iuniverse.com
1-800-Authors (1-800-288-4677)

ISBN: 978-1-5320-8791-2 (sc)
ISBN: 978-1-5320-8792-9 (e)

Print information available on the last page.

iUniverse rev. date: 11/11/2019

ACKNOWLEDGMENTS

Special thanks to Jean Arsenault for helping with the editing process as well as Jim Brown and Mitchell Whitlock for helping with the back cover description and so much more.

CHAPTER 1

Death is a sharp reminder that we all have a legacy. It becomes so easy to go through the motions and not think about what we'll someday leave behind. But then it happens. Someone close to us dies and we're forced to take a more serious look at our own lives. What do we have to show that we ever existed at all?

For some, it's their children. They see the next generation continuing their name, a younger version of themselves. For others, money is their legacy. Property, jewelry, expensive products reflect their hard work and in turn, their value. For an artist, it is a beautiful masterpiece that lives on, carrying their name until the end of time.

But for some, legacy goes much deeper. It's a reputation that carries strength. A name that symbolizes power and a heart that keeps beating long after the body has perished. You may have left the earth but do you ever leave the room?

Jorge Hernandez would never die. He'd someday breathe his last breath but his legacy would continue forever. For his *familia*, in memories of love and loyalty. For those he ripped apart, his dark eyes would forever haunt them. No one doubted that fact. For his heart carried a lifetime of brutal acts and intense moments of love that silently collected together. When you're a man with a legacy, everything matters.

"Paige, this here," Jorge pointed toward a stack of papers on his desk before looking up at his wife. "This here, it is too much. We move into a new neighborhood and now we must deal with rules? Are we not free in this country?"

"We are," Paige Noël-Hernandez replied in a gentle voice. Her blue eyes glanced at the documents they received earlier that day. "However, it seems they want to keep this a *respectable* neighborhood so they're telling us we have to follow the rules."

"In my home in Mexico, this would not be a problem," Jorge huffed, his eyes turning cold. "If I want to walk around nude in my fucking yard, I would like to see any of these people try to stop me. You Canadians, why so uptight?"

"I know," Paige reluctantly agreed. "I guess it's because they want…"

"Conformity?" Jorge finished her sentence and grabbed the document and began to read it again. "Only one pet permitted per household and that pet, it cannot shit in the yard and if it does, it must be cleaned immediately? No toys in the yard? No parties in the yard? Noise kept to a minimum? This here, we have avoided prison, for this?"

Paige laughed as her husband playfully tossed the papers aside. She opened her mouth to say something but stopped.

"We have children," Jorge continued to rant. "Not robots! We cannot keep Maria from practicing her singing and dancing. We cannot stop Miguel from wanting to walk through the yard and sometimes, like last week, it may be naked."

In fact, it was this occurrence that had caused a stir in the neighborhood. While Jorge thought it was a joke when the woman from next door approached him about their 11-month-old child running through the yard naked, it apparently broke a residential rule.

"He's a fucking child," Jorge repeated what he had said to the horrified neighbor at the time. "It is not as if we allow our baby to run around unsupervised but Maria, she was responsible for him at the time."

"She was changing him near the door when her soup boiled over," Paige reminded him. "He pulled himself up and headed outside. In fairness, none of us knew he could open a door."

"But this here, it is us," Jorge lowered his voice. "This is not a normal family. We must be very careful. The doors should always be locked."

The smile slipped from Paige's face and she nodded. The family had found themselves in dangerous predicaments on more than one occasion and although they liked to believed they were safe, the reality was that they'd always be looking over their shoulders. As a former narco, Jorge had made many enemies but none were as vengeful as those he had instigated since immigrating to Canada.

Jorge Hernandez would never apologize for his domination in the Canadian marijuana industry after he ruthlessly took it over, leaving behind a trail of blood and bodies. The authorities simply wrote off most cases as unsolved; while politicians were in his pocket. It became common knowledge that he was not the man to oppose. Jorge and his army of foot soldiers were powerful and since the death of one of their own, he carried vengeance in his heart. It was only a matter of time until someone paid for the death of Jesús Garcia López.

"I wish we could move out of Toronto," Paige quietly confessed. "I'm not sure how I feel about this neighborhood now that we're here. I assumed that people would mind their own business but it makes me very...uncomfortable how *aware* people are of everything we do."

"This here, it does bother me," Jorge admitted as he leaned back in his chair, his dark eyes glancing toward the bulletproof window. "I thought putting a fence around the house - it would be helpful, however, it is apparently not high enough, *mi amor.*"

"The houses are so close together," She replied as a thumping noise suddenly started upstairs. Jorge's oldest child, Maria, was practicing her dance moves. She had recently divorced herself from the idea of becoming a world-famous actress to instead becoming a dancer.

"It is good that Miguel, he can sleep through so much noise," Jorge commented as he pointed toward the ceiling. "This here, will it get us kicked out of the neighborhood."

"It's between 10 a.m. and 8 p.m. and you won't allow us to open windows anymore, so we should be fine," Paige replied as she rolled her eyes and Jorge laughed. "Fortunately, Miguel sleeps through anything. He passed out on the playroom floor again."

The couple rose from their seats and moved out of Jorge's office and headed toward the living room. Their new house was large, expensive and reminded Jorge of his former home in Mexico except it didn't have the same feel to it. Although it was beautiful, he compared it to a model with no soul. The rooms felt empty, despite all the life his family brought to it. To him, there was always something missing but he was never able to put his finger on it.

"The others, what time are they arriving?" Jorge referred to the associates that were his extended family; the people who worked for and with him. Their group had grown smaller over the past year, but if anything, he felt they were stronger than ever before. Tragedy had brought them closer.

"Soon," Paige glanced at her phone and pointed toward the kitchen. "Juliana should be back by then, so she can keep an eye on Miguel. I'm going to make some coffee. Are you hungry?"

Jorge shook his head and glanced toward the large front window. He was just in time to see his nosey neighbor walking by with another woman, both looking in with prying eyes. He gave them the finger.

"Jorge!" Paige attempted to scold him but instead let out a gentle laugh. "Did you give her the finger? Come on, we're trying to fit in here."

"She is lucky it is not a bullet in the head that I give her," Jorge immediately defended himself as he closed the blinds. "Paige, I do not like these nosey *putas* hanging around and watching me"

Paige attempted to suppress her laughter as he continued to rant.

"If my son, he wants to run naked in the yard, he can," Jorge said as he firmly stood his ground. "If I want to get two pets or a pet chicken, I will do so. If I want to have a wild party at 10 PM, I *will*. That lady, our neighbor," Jorge defiantly pointed toward the next house. "She will be smart to stay out of my crosshairs."

Paige sucked back her smile and gave him a serious nod as she headed toward the coffee pot and Jorge followed her into the room, leaning up against the counter.

"That woman, she may go *missing* if she keeps it up," He paused and was about to continue when a thumping on the stairs caused him to clamp his mouth shut. Seconds later, his 12-year-old daughter sprang into the room with Miguel in her arms.

"I can't practice my dancing because Miguel keeps coming in my room," She complained and handed the toddler to Jorge. "I swear, since last week, he thinks it's funny to barge into my room. Yesterday, I was half-naked and-"

Ok," Jorge put his hand up in the air to indicate for her to stop while holding the squirming toddler with his other arm. "Maria, we have been over this. He's a baby. He does not understand why he cannot just walk into a room"

"Or *out* of doors! Remember last week?" Maria spoke dramatically as she swung her hands in the air. "I didn't think a little baby could open a door. He's not even *one* yet."

"Maria, he is a Hernandez," Jorge spoke triumphantly. "Of course, he will progress faster than other children."

"It's annoying," Maria continued to speak dramatically, batting her eyelashes rapidly as she swung on her heels. "Now, I have to get back to work. I'm never going to make it as a dancer if I don't practice."

Jorge gave Paige a look as Maria strutted out of the room.

"Not even 13 yet and we got a diva in the house," He said and shook his head, turning his gaze toward Miguel. "Did she kick you out?"

He gave his son a quick kiss on the top of his head, feeling the soft, black hair against his face. Closing his eyes, a wave of emotion flowed through him as he considered Miguel's namesake, his younger brother who died as a child. He looked like him but yet his spirit was that of his father's. He would be a wild one. Jorge could see it already.

"Ah Paige," He opened his eyes as Miguel relaxed and snuggled against his chest. "I have two perfect children. I have a perfect wife. If only we could forget the outside world, I would also have a perfect life."

"Unfortunately, it doesn't work that way," Paige slipped a package of coffee back into the cupboard. "And I'm not sure any of us are perfect."

"Ah, *mi amor,* that is where you are wrong," Jorge insisted. "This family, we are perfect. I may hate a lot of people including that neighbor of mine but this here…" He looked down into his son's eyes just as he let out a devilish giggle. "They are my legacy. One day, my son, my daughter, they will rule the world. I will make them powerful and strong."

"Can we maybe wait until Miguel is out of diapers before he takes over the world?" Paige spoke smoothly as she moved closer.

"It will be soon," Jorge insisted. "This child, he's the product of two very strong, powerful people. He will be a superhero. No one and nothing will stand in his way, just as nothing and no one has ever stood in our way, *mi amor.*"

"He is a Hernandez," Jorge continued. "And no one is stronger than a Hernandez."

CHAPTER 2

"My son, he is a curious one," Jorge finished his story as the small group followed him into the office. Ignoring the unpacked boxes throughout the large room, he walked behind his desk and turned to see his comrades sit in their usual seats, each showed their personal reaction to Miguel's adventure. "He barges through doors and this here, it is symbolic. It shows that *nothing* will stand in his way."

Diego Silva dramatically rolled his eyes while Marco Rodel Cruz laughed, probably since he had children and was aware of the many antics of raising a toddler. Chase Jacobs looked slightly solemn as a father who rarely seen his kids while Diego's sister, Jolene, appeared much less amused than the others.

"He could've been hurt," She loudly piped up as she leaned forward in the chair, her eyes widening. "What if he…he ran to the streets? What if he….what if someone, they kidnaps him outside? What if…"

"*Kidnapped,* Jolene," Diego abruptly corrected his sister's broken English. "For fuck sakes, you've lived in Canada for how long and you still can't even speak proper English. We aren't in Colombia anymore."

"I am *fine,*" Jolene shot back while the others merely looked amused. "I do not speak perfect English. I get that, Diego, you do not have to lecture me each time, you know?"

"Ok, let's calm the fuck down," Jorge interrupted the argument before it could get in full swing. He glanced up to see Paige enter the room and gently close the door. "Jolene, believe me, we did not know that Miguel could turn a doorknob. Since that day, this house has been childproofed."

"Juliana looked after it," Paige referred to Miguel's nanny as she joined the others at the desk. "He just started to walk so it never occurred to us that he could make an escape too."

"But I am concerned," Jolene was quick to emphasize as she glanced between Jorge and Paige. "He is my godson, so I worry he will be ok."

"He's my godson too," Diego quickly jumped in at the same time that Chase opened his mouth to say something, but halted when the anxious Colombian took over the conversation. Jorge merely grinned. "But I also know that kids do these kinds of things. It's not a national emergency, *Jolene.* He just learned to walk, he wasn't going to start hitchhiking across Canada."

"He could've got into the street, Diego!" Jolene snapped back at her brother. "You do not see the dangers like I do."

"In fairness," Chase Jacobs finally got a word in and everyone turned their attention to the indigenous man. Much younger than the rest of the group, Jorge often saw him as a student that had so much to learn and yet, his loyalty was his most impressive feature. "There's a fence around the house, so I doubt he would've got anywhere and trust me, kids are fearless. Once they get their legs, you can't stop them."

"Get their legs?" Jolene appeared confused, her eyes narrowing in on Chase. "What do you mean by this?"

"Ok, that's it," Jorge cut in and shook his head. "We cannot talk about this all day. Jolene, he means that Miguel has learned to walk. We must move on to talk about other things."

Noting that he had everyone's full attention, Jorge paused for a moment.

"As you know," He began to speak slowly, choosing his words carefully. "Alec Athas has approached me with some concerns. This here is highly confidential since he is now the prime minister of Canada. In fact, our entire conversation had to look casual as if we just happen to see each other."

"It sounds like something out of a movie," Diego piped up. "Did you pretend to bump into each other in a church or at H&M?"

Everyone laughed and Jorge grinned, raising an eyebrow.

"Actually, it was at the Gap," He replied and everyone continued to laugh.

"Everyone is watching him now," Paige referred to the Greek-Canadian they helped get elected. "He's surrounded by staff and the media. Even on his own time, it seems like people are hyperaware of who he's talking to and why."

"What a time to start dating someone," Diego said with wide eyes. "I saw on the news.."

"Ok, so let us get back on track," Jorge cut him off. "The point is his whole life is being watched now so we must be careful. We had a short discussion about his concern. In turn, I had Marco do some research for me…"

Everyone knew that Marco was not only the head of IT for Hernandez-Silva Inc but he also was an effective hacker. He had been able to find crucial information on more than one occasion. At one point, the Filipino accidentally stumbled across a series of emails that prevented an armed man from entering a Toronto area girl's school. Jorge considered him one of his strongest people.

"What's this about?" Diego appeared confused. "We helped him get elected so what's he need us for now?"

"There was some unusual activity that concerned him," Jorge replied. "Athas had a feeling that his dutiful little workers weren't telling him everything about a sudden drop in homeless people in Canada."

"What do you mean?" Chase asked. "That's what we want."

"It depends on why," Jorge corrected him. "It is getting better however, that was the strange part. The cities where it was improving did not have any programs in place that explained such a radical change."

"They weren't shipping them out?" Paige quietly asked. "I think something like that happened when they had the Olympics in Vancouver."

"Ship them out?" Jolene appeared confused. "How do they do?"

"Put them on a bus and move them to another town," Paige replied and turned toward Jolene. Diego was between them and leaned back. "They didn't want tourists and the media to recognize the less pleasant side of their city, so they got them out of sight."

"That does not seem like a solution," Jolene muttered.

"Unfortunately," Marco took over the conversation. "That solution, that was better than what they are doing now."

All eyes were on Marco. His normally joyful expression disappeared causing the room to suddenly feel heavy.

"Sir," He turned his attention toward Jorge. "I have hacked the emails of some of the men you mentioned to me and....I was not able to find anything because, I assume, they must be careful."

"What about the app?" Jorge asked.

"What app?" Diego asked. "Don't tell me you put spying app on their phones or some shit like that?"

"Actually...." Jorge said with a raised eyebrow.

"It's the government," Diego shot back, his eyes widened in excitement. "You can't do that."

"You can when it is your prime minister asking for such," Jorge insisted. "Trust me, the proper government agencies, they know. The people carrying the phones, they do not."

"Is that allowed?" Paige asked.

"It is my understanding that...the government, they often do things that are less than...." Jorge wasn't sure how to finish that sentence. "The people with this app, they believe it is for something else but it allows them to be monitored."

"Wow!" Diego shook his head.

"So, Marco, you found something?" Jorge returned his attention to the Filipino. "You do not look pleased."

"Mr. Hernandez, this here, it is bad," Marco replied and paused for a moment. "Two members of parliament, they were joking in text messages about how they are 'cleaning up the big cities'. When I tracked their conversations and followed some leads mentioned in the messages....well, I will send you what I have found."

Everyone in the room grabbed their phones and began to scan through the information sent to a secure email site. Paige was the first person to react with a gasp.

"Is this here….am I understanding this correctly?" Jorge doubted his English for a moment. "This cannot be right."

"Sir, I'm afraid that it is," Marco shook his head.

"They're purposely putting fentanyl on the streets to kill people," Paige calmly replied. "They know homeless people are vulnerable. If they die, they assume the public will think they're addicts and will think nothing of it."

"They can't do this," Chase spoke up. "These people need help."

"It is an easy solution," Jorge quickly got up to speed. "It is cheaper to have them die than to get them help. Slaughter them like sheep."

"Also, people become desensitized and aren't surprised when they hear about fentanyl deaths in the news." Paige added.

"We do not hear these stories as much," Jorge observed and exchanged looks with his wife. "But this here, it says it happens every day."

"Yup, every day," Diego said and shook his head. "Fuck! So these numbers, are they right, Marco?"

"Yes, sir," Marco replied with a troubled look on his face. "Hundred of people every week, across the country but they try to spread it out so that it's less obvious."

"And Athas, he didn't know about this?" Chase asked. "I mean, he's the prime minister. Isn't it his job to know everything?"

"He's not accountable if he doesn't know," Paige commented. "Somewhere along the line, you'll see reports on television about how the numbers are going down and the media will find a reasonable explanation for that change. No one is the wiser."

"His staff is taking care of it behind his back," Jorge added.

"Alec would never allow this," Paige insisted. "But I'm not surprised it's happening. One of the easiest ways to get rid of someone is to have them OD."

As one of the world's best assassins, Paige Noël-Hernandez was definitely knowledgeable on how to make a murder look like a suicide or an accident. In fact, Jorge met his wife because of a mix-up that brought her to his wrong room. Although he saw the humor in the story, Paige did not. The fact that she could've accidentally killed the man she would eventually marry was horrific to her.

"No one would be suspicious," Chase said as he glanced toward Paige. "How often does this happen?"

"I've heard," Paige began to reply. "That a stagnant musician sometimes is found dead as a way to regain interest in their work. It's been known to help out a few labels when they weren't going to hit their target for a quarter."

"So kill off the rock star," Chase spoke up. "Make it look like an OD, his music sales go up…"

"Exactly," Paige replied. "Don't think it hasn't happened."

An uncomfortable silence followed. Music was a very personal affair between the artist and his listener.

"So, what do we do?" Chase asked in a troubled voice.

"We must share this information with Athas," Jorge replied and hesitated for a moment. "It is up to him at that point."

"But he's not supposed to know," Diego offered. "What *can* he do?"

"My guess is the opposition will suddenly find out before the next election," Paige suggested. "Remember what happened with the former prime minister? He wasn't aware that his own staff ignored the alerts that a fire was heading toward that indigenous community but people still blamed him and he had to step down."

Everyone fell silent again. This tragedy had a rippling effect throughout the country and caused protests and heartbreak as a result. Jorge Hernandez had managed to swoop in and save the party before deciding to step back and put Alec Athas in the spotlight.

"It is good," Jorge began and leaned on his desk. "That I did not become prime minister because if my staff did something like this behind my back…"

There was no need of him finishing. They knew. As did so many who had crossed Jorge Hernandez in the past.

CHAPTER 3

Having a meeting with Alec Athas was no longer as simple as sliding into a booth at a nearby coffee shop. The prime minister was often traveling and spent the rest of his time in Ottawa, the nation's capital. Even when he was in Toronto, there would be too much attention if they met. Fortunately, over 20 years in the cartel had taught Jorge about secretive methods to contact someone.

The secure phone call took place the following morning from the privacy of his office. Jorge told him everything Marco was able to learn, pausing a few times to see if Athas had a comment, but he remained silent. When everything was revealed, he finally spoke.

"My *own* party has done this behind my back?" Alec quietly asked. The disbelief rang through his voice. "Are you sure?"

"I got proof to back it up," Jorge insisted as he glanced at some documents on his desk. "It is all here and I can give it to you."

Alec sighed loudly.

"Look," Jorge continued. "I do understand. You must rely on your people to be loyal and trustworthy just as I must with my people."

"Yeah, but your people know the consequences if they don't fall in line with you," Alec reminded him. "Politics, it's a whole other game."

"Yes, but who says the rules must be different," Jorge suggested. "This man, from what I see in my documents, it was his idea. While you are out being the official face of Canada, he has worked behind your back to potentially bring down the entire government, if this gets out."

"It's not even that I'm thinking about," Alec explained. "It's the people. I worked with these people when I was in social work. I *know* their stories. They aren't on the streets because they chose that lifestyle. They're on there because of an unfortunate chain of events that was often no fault of their own. And even if it was because of a stupid decision, does that mean they deserve to be killed off like a herd of animals?"

"This here," Jorge replied. "Is not acceptable. However, do you think it is the first time a government did such a thing? Do not be naïve, Athas. This perhaps was happening before you were even in the picture."

"I should probably go and think about what to do about this…"

"Alec, may I make a suggestion?" Jorge spoke up. "First and foremost, you do not want to be linked to this situation. I agree. It must change however, you also can't have your name associated with this if it ever *does* get out. Perhaps you can announce a study to explain lowering numbers and meanwhile, I can easily take care of the man who was disloyal to you."

"Jorge, the way we deal with things in government isn't exactly like the cartel," Alec nervously reminded him. "We can't kill off the people involved…"

"I have to disagree with you," Jorge replied, showing no judgment. "This here is no different from the cartel or any line of business. If those who work with this man sees that he gets away with it, nothing is stopping them from also doing what they want behind your back. They see that you are easy. They see they can get away with it. Then if the truth ever comes out, you look like a fool if you weren't aware of what was going on in your own government. People won't believe it and even more important, they won't care. Look at the former prime minister. He knew nothing of the indigenous community that burned to the ground but it did not stop the people from hating him, wanting him to step down."

There was silence on the other end of the line.

"I am telling you, Athas," Jorge continued. "You must cut the blood off right now or this here situation will have a life of its own."

"I….let me think about it," Athas replied

"Don't think too long," Jorge suggested. "This here, it is not going to get better. The man dies and you gather the ones who worked with him for a private meeting. Supposedly it is to discuss how to move forward, a replacement, that kind of thing but you must also tell them outright that you know what this man was doing behind your back and you were about to expose him. Make it clear that you are *protecting* them by not allowing the truth to get out since clearly, the Canadian people will want someone to pay. I assure you, none of these people will want to take the fall for another's stupidity. I also assure you that deep down, there will be a part of them that doesn't, for a moment, believe his death was a coincidence."

"And you're sure that he's guilty," Athas seemed to regain his confidence. "You have solid proof."

"*Amigo,* I can have this to you as soon as you wish," Jorge insisted. "However, there is no mistake. This is a conversation that has taken place and you know yourself, you were already suspicious for weeks when you brought this to my attention. On some level, did you not know already that something was wrong? This man, can you see him doing what I have told you?"

There was a slight pause before Alec Athas answered.

"I can," His voice was unpretentious and gentle. "I hate to say it, but I can."

"Then you must take care of this immediately," Jorge insisted. "You cannot let it go further."

"You're right," Alec admitted.

"Am I not always right?" Jorge asked. "This here, we can take care of. I can do it but Paige, she is your best bet. She is already aware of the situation."

"Ok," He replied with some reluctance and then appeared to regain his composure. "Ok, yes, you've never steered me wrong. If you think this is what must happen, let's do it."

"Very good," Jorge replied and thought for a moment. "I would like you to have a copy of these conversations. The people you will be having a meeting with following this unfortunate death need to be reminded of their part. It is a way of assuring their silence and of course, showing them that they are being monitored."

"That would be perfect, thank you."

"*Adios amigo,*" Jorge replied. "The next time you hear from me, we will have a quick discussion about…..my son's first birthday party. We will be inviting you. When you receive this call, it does not matter what you reply. All that matters is you know that the deed has been done. This man, he will no longer be a problem."

"Understood."

Jorge ended the call and looked around his office. Athas had to be careful. His trusting nature made him vulnerable to many things. This was a test and he had to pass. He needed to be strong, yet very much a sheep in public while in the background, Athas had to become a wolf. It was vital.

After giving each of his sleepy family members a quick kiss on his way out the door, Jorge rushed to his SUV with a coffee in hand. He noticed his neighbor was looking out the window and ignored her. Jumping behind the wheel, he wasted no time tearing out of the driveway and heading down the street. Glancing at the clock on the dash, he noted it was only 7:04.

Knowing that Chase would be at the company's club receiving orders and organizing his week, Jorge made his way to *Princesa Maria*. Traffic was already backed up but Jorge didn't care. He fixed his tie in the mirror, drank his coffee and thought about everything he wished to do before noon. It was a lofty list but he was a busy man. This was his life.

A text message from Marco interrupted his thoughts.

There is something we must discuss when you have time.

Marco, I am heading to the bar. Meet me there.

Very good sir.

Feeling his stomach rumbling, he replied.

Bring some food.

Arriving at the club, he swung into a parking space and jumped out of the SUV. Glancing around, he entered the building, careful to lock the door behind him. He was met by the aroma of fresh-brewed coffee and wasted no time heading toward the bar.

"Morning, *amigo,*" He called out as he reached for a cup and proceeded to help himself. "*Cómo estás?*"

"Hey!" Chase walked out of his office behind the bar, appearing tired, yet professional in a suit and tie. Jorge insisted his associates always look the part of the business class. "You're early this morning."

"Yeah, well, I have been up since….5? Something like that," Jorge replied. "I had to talk to Athas first thing and he's a hard man to catch."

Chase nodded.

"Has Clara been in?" Jorge asked, referring to the company's 'cleaning lady'. Clara checked for listening devices or anything suspicious in both their offices and homes.

"Yup."

Chase gestured toward his office and the two men went inside, closing the door behind them.

"I'm never as certain about the bar," He admitted. "I'm sure it's fine too but I feel safer talking business in here."

"Sure." Chase agreed. "So, you told Athas what we know?"

"Yup."

"You gotta plan?"

"Yup."

Chase nodded just as his phone beeped.

"Marco is here."

Jorge laughed. "I barely sent him a message."

"He gets around fast on that bike of his," Chase reminded him as he headed toward the door. "He avoids so much shitty traffic."

Moments later, the three men gathered in the office. Marco brought bagels.

"Sir, this was the first thing…"

"That's fine," Jorge waved his hand as he grabbed a chocolate chip bagel from the bag and shoved it in his mouth while Chase grabbed one and went behind the desk.

"What you got?" Jorge spoke with his mouth full.

"Sir, you asked me about your neighbor that concerns you," Marco reminded him as he sat down beside Jorge. "I found something that makes me uncomfortable."

Jorge continued to chew but exchanged looks with Chase before returning his gaze to Marco.

"This woman, you say you don't like," Marco continued. "Next door to you, she does not live there, sir."

"Excuse me," Jorge was finally able to talk again. "What do you mean?"

"This woman, she is renting the place and arrived only days before you and your family moved into the neighborhood," Marco paused. "I do not have to tell you that this is most suspicious."

No one said a word. The three men exchanged looks and Jorge nodded. This was no coincidence.

CHAPTER 4

"It's not even noon and you're already talking about murder," Paige calmly remarked after Jorge arrived home and ushered her into the office. She appeared tired as she glanced toward the bulletproof window. "I thought we were talking about separating ourselves from all of this since…"

"Paige, this, I would like," Jorge lowered his voice. "But sometimes, there is no other way."

She didn't respond but her blue eyes were curious.

"This man," Jorge gently continued. "The one who works for Athas? He is crucifying people like he's head of a cartel. It is not as if he is a saint. Do you think he should be allowed to live? It is also important that Athas sends a message to the others. This man, he was the mastermind but he did not work alone."

Paige slowly nodded before finally speaking.

"It will be high-profile. The media will be all over it."

"And they will find nothing," Jorge insisted. "The man, maybe he had troubles and committed suicide?"

"But none of this can get out," Paige replied. "If it does, people will blame Alec even though he didn't know."

"It will not get out," Jorge reminded her. "Do you think the others involved will admit it? Do you think they want to go to prison or end up dead too? This is our insurance and we must use it."

"Ok," Paige appeared sold on the idea. "So when do I do it?"

"Paige," Jorge shook his head and hesitated. "This is not for you. We must have someone else do it."

"Like who?" She shrugged while a faint smile crossed her lips. "Who are we going to send? Diego? Chase? Jorge, you know I'm the only one that can do this and make it look like a suicide."

"I do not like you getting involved."

"It's not as if I haven't killed before," She reminded him. "Many times."

"But now, Paige," Jorge said as he leaned back in his chair, his eyes averted to the ceiling. "I do not like you going out of town alone and dealing with this situation."

"You can come with me," She suggested. "Or Diego."

"I think what must be done," Jorge spoke thoughtfully. "We must first research this man. What is the state of his health? What is his routine?"

"Wouldn't it be interesting if *he* died of a fentanyl overdose?" Paige asked as a look of passion-filled her eyes, causing Jorge to get swept up. "We need to find a way to get it into his system."

"This here, it should not be difficult," Jorge reminded her. "In fact, this sounds like the easiest thing to do."

"Maybe he had an issue…"

"As if the police could prove otherwise," Jorge reminded her. "As if they would even try."

Paige nodded with a gentle grin on her lips.

"Perhaps you and Marco," Jorge suggested. "You can do some research together. I am sure between the two of you, you will have this man's life figured out very quickly."

"You can tell a lot by someone's emails, text messages, and scheduling," Paige observed as she grabbed her phone and began to tap. "I'll see if Marco is available this afternoon to help."

"Also, *mi amor,* the neighbor lady….."

Paige hesitated and looked up. The two shared a silent look.

"You said she doesn't own the house?" Paige finally confirmed. "She's just…staying there?"

"It is one of those short-term rentals," Jorge attempted to find the words in English. "The house, it is owned by a family that buys homes and rents them on a site for days, weeks....this woman, she does not even own the couch she sits on let alone the house itself."

"And she moved in at the same time as us?"

"*Si,*" Jorge nodded. "I thought maybe she was a cop but Marco, he does not think so. We must find out who she is…"

Paige didn't reply but appeared lost in thought.

"I did not think that short-term rentals were popular now since," Jorge said with an evil grin on his face. "You know…..that exposé about the porn site that posts videos of unsuspecting tenants."

"Oh yes!" Paige said with laughter in her voice. "Yeah, that whole industry took a nosedive after it came out that people were putting cameras throughout their home and secretly recording their tenants. Turns out owners said their cameras were hacked and it was difficult to prove otherwise."

"Like the police were really looking," Jorge joined her in laughter. "A smart business person saw an opportunity and took the risk. His site, it only grew in popularity once that news broke. He might be in hot water but it is hot *million dollar* water."

"People enjoy voyeurism," Paige added as Jorge continued to laugh. "The industry hasn't been the same but a lot of people made money on their rentals *and* the sex tapes. They just blurred out the faces. Maybe the neighbor lady isn't aware…."

"Yes, well, *mi amor,*" Jorge countered. "Either way, her rental agreement is about to end."

Paige nodded.

"Let us first find out what she is doing," Jorge suggested. "And we'll act accordingly."

"Sounds good," Paige replied as she rose from the chair and glanced at her phone. "I have a few things to do before I meet Marco. Between the two of us, I think we'll have everything we need."

"It will work out perfectly, *mi amor.*"

After Paige left, Jorge found the silence overbearing. So much had changed since Jesús died. He continued to show strength to the others even though most days, it simply wasn't in him to do. There was an empty spot when they sat around the table and time refused to heal the wound.

A wave of emotion suddenly overwhelmed him, causing Jorge to jump out of his chair and head to the door. It was necessary that he left that room and got out of the house so he wouldn't fall down the rabbit hole of despair. He had spent too many days locked in his office, a bottle of tequila on the desk while he thought back to the many memories of Jesús and the guilt he felt for his murder. It was necessary to escape the ghosts that haunted him.

In the SUV, he sat behind the wheel for a few minutes before finally backing out of the driveway and on the street. He mindlessly drove until he found himself back at the *Princesa Maria.* Jorge located his key and headed toward the door. He welcomed the silence but instead found Diego and Chase in a lively discussion at the bar.

"I know it's not the same," Diego was speaking dramatically with his arms waving in the air. "But I'm telling you, you gotta let it go."

"What's going on?" Jorge spoke with a strong voice even though he felt apprehensive to join the conversation.

"Oh, Chase is paranoid cause his son is oddly attracted to the color pink," Diego spoke flamboyantly as he crossed his legs and sat up straighter. "I told him, it don't mean he's gay and so what if he is?"

"Your son, he is gay?" Jorge asked. "Isn't your son just a child?"

"But *we* know when we're young," Diego leaned forward as if confiding something to Jorge, with his exaggerated expression. "That's what I'm telling him."

"My son isn't gay," Chase clarified as Jorge headed behind the bar and reached for some tequila. "He just…really likes pink and my ex, she's making a big deal about it."

"Of course, in your little redneck town," Diego quickly jumped right in. "They don't like the gays."

"Audrey's not like that but she's worried about other kids," Chase insisted. "And he's not gay."

"Denial," Diego teased and turned his attention to Jorge. "Hey isn't it early in the day for a drink?"

"It's been a busy day," Jorge said and knocked back the shot before placing the glass on the counter and returning to the other side of the bar, where he sat beside Diego.

"I heard about the neighbor thing," Diego nodded toward Chase. "He told me. Is she a cop or what the fuck?"

"Not a cop but we do not know," Jorge replied. "Paige is meeting with Marco to figure it out this afternoon…"

"Paige, she's at the office?" Diego spoke excitedly and jumped off the stool. "I'm *so* going to surprise her with coffee from that shop she loves! Oh, it's gonna be a great afternoon."

"And just like that, you leave us?" Jorge teased.

"I have *hardly* seen Paige lately," Diego started toward the door. "You got me working around the clock."

"See you, Diego," Chase said with humor in his voice as the door closed. "He wasn't even here for a half hour and I'm exhausted."

"This is Diego," Jorge reminded him. "At least, he is not depressed anymore."

"At least we *all* aren't," Chase countered as he ran a hand over his short hair. "The last few months have been rough."

"It is about to get rougher too," Jorge predicted. "Just this time, not for us."

"Oh yeah?"

"Yeah, but let's go to the office," Jorge suggested as he stood up. "Your staff will be here soon."

Once inside the small room, their conversation continued.

"So what's going on?"

"We might give Athas' man a taste of his own medicine…literally," Jorge replied as Chase went behind the desk and Jorge grabbed the first available chair. "And it ain't going to taste good."

"Medicine often doesn't," Chase quickly caught on. "Who's gonna take care of it?"

"I don't know," Jorge replied. "I was thinking Paige but I would rather keep her out of it."

"I can."

"You?" Jorge was surprised. Although Chase had stepped up in the last few months, he wasn't a murderer. "You want to do this?"

"Tell me how to do it and consider it done."

"Are you sure?"

"I said I wanted to go all-in," Chase replied as he sat up straight. "And I meant it."

"It's not that easy," Jorge reminded him. "You have to get to the guy…."

"I can bring Jolene with me," Chase suggested. "She can get to *any* guy."

Jorge considered the voluptuous Colombian woman who had used her looks to bewitch many of their victims and nodded.

"We will see. Let us get more information first."

"I've got this."

Jorge opened his mouth to reply but stopped.

Chase no longer had the naïve eyes of a boy but the determined glare of a man. It was a new day.

CHAPTER 5

"Are you serious?" Paige asked as Jorge ushered her into the office later that afternoon. "And why do we have to come in here? Juliana is upstairs with Miguel and Maria is practicing dance moves."

"*Mi amor,* I would rather that we keep our business away from the family," Jorge insisted as he closed the door and started toward the desk. "There has been too much for them to see in the last year."

Paige fell silent, her expression sober. She followed him to the desk and took a seat across from him.

"So today, you learned much?" Jorge restarted the conversation and watched his wife nod her head. "Do you think this will be difficult?"

"No, quite the contrary," Paige replied with the same self-assurance that had first drawn him to her. There was something in her voice when she talked of murder that sent a fire throughout his body. "This one will be easy. As it turns out, he enjoys a little cocaine on the weekend to take the edge off….of course, we're going to make sure that there's something else in it."

"I do like this idea," Jorge said as he watched his wife with interest as his desires began to churn. His eyes fell on the curve of breast underneath the fitted red blouse she wore. "So simple but I must ask how you will get the two mixed."

"He always has a supply at home," Paige replied with ease, her voice as smooth as honey which highlighted her dangerous side. "I just have to get into his condo, add a concentrated amount to the coke and leave. Easy peasy. Marco will make sure to hack the security in his building and no one will know I was even there."

"So this problem will take care of itself," Jorge spoke in a husky voice as he stared into her eyes. "Except, of course, I do not want you to do this yourself."

"Jorge, I know we must be extra cautious but…"

"But I will do anything to protect my *familia,*" Jorge reminded her. "This includes not having you in any dangerous situations."

"I'm not in danger," She countered and sat ahead in her chair and he felt his libido sparked by the passion in her eyes. "But I have to do it. This has to be done carefully because fentanyl is very dangerous plus I know how much to use. You can't send Jolene and Chase. It's too risky."

"Perhaps you should teach them everything you know," Jorge suggested and felt his desires continue to climb. "Chase, at least. Jolene, I'm not sure about but Chase, he wants to learn everything you know."

"Everything I know?" Paige countered, appearing to pick up on the lust in his eyes. "Could he handle everything I know?"

His mind swirling, he watched as his wife rose from the chair and walked to his side of the desk. Leaning down, her lips met with his and Jorge wasted no time pulling her close, his hand working to open her blouse while her hand moved toward his groin. He felt pleasure quickly building after her fingers reached inside his pants as he closed his eyes and leaned back.

There was a momentary pause and his eyes sprang opened to see her remove her pants. She was wearing no underwear. That one fact stalled his thoughts as she continued to undress, until he suddenly realized he needed to do the same. Pulling down his pants and boxers in one swift move, he watched her move closer once again, his hand reached out to pull her close.

"The door, *mi amor,* is it locked?"

"Yes," Paige spoke breathlessly as he sat back down on the chair. Her legs straddled each side of the chair as she eased herself on top of him. After some long, drawn-out kisses, she slowly moved him inside of her causing him to tighten his grip around her back.

The next few minutes flew by as she moved frantically, loudly gasping as his hands continued to clamp on her hips as his excitement intensified so quickly that he thought he would lose his mind. He wasn't sure if it was the rapid movements or the way she tightened her lower body that caused the waves of pleasure to be so fierce that he let out a noise a little louder than he would've liked with others in the house. His orgasm was so strong that he felt weak when she finally collapsed against him and they held each other close. Heat rose between them as his fingers gently caressed her back.

"Oh Paige, I do not know what you did but I cannot remember the last time I felt like this," Jorge commented in a low voice as she began to stand up. "There are towels here. Can you pass me one?" He pointed toward the bottom drawer of his desk.

"I'm glad you enjoyed it," She said while passing him a towel before picking up her clothes, only stopping to give him a brief kiss before heading toward the small bathroom connected to his office. "I tried something I read about online…I guess it worked."

"Mi amor, I do not know what you did," Jorge replied as he tapped the towel against his groin. "But it definitely worked. I hope I was not loud."

"You were but Maria has her music on."

It took a minute for him to realize she was right.

"Perhaps we need a couch in here," Jorge commented. "You know, it would be nice for when….more comfortable."

"We should," Paige replied as she closed the bathroom door and Jorge rose to pull up his pants.

"Perhaps I will look into it tomorrow," Jorge spoke more to himself than Paige.

Five minutes later, they were back to their original conversation, although Jorge now felt a rush of endorphins flowing through his body. Work suddenly felt less important, his original reservations dropped.

"Paige, if you must go…"

"I must but if it makes you feel better, I can bring someone with me," She offered.

"Yes, Paige, this would make me feel better," Jorge admitted. "I do not like the idea of you doing this at all but if you must, please bring someone with you."

"So, what's this about Chase wanting to learn what I do?" Paige began to laugh. "It's not exactly a community college course you can take two nights a week."

"Obviously, *mi amor,* but he has expressed interest in some of the work you do and I think this is a good thing," Jorge insisted. "It is time to teach him more."

"But maybe we're going about this the wrong way," Paige countered. "Maybe we should move away from all of this insanity. The more we fight, the more people will fight back…"

"But this here with Athas, someone has to take care of," Jorge reminded her. "This must be done carefully. I feel Chase can do so. I am not saying train him to be a sniper but why not show him some things…you know, like this man who deceives Athas? It is not complicated so it is a good place to start."

"He has stepped up a lot since Jesús died…"

"And *mi amor,* he wants to step up more," Jorge insisted. "I know, you do not normally like to teach these things but we cannot be out there forever. We need to teach the soldiers."

Paige nodded slowly. "It's just…Chase, he's so…"

"But he has changed," Jorge reminded her. "He is not the same boy next door he used to be. The only thing you must be careful of is to not fall in love with him like everyone else in my family seem to…"

Paige rolled her eyes and laughed.

"I am just saying….Maria, Jolene…Diego…."

"Ok, well I'm not them," Paige reminded him. "I can easily teach Chase some of these skills without that being an issue."

Jorge grinned and winked at his wife. He loved teasing her.

"I assume this weekend is as good of a time as any," Paige continued. "We're what….Wednesday."

"This weekend, we should do it," Jorge agreed. "It will not take long. You and Chase, you can go on a day trip and take care of this…..I figure by Monday, we will hear something on the news."

Paige nodded and glanced at her phone.

"Does he have anyone who would be looking for him….a wife, girlfriend?"

"A maid," Paige said and looked up from her screen. "Both his wife *and* girlfriend live in other cities and neither is planning to go see him this weekend. It seems he's kind of pissed off both recently...."

"Ah, yes, it makes sense that he might go headfirst into the cocaine this weekend," Jorge said with a grin on his face. "So the maid, she will be in?"

"Every Saturday."

"Perfecto."

"Now about the neighbor....."

"Oh fuck," Jorge automatically changed his disposition. "She was watching me when I returned home earlier today."

"She's not a cop."

"I did not think she was but then again..."

"No, she's an associate producer of one of those gossip type shows," Paige continued and sat up a little straighter. "You know the kind you hate?"

"Ahh!" Jorge rolled his eyes at the sky. "If I see Maria watch those shows one more time.."

"I know," Paige replied and put up her hand. "It seems that she wants to write an exposé about you since you dropped out of politics. By being next door, she's purposely attempting to instigate issues so she can catch you raging at her on camera or take pictures."

"Please tell me she has none so far?"

"She has..." Paige paused for a moment and put up her hand. "Don't freak out and do anything stupid."

"Oh fuck!" Jorge said and closed his eyes. "What does she have?"

"Marco hacked her phone and she has a few pictures...of the kids."

"What!" Jorge jumped up from his chair. "That lady, she is dead."

"Calm down," Paige swiftly stood up. "We have to be careful, remember, she's talking to people at her network about the work she's doing. If she suddenly turns up dead..."

"Then the others, they will keep the fuck away," Jorge rushed toward the door.

"Not necessarily," Paige reminded him. "We're going to *act* not *react*. Calm down."

Jorge stopped at the door and turned toward his wife.

"Paige you know me," Jorge replied. "When it comes to my family, especially my children.."

"I know," Paige replied. "But, she's keeping everything close to her chest so the network has nothing. She wants to gather more information before sharing anything."

"So everything she got is in her home?"

"Yes."

"So we must remove it," Jorge replied.

"Already done," Paige insisted. "Unless she has it on a backup, we got everything."

"Ok," Jorge found himself calming. "So now, what?"

"I have a plan," Paige spoke in her usual calm voice. "This one's going to be easy."

CHAPTER 6

"You know, Diego," Jorge's voice echoed through the boardroom of Our House of Pot. "This here, it has been too much of an adjustment for me. Jesús died, what? Six months ago and I believe I feel worse than I did then. This is not me."

"We worked closely with him for years," Diego said while fixing his tie and leaning back in his chair. "Of course, this is going to affect you."

"I know Diego but I have seen so many die over the years," Jorge reminded him as he stared into space for a moment. "It is as if my head is on backward, you know? I wake up in the morning and I feel...I feel like what is the point?"

Diego's eyes widened as he listened from the head of the table but he remained quiet.

"Wait," Jorge hesitated. "Was Clara in today?"

"We're clean."

"All that we do," Jorge continued. "What is the point? I control most of the pot business in Canada, I control the politicians and yet, I could not stop one of my closest associates and friend from being killed."

"Jorge, you are *not* God," Diego reminded him as he anxiously leaned ahead on the table. "I know you *think* you are but you are not..."

"Diego, I have never once thought of myself as *Dios,*" He replied with a smooth grin. "This here is not the problem."

"You know what I mean," Diego sputtered out a reply, his forehead wrinkling in frustration. "You can't control everything. We didn't see it coming."

"What else do we not see coming, Diego?" Jorge countered just as Tom Makerson arrived. The young editor for *Toronto AM* seemed hesitant as he entered the room. "This is the problem."

Diego didn't reply but looked troubled.

"Good morning," Makerson interrupted with some reservation as he closed the door behind him. "Sorry, I'm late. Traffic was backed up…

"This it is fine," Jorge cut him off and shrugged. "You do not have to tell us about the traffic this morning."

"Guess I'm not the only one," Makerson glanced around the table as he sat across from Jorge. "Or is this it for today?"

"Paige and Chase, they are on a…..mission," Jorge said and glanced at Diego, who had a grin on his face. "They will return later today. Jolene is tied up at the warehouse but this here, it does not concern her anyway."

"Oh?"

"It has to do with our new neighbor," Jorge continued and watched Diego make a face. "She is a problem."

"Yes, I've heard you mention her in the past but I'm not sure how I can help," Makerson said but appeared intrigued.

"As it turns out," Jorge continued. "This woman, she makes her living doing those gossipy, exposé news shows."

"And she wants to do one on you?" Makerson guessed, suddenly appearing more relaxed. He ran a hand through his strawberry blond hair. "What's her name?"

"Christina Hampton," Jorge replied and watched Makerson roll his eyes. "You know her?"

"Yeah, well, I know never to call her *Chrissy*," He said shaking his head. "I made that mistake at an event a couple of years ago and she nearly ripped my fucking head off."

"Ah, so, temperamental?" Jorge asked.

"To put it mildly," Makerson answered and cleared his throat. "So she moved next door to get a story? Is that what's going on?"

"It appears so," Jorge replied with some hesitation. "Her place, it is a short-term rental and she was attempting to collect information on my family. It has since been lost in an unfortunate technical issue…"

"Ah, I see," Makerson grinned. "Did she have anything…"

"No, not really," Jorge replied. "However, she did have pictures of my children and to me, that crosses the line."

"How long was she there?"

"Not long," Jorge replied. "She moved in just before we did."

Makerson paused for a moment.

"So, she didn't have anything?" He confirmed. "Because as a journalist, I know that we need results quickly or the story gets dropped. She must've had a basis to go to this trouble."

"From what Paige said," Diego said. "She got nothing. Just notes on a few confrontations with Jorge but that's it."

Makerson looked troubled.

"What do you think?" Jorge swiftly asked him.

"I think it's strange she's doing this herself and doesn't have some low-level employee watching you," Makerson replied. "Why is *she* doing this? She's a little high up in the food chain. What does she want?"

"That's what I said," Diego abruptly replied. "Jorge, this is big or she wouldn't bother."

"But she got nothing," Jorge reminded them both. "She can think or suspect whatever she wishes but without proof, this is in her head."

"If she knows anything," Diego cut in again. "Why would she be stupid enough to get in your crosshairs?"

"Money?" Makerson attempted. "Maybe the network offered her a bonus to get you under fire."

"Who owns the network?" Jorge countered.

"Hers?" Makerson thought for a moment. "You're asking the wrong question. That doesn't matter. They just want ratings but what you have to look at is her advertisers."

Jorge and Diego exchanged looks.

"You find out who they are and then you're on to something," Makerson said as he pulled out his phone and started to tap on it. "I will tell you this much, I'm pretty sure Big Pharma keeps that show on the air."

Jorge felt the tension building in his head.

"So, what is probably going on," Makerson continued before pausing for a moment to read something before nodding. "Yeah, I was right. So this means they're trying to get some dirt as a way to pull your company down."

"Well, this here, it is not happening," Jorge gruffly insisted and glanced at Diego. "So, do we slaughter the sheep or the farmer that owns them? That is my question."

"If you slaughter the sheep," Diego replied. "The farmer is going to find someone else."

Jorge thought for a moment.

"Diego, I do think that actually," Jorge reached for his phone and glanced at it. "Once Paige and Chase have completed their mission, we might be able to kill two birds with one stone."

Makerson looked intrigued.

"I have not been in the media in months," Jorge continued as he glanced at the editor. "Perhaps it is time we do a little interview discussing my concerns for the dangerous pharmaceuticals that kill people on our streets. There's been a rise in fentanyl-related deaths in recent months. Perhaps the families of these people could gather to tell their story."

"Class action lawsuit," Diego suggested.

"It's happened before," Makerson replied with a grin on his face. "As the CEO of House of Pot, this is obviously a concern to you."

"Well, yes, I am concerned that we are being connected and it is very important that we remind people what we sell is mild in comparison," Jorge continued. "I have a feeling that this here, it will work."

"And Christina Hampton?" Makerson asked.

"I wonder how much that house is worth?" Jorge mused. "I wonder if the owners would be willing to sell?"

"I'm looking for a house," Diego lurched forward with excitement in his eyes. "This would be perfect! We could be neighbors!"

"I am starting to think I would rather the television bitch," Jorge teased. "Yes, Diego, this would be a suitable home for you. You can pack up all your lime trees and move in."

"Lime trees?" Makerson asked. "Do you really have lime trees, Diego?"

"Don't ask," Jorge suggested but Diego was already ignoring them both as he tapped on his phone. "Our neighborhood, it is about to go to hell."

"But will this stop her from investigating you?" Makerson asked.

"It might if I come up with a creative going away present," Jorge smirked and didn't reveal anything else. "It is about timing. Everything must happen at once and I believe, this will send her a message."

"Speaking of messages," Diego suddenly looked up from his phone skeptically. "Have you heard from Paige."

"Not yet," Jorge glanced at his phone and noted the time. "They should be contacting us soon."

It wasn't for another hour before the text arrived. Jorge was waiting for his daughter outside the school when a quick message told him everything he had to know.

I'm going to be late for dinner so start without me.

Jorge grinned and replied.

We will get take-out. I will see you soon, mi amor.

He looked up in time to see Maria rushing toward the SUV. Unlocking the door, he watched as she reached for the handle and pulling it open.

"You never come to get me, *Papa,*" Maria asked suspiciously. "Where's Paige?"

"I do come to get you, all the time," Jorge countered as she climbed in and closed the door. He immediately locked it again. "It is usually Paige who has the time to do so. I am sometimes in meetings."

"Where is she?"

"She is busy and will be home later," Jorge spoke hurriedly. "Maria, what do you want for dinner? I told Paige I would pick up something."

"McDonald's."

"Paige will kill us if she knows we get fast food," Jorge teased. Maria giggled as she fastened her seatbelt and they drove out of the parking lot.

"That's why we get her something else," Maria suggested. "I could go for a cheeseburger right now and Miguel loves their fries."

"Miguel loves *all* fries," Jorge countered and grinned. "Mostly he loves throwing them on the floor."

"We can clean them up before Paige gets home," Maria suggested with a gleam in her brown eyes. "What do you say?"

"Maria, for tonight, yes we can have burgers and fries," Jorge replied as his stomach rumbled. "But if Paige asks, it was *your* idea."

"It *was* my idea," Maria reminded him. "She always complains I don't eat enough but tonight, I could eat everything on the menu."

Jorge glanced at his daughter's petit figure and grinned.

"Your eyes, *chica,* they are bigger than your stomach," Jorge decided to switch gears. "How was school today?"

"It was ok," Maria shrugged. "I'm glad the year is almost over."

"I thought you liked this school."

"It's boring,"

"What about your dance?"

She shrugged.

"Papa, I think it is time I move on."

"Move on?" Jorge asked. "What do you mean?"

"I think I need to consider other options for next year," Maria insisted. "I'm almost 13 and I think it's normal that I go to a school with both boys and girls. I find being around other girls all day….Insufferable."

"Insufferable?" Jorge repeated. "But what do you mean?"

"I find other girls…catty and mean," Maria spoke firmly. "Plus, you don't want me to turn lesbian, do you?"

"What?" Jorge attempted to find the words but couldn't. "I…

"That's what happens," Maria insisted with wide eyes. "When you're around girls all the time….at least that's what they tell me."

His phone beeped causing a welcomed interruption.

CHAPTER 7

"We were extra careful since he's with the government," Paige reminded Jorge as they both got into bed later that night. "Cameras were off in the building and his apartment but we also had to think of surrounding areas. He's a big shot so the police will make an effort this time."

Jorge grunted and rolled his eyes.

"It's too bad that all the people on the streets dying from fentanyl don't deserve the same courtesy," She remarked in her usual calm tone as she stretched, temporarily distracting Jorge with her long, lean body. "But even in numbers, they don't get police attention."

"This here, does it surprise you?" Jorge asked and watched Paige shake her head. "They are merely an inconvenience in the first place. Plus, who do you think the police work for?"

"Good point," Paige replied as she nodded. "Hopefully the homeless deaths will slow down soon."

"They will, *mi amor*," Jorge replied as he moved closer to his wife. "As I said, I plan to have an interview with Makerson in the next few days. It will line up with this high-profile death and my concern for the many on the streets. I hope it will send a message of what happens if they go behind the back of our prime minister."

"I think it sends a strong message," Paige leaned in close to her husband. "If you fuck with Alec Athas, you fuck with Jorge Hernandez. I don't think anyone wants to get on your bad side."

Their lips met and their conversation quickly halted.

Jorge awoke early the next morning. Despite that it was a Saturday, his phone didn't stop beeping as his troops checked in. The first person to chime in was Marco, who asked to speak with him at his earliest convenience. Jorge insisted he drop by the house for a brief conversation.

"Sir, I have something for you," He spoke excitedly as soon as Jorge met him at the door. The Filipino pointed toward his laptop bag as he walked into the house, politely ignoring a crying baby upstairs and the loud music that flowed from Maria's room.

"We will go to the office," Jorge said as the men walked. "Please, you must ignore this noise, Marco. My daughter wants to be an entertainer… of some kind and my son, he's getting his teeth."

"I do not pay attention to such things, sir," Marco said with a grin on his face as the two men entered Jorge's office, where he closed the door. "This is my house every day."

"How are you enjoying your new home?" Jorge asked with interest as he walked behind his desk and Marco sat across from him. "Nice neighborhood?"

"Sir, I will never know how to repay you for your kindness," Marco spoke appreciatively. "When I think of the home we had even two years ago…"

"Marco, you know I like to invest in my employees," Jorge replied and sat back in his chair. "This is what we do in Mexico. We remember the people who make our organizations strong and you, *amigo,* you contribute a great deal to my success."

Marco gave an appreciative nod.

"So, you found something for me?"

"Yes, sir," Marco hurriedly pulled the laptop out of the bag and turned it on. "I think this is something that will….put this woman's reputation on the line."

After hitting a few keys, Marco turned the laptop around to show a video of Jorge's neighbor naked, on top of a much older man. He briefly wished the sound worked along with the camera Jorge had recording her over the last few days.

"It was a busy Friday night," Jorge laughed at his joke. "This here should take care of one of my problems."

"Do you plan to blackmail her, sir?"

"I plan to send this here," Jorge pointed toward the laptop, ignoring the image of the young woman reaching for a sex toy. "To a site that specializes in short-term rental porn. It is a *thing*, Marco."

"I had heard of such, so this here is true?"

"Our nosey neighbor, she will regret spying on us and taking pictures of my children," Jorge insisted. "You do not mess with a man's family."

"I agree, sir," Marco nodded as he pulled the laptop back toward him. "Would you like me to post this video on the site you mentioned. I can do so and it will be untraceable."

"This would be perfect," Jorge said and thought for a moment. "But first, I want Makerson to see it. He's on his way here. We are planning an interview for perhaps tomorrow or the next day."

"A live stream?"

"Yes, we wish to talk about our concerns over the rise in fentanyl deaths on our streets," Jorge spoke casually and glanced at his phone. "I wonder if he knows the man in the video."

As it turned out, he did.

"Oh, my fuck!" A smile lit up his face shortly after his arrival when Jorge showed him the video. "You got this next door?"

"Yes, we decided to turn things around on Christina Hampton," Jorge said as he glanced toward the laptop and watched Makerson's eyes as they studied the video. He hit some buttons on the keyboard while beside him, Marco leaned in.

"I know this man," Makerson said and nodded, looking over the laptop at Jorge. "I know this man!"

"Really?" Jorge asked with interest.

"He's the producer of her show," Makerson replied. "I guess now we know how she got her job….spreading her legs."

"Yes, well," Jorge said as pushed his chair closer to the desk. "You can only spread your legs so far apart before they snap and this lady is about to hear a very loud pop."

"Would you like me to upload the video now, sir?" Marco asked enthusiastically.

"To where?" Makerson asked cautiously. "You don't want her to trace this back to you…..do you?"

"It is the site that posts short-term rental videos," Jorge said and watched Makerson grin in response. "Sometimes, I hear, these cameras are hacked…"

"There's big money in those videos," Makerson reminded them. "The more hits they get, the more money contributors make."

"Ah, the world we live in today," Jorge said with a sanctimonious grin.

"I'm not even sure of the legalities," Makerson replied while shaking his head. "But I think in court, Hampton would have to prove that she *didn't* post the video herself and let's face it, she can't. You'd be surprised how many people record themselves to make money, then act as if they had no idea. Anything for money."

"Poverty," Jorge said with a grin. "It does not make for popularity."

"People are willing to pay for this," Makerson replied as Marco pulled the laptop toward him and began to work. "Are we posting her name with it?"

"I do not think we can for legal reasons," Marco replied. "But this is not to say that someone cannot discover it and put it on Twitter, stating that it looks like her. Maybe add a hashtag?"

Impressed, Jorge nodded and exchanged looks with Makerson.

"This here is my favorite employee right now."

The two men laughed.

"By noon," Makerson predicted. "This woman's reputation will be down the toilet."

"Hey, it does look like she has some skills," Jorge pointed toward the laptop. "Perhaps, it is a mere career change for her."

Marco finished his task and Jorge insisted he take the rest of the day off. After a brief discussion with Makerson about their upcoming interview, scheduled tentatively for the next afternoon, he concluded their meeting.

"This is a good day," Jorge commented as he walked Makerson to the door.

"The house is much quieter from when I arrived," Makerson glanced around. "No crying baby, no music…"

"Yes, that has been all morning," Jorge said as they arrived at the entranceway. "Paige took the kids to an amusement park. I believe Jolene, she will be joining them."

"What will you do with the house so quiet?"

"It won't be quiet much longer," Jorge said while opening the door. "Diego will soon be here for a meeting."

Makerson laughed as he left and Jorge took a breath. He felt someone's eyes on him and turned in time to see his neighbor walking by and he laughed. Her world was about to take a sudden, unpleasant turn.

Diego arrived shortly after with Chase in tow.

"I got the house!" Diego announced before Jorge could even say hello but stood back as his *hermano* swept in while Chase followed, a sheepish grin on his face. "We'll soon be neighbors."

"Just like that?" Jorge asked as he closed and locked the door. "No hassles, negotiations…."

"I gave them an offer they couldn't refuse," Diego said and clapped his hands together. "Isn't this exciting?"

Jorge mocked a horrified expression, which Diego ignored and trotted toward the office.

"This is about to become a very interesting neighborhood," Chase quietly commented as the three men went into the office and closed the door. "But at least you'll have the nosey lady out."

"Yeah, I ain't living with her," Diego announced as he sat down and fixed his tie. "She's got to get her ass out. They tell me her contract is on a week-to-week basis so by next Saturday, that bitch is on the street."

"She will not be a problem much longer anyway," Jorge predicted with no further explanation.

"Am I gonna have to clean up blood in my new place?" Diego glared at Jorge. "Cause if you're going to.."

"No no," Jorge laughed. "Murder, it is not always the answer. I have a little video circulating with my neighbor. She will not be bothering us again."

"A video?" Chase asked.

"I will show you later," Jorge said and shook his head. "Trust me, the neighbor, her career is over. What you guys got for me?"

"We took care of the MP," Chase referred to the previous day. "I'm sure Paige told you everything."

"Yes, and she said you did well," Jorge spoke appreciatively. "Paige was quite impressed with your help. Let us hope the fucker dies."

"I said I wanted to do more and I meant it," Chase spoke confidently. "Whatever you need."

"I will keep this in mind, thank you," Jorge replied and turned to Diego. "And you, what else you got?"

"I just wanted to tell you about the house," Diego spoke dramatically and crossed his legs. "Oh, wait, there is something else."

Jorge shrugged.

"There's some guy who keeps calling the office looking for you," Diego informed him. "I didn't think anything of it but the receptionist said he's pretty pushy."

"This here, it could be anyone," Jorge replied with a shrug.

"It sounded suspicious so I said next time to redirect the call to me."

"You got a name?"

Diego made a face and shook his head.

"See who it is and what he wants," Jorge said and thought for a moment. "Just in case. I don't like surprises."

"Will do." Diego appeared unconcerned. "It's probably nothing."

"Let us hope," Jorge replied and raised an eyebrow. "Let us hope."

CHAPTER 8

"There's more than one way to skin a cat," Paige commented with a smirk on her face as her fingers roamed across the keyboard to scan through comments about Christina Hampton's video. "It went viral fast."

"What do you expect? People, they know her face from tv," Jorge commented as he glanced at Makerson rushing around the office, preparing for their live interview that would stream on social media. "And now, they also know some of her other body parts too."

Paige laughed and Makerson merely grinned as he adjusted the lighting near where they would sit.

"I suspect she will be moving soon," Paige commented as she closed her laptop and pushed it aside.

"She has no choice," Jorge reminded her. "Diego bought the house."

"The funny part is that she blames the homeowners for recording the video," Makerson commented as he walked back toward the desk and turned on his laptop. "And they say that it's her that recorded it since there are no cameras in their house."

Jorge and Paige exchanged looks.

"What can I say?" Jorge finally responded, "I have a very good team."

"Ok, so," Makerson seemed to switch gears as he tapped on his keyboard. "I think we should keep this relatively short and to the point. It's more about making a statement and Athas, he knows you're doing this?"

"Yes," Jorge nodded. "He has a press conference in the morning about the 'suspicious death' of the member of parliament. He must try to explain the mixture of fentanyl and cocaine found…"

"About that," Paige cut him off. "He won't mention the cocaine. He'll just say there were 'traces of fentanyl' found at the scene because there are already rumors swirling."

"This is true," Jorge nodded. "They will make him look like an innocent victim."

"In fairness," Makerson cut in and exchanged looks with the two of them. "Athas will have to keep his cards close to his chest."

"Yes, we must protect the rich," Paige spoke sarcastically.

"And powerful," Makerson added.

"Except we won't be doing that this time," Jorge reminded them. "Athas, he has an emergency meeting planned for his troop of clowns. Let us hope they now see he is not the person to cross and soon, we will make sure the real story is leaked."

"Just tell me when," Makerson reminded them.

"We will talk about the rumors of fentanyl in this interview than later tonight, I suggest you say 'a source' claims there were also traces of cocaine found," Jorge thought for a moment. "And I think that will be the opening Athas will need in the press conference tomorrow. He may not admit everything but at least, it will cause speculation."

"That's all we need to get the vultures circling," Makerson said then briefly paused. "And regarding the homeless.."

"After our interview, you will do some *extra* investigating and discover that those deaths have increased dramatically in the last few weeks and months," Jorge commented. "You will then question why this information wasn't given to the public."

"Perfect," Makerson grinned. "Oh, did I tell you that I'm up for a journalism award this summer? All these tips you give me, they're paying off. For a newspaper, we're striving in a time when others are flopping."

"*Amigo,* you just have to give people what they want," Jorge reminded him as Makerson gestured for him to sit down across from the computer, surrounded by soft lighting. "And the people, they want the truth."

"Oh yeah and they come to expect it from us," Makerson replied as Paige listened from the other side of the desk. "I mean, our online following has *doubled* since last year. That's social media, newsletter signups, everything."

"Sounds like you've assured of job security," Paige spoke in an even tone.

"You, my friend, you always have job security when you work for me," Jorge assured him. "This, I can tell you."

Makerson nodded appreciatively.

"So let us, as they say," Jorge pointed toward the laptop. "Get this show on the road."

A few minutes later everything was ready and the interview started. After introductions and some casual talk as Makerson glanced at his iPad to see how many people were watching live, he finally started to discuss the main event.

"With the shocking death of a member of parliament announced earlier today and rumors that fentanyl was found on the scene," Makerson smoothly switched gears, pausing a moment to take a breath, as if lost in thought. "I'm curious what you think? I know you've mentioned the fentanyl issue many times last year while running in the leadership race, so it's a bit of a hot topic with you, Mr. Hernandez."

"It is because this here, it is a deadly drug," Jorge jumped in as Paige nodded in the background. "And we must ask ourselves why it has become so…prevalent in these times? It is not a new drug. Fentanyl has been around for years and now, suddenly, it is killing hundreds of people in this country."

"Why is this a concern to you?" Makerson asked bluntly. "You're the CEO of Our House of Pot, a nationwide chain of cannabis stores so why is the subject of fentanyl always coming up?"

"I keep seeing in the media that people, they sometimes put our drugs in the same category," Jorge replied and glanced toward the red light on the laptop. "And I assure you, they are not the same. We are an ethical company that provides a natural product that people enjoy, that people use for medical purposes and this here….it is so very different from the devastation that fentanyl has created."

"I think a lot of people are confused about where it's suddenly coming from," Makerson threw in. "I mean, as you stated earlier, it's not a new drug. Fentanyl has been around for years so why is it suddenly on the streets?"

"My understanding is that it is cheap," Jorge replied as if he had no idea. "It creates a stronger high, so in essence, this allows drug dealers to stretch out products *like* cocaine and make more money. I do not know, this is what I hear."

"But where do you think it's coming from?" Makerson pushed. "I know in the past, you've mentioned that you've spoken to a lot of people in both law enforcement and of course, other government officials on the matter. What are you hearing?"

"I am hearing a lot of talk about it coming from labs in China," Jorge paused and shrugged. "I do not know if this is true. I do wonder, however, why this does not seem to concern Big Pharma. Otherwise, would they not try to stop such labs that are counterfeiting their product? It would make sense to me that they would have a vested interest in stopping this epidemic but it does not seem that way."

"What do you think Big Pharma has to gain from this?" Makerson asked innocently as if the two hadn't planned this interview in advance.

"Well, money," Jorge began to laugh and Makerson joined in. "Obviously, this here is the most important thing to them. I mean, do not think they are not aware of how powerful these drugs are and how they cause addiction and death?"

"But of course," Makerson cut in. "They're used for good too. Late stages of cancer, for example, many of these drugs provide relief for those suffering."

"Of course they do," Jorge replied. "But why are they so easily accessible? Tell me that. If the rumors are true regarding the tragic loss of a man who was part of our government, this perhaps will make people see that it is not just a problem of those living in poverty, on the streets. This is and always should have been, a Canadian problem. We must ask the difficult questions and make sure that the proper people are accountable. It is time that something is done."

"What can we do?"

"Find solutions," Jorge recommended. "I have decided that Our House of Pot will do what it can to help. My plan is to talk with those who are on the frontline dealing with addicts to come up with positive solutions and of course, help finance these organizations. I know we cannot resolve everything but I hope by getting involved, we also encourage other businesses in this community to do the same."

The interview ended shortly after with thousands watching. Comments poured in; some positive, others bashing Jorge Hernandez and referring to him as 'Canada's biggest drug dealer', something that only made him laugh.

If only they knew.

"This here is good, no?" Jorge asked Makerson after the final light was turned off and the two men moved his desk back into place, while Paige continued to monitor the comments on her laptop.

"I think you got a leg up on Big Pharma," Makerson replied. "And what if they were investing in these counterfeit labs on the sly? Ever think of that?"

"This is what I'm also wondering," Jorge replied. "There is a big difference between a drug that allows you to escape and a drug that can kill you immediately. There is something not so fun about that one."

"I still think we should've brought up CBD oil..." Makerson commented and quickly continued. "I understand why you didn't want to since it makes it look like your motive was to push a product from your company rather than help. I think it's important that people see that the less traditional methods are sometimes more helpful."

"This here is a conversation we can have in the future," Jorge reminded him. "After the dust settles. I will perhaps donate a certain amount of my company's CBD oil to the cause to help those recovering from addiction. We must think of longterm goals as well. It will work out."

"I'm glad Clara was in before we started talking about this," Paige reminded them both. "Especially since this office had devices in the past."

"I have her in more regularly now," Makerson confessed. "That fucking freaked me out. I get her in on Sunday night to check after everyone including the cleaners are gone. Having Marco install those cameras also gives some peace of mind. If anyone's ever in again, we can at least find out who it is."

"Welcome to our world," Jorge said and waved his hand in the air. "It is...how you say, inconvenient at times but necessary. It helps us all sleep better at night."

"I thank you," Makerson gave him a nod, a relaxed smile appeared on his lips.

"I also extend my gratitude," Jorge commented and glanced at his wife. "Paige, she reminds me of the importance of being gracious to those who help us."

"My paper is thriving…"

"Yes, but that is your work," Jorge reminded him. "You will be receiving a surprise from me tomorrow. It is a good one, I assure you. It will….ease your financial burdens."

Paige and Jorge left a stunned Makerson behind as they headed for the elevator.

"You shouldn't have told him," Paige commented in a low voice. "He would've been more surprised."

"Ah, *mi amor,* but there is something about the anticipation that adds to the satisfaction," Jorge spoke seductively as the elevator door closed. "Do you not think?"

"I do," She commented and eased closer to him. "Having his condo paid off, that's pretty big."

"I treat my employees well," Jorge commented. "Marco, Makerson… Diego…"

"You're like Oprah when she gave away cars," Paige joked. *"You get a house! And you get a house…"*

Jorge laughed. "This reference, I do not understand. Oprah, she gives away cars?"

"At one time, she did," Paige replied. "But I love that you're doing it. As long as the government doesn't ask too many questions."

"Paige, we can now show on paper that we're legit. The government, they do not have to know a fucking thing. The CRA, they worry about the middle class, they do not ruffle rich feathers. They know better."

The elevator stopped on the ground floor and they got out. Walking toward their SUV, Jorge took his wife's hand and squeezed it.

"Now, if only we could spend the rest of the day together, *mi amor* but what do they say….." Jorge stopped in the middle of the parking garage and pulled her close. "No rest for the wicked."

"That is what they do say," She muttered and moved in to kiss him.

CHAPTER 9

"Everything blew up overnight," Paige spoke calmly the following morning as the two sat at the kitchen table, drinking coffee and leaning in on his MacBook. "Makerson's comment on speculation of cocaine on the scene got hundreds of retweets and comments."

"This here, it is on fire," Jorge sat up a bit straighter, a smooth grin crossed his lips. "Athas will have to address the rumors in his press conference this morning."

"Have you spoken to him?"

"Not yet but we will talk again soon," Jorge replied and seemed to relax. "It does not matter because we already had this planned. He will go out, speak of the loss of such a *valuable* member of his team, send his sympathies to the families, that kind of thing. Reporters will push, so he will give vague details regarding the fentanyl."

"Knowing Alec, he'll avoid talking about the cocaine for now," Paige considered for a moment as she stared at the screen. "It's a sensitive time but it doesn't matter, all we need is that speculation."

"The rest, it will take care of its self, *mi amor.*"

"What about your interview?" Paige muttered as the sound of feet hitting the stairs caught both their attention. "Crazy comments still?"

"Paige, I do not read the comments," Jorge said as he shook his head and made a face. "These here, are of no importance to me."

"I noticed there were a lot of views this morning," She added in a low voice as Maria entered the kitchen carrying a bag.

"This here is what we want," Jorge said and turned his attention to Maria. "School, it is almost done for you, is it not?"

"Almost, just a few weeks left before exams," She replied. "I can't wait. I'm looking into a dance program to take over the summer."

"Well, this here might be good for you," Jorge replied. "Just remember, nothing on YouTube."

"I won't, *Papa,*" She replied with some attitude in her voice. "I told you I wouldn't do that again."

"We continue to keep our lives private in this house," Jorge reminded her. "Do not forget that."

Paige and Maria exchanged looks.

"What?" Jorge was suspicious. "What is going on?"

"*Papa,* this boy invited me to this school dance…"

"No!"

"*Papa!*" Maria's face was full of shock. "You didn't even let me explain. He's from our sister school and…"

"Maria, you are 12 years old," Jorge reminded her. "You're much too young for such things."

"But I'm almost 13 and other kids.."

"You, Maria, are not other kids," Jorge grew frustrated. "You are too young for dating. We do not know this boy or his family."

"Jorge, maybe we should discuss this later," Paige cut in. "We don't need to fight first thing in the morning. I think you need to hear this. It's a school dance, there will be chaperones…."

"I do not care," Jorge insisted. "My Maria, she is much too young for boys and dating."

"It's just a dance," Maria began to cry.

"Let's calm down," Paige put her hand in the air. "Please. Can we talk about this tonight?"

Jorge felt his heart sink and nodded in silence.

Paige put her arm around Maria who continued to sniff.

"Jorge, you and I will talk about this more later," Paige calmly suggested. "Then tonight, we'll all talk about it."

Maria nodded and Jorge reluctantly agreed. Rising from his seat, he silently crossed the room and hugged his daughter.

"*Bonita,*" Jorge said with some hesitation. "To me, you will always be a little girl. I am sorry if I sometimes overreact."

"I know," She whimpered and Jorge felt love flow through his heart as he started to let her go and she moved away. It was then that something outside caught his eye.

"What…." He walked toward the window and Maria and Paige followed him.

"Wow, it looks like our neighbor is moving," Paige spoke in a sunshiny voice. "Lots of suitcases!"

"Ughh….finally," Maria complained. "She was a weirdo."

"This is true, Maria, she *is* a weirdo," Jorge said as he leaned in and kissed the top of her head. "I must go and say a final goodbye."

"Jorge, you…" Paige started.

"No no, *mi amor,*" Jorge said as he moved away from his daughter and toward the door. "You know me, always a gentleman."

His wife and daughter looked equally horrified.

Outside, the sun instantly touched his face and feeling smug, Jorge fixed his tie and approached Christina Hampton. She was placing a suitcase in her trunk.

"Do not forget your video recording equipment," Jorge sang out in a cheery voice. "It has, after all, made you famous."

Receiving a dark glare in response, the phrase 'if looks could kill' crossed his mind. Of course, this didn't affect him.

"I find it interesting that a lady who had an issue with my toddler running out of the house naked was so quick to show off her…"

"You did this!" She immediately accused, causing Jorge to step back in mock disbelief. "You did this to me. You found out I was in television and you did this!"

"Ah, yes!" Jorge played along. "I asked your…what was it? Producer to fuck you. I sent him there at that exact time, then brainwashed you into thinking you should set up cameras and jump on his dick. Yes, *senorita,* this is all me. I am *that* good."

The color drained from her face.

"You know, sometimes it is good we take responsibility for our actions," Jorge continued as he started to walk away. "Rather than to blame others."

"I know you're a dangerous man," She countered. "And I plan to prove it."

"Lady," Jorge approached her again, this time getting in her face. "I think your reputation, it is not so good these days. If I were you, I would be happy that's all you lost."

After staring into her eyes long enough to communicate that it was time she cut her losses, he could see that the sheep had recognized the wolf. Rather than reply, she simply nodded but the fear in her eyes was unmistakable.

He returned to the house just as Paige and Maria were driving out. Both waved as he walked toward the door. Christina Hampton got in her car and drove away. It had been a successful morning already.

Jorge barely got back into the house when he heard his office phone ringing. Rushing into the room, he quickly closed the door and grabbed the receiver.

"*Hola!*"

"Good morning, Jorge," Alec replied, his voice sounding tense. "I wanted to give you a quick call before the press conference. You certainly added fuel to the fire last night."

"What can I say, I do enjoy a good fire," Jorge replied curtly. "It is what we said we would do."

"I had a meeting with the others last night," Alec spoke in a low voice. "It was very productive. I feel that my point was pretty clear."

"And that point is?"

"Don't fuck around behind my back," Alec muttered. "I told them that I heard what was going on without my knowledge and it wouldn't be happening again. No secrets."

"And there have been many…"

"I like the part where you said your company would help."

"That there, it was a last-minute decision," Jorge replied. "So tell me, you feel your confrontation, it was a success."

"I think I may have opened the door to a shitstorm," Alec confessed. "It's like being married to someone and suspecting they're having an affair.

You think you want the truth but when they tell you everything, you regret asking."

"Is that right?" Jorge asked. "Do you mean..."

"As it turns out there's been a lot going on behind my back," Alec replied. "I hadn't expected everyone to be so forthcoming."

"Well, when you consider that the last man who conspired behind your back has suddenly turned up dead," Jorge reminded him. "People, they tend to wish that this is not also their fate."

"I guess I didn't think so much would be held back from the prime minister," Alec spoke naïvely. "I always thought that the person running the country would be privy to everything happening here. That I'd know all the secrets."

"So, may I ask what you learned," Jorge asked. "Or is this too much?"

"It's pretty bad," Alec sounded emotional. "Some of the stuff....It's horrific. Canadians have no idea how much is hidden from them. I mean, I've known that to a degree since being elected but there are some things...I don't know how people sleep at night."

"You are perhaps not talking to the right person about this," Jorge reminded him. "I have slept many nights on a mattress built of evil."

"I think that's why I feel I can tell you this," Alec hesitated again. "Remember that fire last year? The one where the indigenous people died? The community that could've been saved but they instead let the fire go?"

"Yes," Jorge spoke quietly and sat down. "Even me, I see this is a horrific tragedy and some, they have called *me* the devil. Why do I have a feeling it is much worse than I originally thought."

"It is," Alec spoke with a bitter tone. "It was planned."

Jorge remained quiet and leaned against his desk.

"They said the indigenous people were getting too vocal," Alec spoke with emotion in his voice and paused, creating a heavy moment through the phone line.

"And they wanted to send a message," Jorge finished his sentence. "Shut up or this could happen to other communities too..."

Alec replied with barely a whisper.

"Yes."

CHAPTER 10

"It should be at your place," Diego spoke loudly as he leaned forward at the end of the table while the others watched him attentively. "Clowns. Animals. Bouncy castle…whatever the fuck that is…"

"Diego, this here, it is not our priority today," Jorge cut him off before the entire meeting got off track. "We can plan Miguel's birthday party afterward but now, we must talk about other things. There is so much today…"

"But this is important too," Diego insisted as he turned his attention to Paige. "This is my *godson's first birthday!* We must plan!"

"Diego," Paige calmly replied. "I think we need to plan something but it can wait until later."

"And bouncy castle? Clowns?" Jorge shook his head and reached for a donut in the middle of the table. "We do not need this."

"And clowns…." Jolene spoke loudly over the others. "They are creepy!"

"Oh, yes sir," Marco spoke up from what was once Jesús seat at the table. "My kids, they are frightened by clowns. My daughter, she cries when she even sees one on television."

"Did you hear about that clown that was a pedophile?" Chase cut in and shook his head. "Ughh…."

"You know," Paige jumped in just as Jorge was getting at his wit's end. "Let's keep it simple. He's just a little boy. He doesn't have any friends yet so we don't need a huge party. Maybe some cake, ice cream…"

"Gluten-free cake, right?" Diego cut in as his eyes grew in size.

"Diego, we got your gluten-free…." Jorge pointed in the middle of the table at a dessert. "Whatever the fuck that is…and you barely touched it."

"I'm watching my sugar intake."

Jorge didn't respond at first, merely giving Diego a look.

"Cake, ice cream," Paige repeated and glanced toward Diego. "And a gluten-free cupcake for you."

"Fair," Diego nodded.

"Good!" Jorge said and put his hand in the air. "That is enough! We have wasted 10 or 15 minutes talking about a birthday party for a child who is too young to even know what a birthday *is*. Great job, Diego."

"It *is* important."

"We will plan the time later," Jorge said and shook his head. "Now, we got a lot of important things to talk about."

Diego waved his hand in the air as if to encourage Jorge to go on.

"First of all," Jorge started. "Thank you, Marco, for your help with my neighbor situation. She is gone. *Terminado.*"

"No problem, sir," Marco said with a huge smile. "It was quite simple. I hope this means she will no longer be investigating you."

"I think she got a clear picture of what would happen if she did."

No one commented but shared a knowing smile.

"Makerson's story about buddy in Ottawa was pretty explosive," Chase commented as he glanced at his phone. "There are hundreds of comments on here."

"People, they must see the truth," Jorge remarked. "Plus it will put pressure on those who work for Athas to be more….direct with him. It also allowed us an opportunity to have Makerson expose the homeless deaths that his staff attempted to hide from him."

"I always thought the prime minister knew everything," Chase said as he shook his head. "I can't believe they were purposely killing those people."

"Tourists, they do not like to see these things, you know," Jorge remarked as he finished off his donut. "And tourist season, it is coming up."

"This, it does not surprise me," Jolene replied as she removed her reading glasses and turned her phone off. "When you say that the government kills people secretly, I am not surprised. Governments, they lie. I do not care what country it is."

"This, we agree on," Jorge replied and glanced at Paige. Their eyes met and she nodded.

"Unfortunately, it does get much worse," Jorge continued with some hesitation. "I recently had a conversation with Athas and he….encouraged his people to tell him everything. Apparently, much is hidden from the prime minister for 'his own good' as they say."

"What did he learn?" Jolene asked with big eyes.

"It's bad," Paige replied before Jorge could continue. "It's really bad."

"She is right," Jorge said and glanced at his wife and then at Chase. "The fire, last year? The one that killed the indigenous people?"

"You mean when the government *knew* it was headed their way and did *nothing*," Chase spoke bitterly. "What? Did they fucking set it too?"

Jorge opened his mouth to reply but no words came out.

Although the realization came quickly, it was almost as if time briefly stopped as the naïvety slipped from Chase's eyes once again. Crestfallen, he leaned back slightly and began to shake his head.

"I am afraid," Jorge finally continued to a still room. "That this here, it is true. It was set."

Reactions were mixed around the table but a wave of realization swept over them, quickly removing sorrow and shock, pulling them into a storm of fury.

"I cannot believe…" Jolene spoke sharply with her hands swinging dramatically in the air.

"But, why?" Marco appeared equally angry but confused by this news.

"Are you fucking kidding me?" Diego shot out at the end of the table. "Racist fucks!"

Paige remained silent but had already said everything the previous night after first learning the news.

Chase shook his head and avoided making eye contact with everyone. Much to Jorge's surprise, he stood up from the table and walked out of the room.

"This, it is his people," Jolene muttered once he was out of the room. "This is, as they say, close to home? Is that the expression?"

"Yes, Jolene," Diego snapped.

"You do not have to be nasty, Diego," She snapped back. "I just ask question."

"Maybe one of us should talk to him," Paige offered as she pushed her chair away from the table and Jorge nodded.

"Jolene is right, he is half indigenous so this is his people,"

After Paige left the room, the group fell silent. Jorge attempted to think of what else he had to say but his mind went numb.

"So, Alec, he needs our help," Jolene offered. "Or do they tell him truth now?"

"He said he learned a lot of hard truths," Jorge welcomed the break in silence. "Secrets, manipulation of the media, they kill bills...."

"Who is Bill?" Jolene asked and squinted her eyes. "Is he someone who works with Alec?"

"It is..."

"A bill, Jolene," Diego jumped in. "That means someone creates a bill they want to be passed and rather than letting it go through, they make sure it's tossed out."

"So, like a law?" Jolene asked.

"Yes," Diego nodded.

"I see..."

"Anyway," Jorge picked things back up. "There is so much more that Alec has not told me yet. I want to have a private meeting with him but it is difficult because of his role. He is watched and everything is documented. I am thinking the day of Miguel's party, he can come as a guest and we will use this opportunity to speak in my office."

"Good idea," Diego encouraged. "It'll look like he is just there for the party."

"Now that the neighbor is gone," Jorge continued. "We are less likely to be watched."

"Sir, I am still checking your other neighbors," Marco jumped in and glanced at his iPad. "So far, everything seems normal. Most people are busy with their lives."

"That is good," Jorge replied. "It is exactly what we want."

"And you'll soon have me as a neighbor," Diego reminded him, appearing almost giddy as he talked.

"I want a house too," Jolene insisted. "Everyone, they are moving and I am still a million miles away from you all."

"You're close to Chase," Diego pointed out.

"He does not talk to me much," Jolene commented sourly. "We should live near one another."

"There is a house available down…." Marco started then glanced up at Jorge. "I mean…"

"If there is a house available in their neighborhood, I want to know."

"I don't even like the neighborhood," Jorge confessed. "I feel like I'm smothering."

"But if we live closer to one another," Diego reminded him. "We can keep an eye on each other too. After Jesús…."

Everyone seemed to agree.

"This here, I will think about…." Jorge said and took a deep breath. "What I wish for is to leave Toronto altogether."

"To go where? The boonies?" Diego asked.

"Maybe," Jorge admitted. "Away from the city. This time last year, I was thinking about living a simple life and yet, it gets more complicated every day."

"Where is this house?" Jolene asked Marco, ignoring Jorge, she was staring at her phone.

"Anyway, is there anything else?" Diego asked hurriedly as if to cut off Jolene. "I got an appointment this afternoon."

"Calm down, Diego," Jorge continued and noticed Paige approaching the door. She was alone. "I was also going to say that in the future, I want Our House of Pot to be working with addiction centers and specialists with CBD oil as a way to help addicts. I do not know the details yet but it is something that we will be doing to spite Big Pharma as well as increase our public perception."

"Plus once these former addicts start using our product," Diego continued as Paige walked in and returned to her seat. "They'll continue on their own dime."

"Or the government's," Jorge added as he turned toward his wife. "Either way, we get paid. So, Paige, tell me what happened…"

"We talked and I managed to calm him down a bit but not much…" Paige admitted as she pulled her chair ahead. "He's infuriated, as you can imagine. Now, he's thinking back to other things that have happened to indigenous people and wondering…."

Her voice trailed off but it wasn't necessary that she finish.

"You know what?" Diego jumped in. "I don't blame him."

"It is reminding me more and more of Mexico," Jorge added and reached for his coffee. "But the government here, they keep their hands clean."

"Do you think Makerson will be in danger if he sticks his nose in too far?" Paige suddenly asked. "I mean, Alec is on top of things but what if….."

"I think he will be ok," Jorge replied. "I will discuss this with Alec. But it is too easy for them now. They can blame the entire homeless situation on a dead man and people will feel good, you know, because this man also died from fentanyl. They will say it is karma."

"Karma is a thing," Paige reminded him.

"I will leave that for you and your yoga mat," Jorge teased and the mood lightened. "At any rate, Chase is ok?"

"He is but I can't help but think this might be the straw that broke the camel's back," Paige replied. "We talked more about how he wants to step up."

"Yes, in the past, he has played more of a background role."

"Not anymore," Paige replied. "Even the day we went to Ottawa, he was in with both feet."

"But for me, I also want to do more," Jolene reminded them. "I always tell you.."

"You will be, Jolene," Jorge assured her. "We are a smaller group than we once were. I need all my people."

"I want to get Chase into some different forms of fighting," Paige continued and hesitated. "Something more brutal than what he's been trained in."

"Hey, what is it you do again, Marco?" Jorge asked with interest. "Knife fighting?"

"It is called Arnis but I have not been doing as much lately," Marco confessed. "I would like to get back into it but also, I would like to do Brazilian Jiu-Jitsu."

"I hear that's powerful," Diego commented with wide eyes. "Maybe I should learn this stuff."

"There's a lot of self-discipline involved," Paige said.

"Yeah, I'm not into that," Diego shook his head. "I'll keep going to the gym and using my baseball bat. It works well too."

"And your taser," Jorge added. "Don't forget your taser."

"Best Christmas gift ever!" Diego insisted.

"I want Chase to try something called Line fighting," Paige gently continued. "It's very brutal….if you look it up, you'll see what I mean."

"Sounds like it would be a benefit," Jorge said as he reached for his phone.

"Chase would get a lot out of it," Paige nodded. "And with his size, previous experience with boxing, combined with this…."

"I have heard of this," Marco spoke up as he scrolled through his phone. "It is quite deadly if performed properly."

"Very deadly," Paige agreed. "The US marines used it."

Jorge did a Google search.

"So, he could literally beat someone to death?" Diego asked for clarification.

Paige nodded.

Jorge looked up from his phone and shared a look with his wife.

CHAPTER 11

"Revenge, it is a dish best served cold," Jorge reminded Chase as the two men sat in his office. On the other side of the door, voices could be heard as others gathered at the house to celebrate Miguel's first birthday. "I think you will agree?"

Chase simply nodded. He was a man of few words which in itself was powerful. When he finally did speak, it usually meant something and people listened. Jorge didn't share his restraint.

"Now," Jorge leaned forward on his desk. "Of course, I will learn more when Alec arrives a little later for the party. The day we spoke, he was not in no mood to get into details so perhaps now, he will offer more information."

"I want to know who's idea it was," Chase spoke tensely. "Who thought it would be ok to kill those women and children…knowing they had no way out."

"*Amigo,*" Jorge said as he leaned back in his chair. "I agree. That fire was horrific but it does show the prejudice of the Canadian government. They may talk multiculturalism and diversity but yet, here we are."

"Here we are," Chase repeated. "And all this, to send a message to the indigenous community…to *my* people to keep our mouths shut."

Jorge observed Chase. The pockets of naïvety in his eyes were now a lake of polluted waters that overflowed, hardening his features. There was a tension that tightened his entire face like that of a man ready for a battle. This was what he needed to enter the war zone.

"Chase, I have spoken openly since Jesús passed," He hesitated and glanced at his phone. "I have spoken openly about legacy and what is important to leave behind. My son, out there, my daughter, they are my legacy. My company, it is my legacy but yet, even more important, is my strength, my power, my force…this here, it is who I am and even in my death, it is important that everyone knows what I stood for and what I stood up against."

Chase's face softened and he nodded.

"We will have many battles in the upcoming months," Jorge said as he checked his phone. "For you, this here, it is a battle and we will learn who was responsible. For me, for all of us, we must focus on finding the person who had Jesús murdered. I promised Paige at the time that we would end the war but I simply cannot let this one go because if the tables were turned, Jesús would seek revenge for me."

"He would've killed your killer," Chase spoke quietly, his head tilted down and his eyes focusing up. "Which you have done, so who are you going after?"

"There are others because this man, he was not a lone wolf," Jorge insisted. "It is important that we take care of the people who have hurt our family. We will find them and take them down in one, huge swoop."

"How?"

"This is not something I have figured out yet," Jorge replied. "I have asked Marco to do some research. We do know a couple of key members. He will learn more about them, who else is involved and a location we can get them together. This here is key to avoid retaliation."

Chase nodded and looked away.

"Unfortunately, my fear is that some innocent people may get in the crossfire," Jorge admitted. "As innocent people often do. But we are trying to learn more before we strike and it is my wish that we can do so with as little collateral damage as possible."

"I want to avoid that," Chase spoke honestly. "I don't want to hurt innocent people."

Jorge nodded but his own thoughts were elsewhere. Glancing at his phone again he started to rise.

"Alec, he is here," Jorge commented. "Turn off your phone."

"Do you want me to leave?" Chase started to stand.

"No, not yet," Jorge replied as he headed toward the door to find Alec on the other side. Without saying a word, he rushed past Jorge and glanced at Chase.

"This feels wrong."

"What?" Jorge asked as he gestured toward his desk to indicate they sit down. He noted that Chase nodded at Alec who returned the gesture as he found a seat. Closing the door, he returned to his desk.

"Your son's first birthday," Alec said with a shrug. "And we're in here talking about…"

"Believe me," Jorge said as he sat behind his desk. "My son, when he is a man, he will understand why this conversation took place today. And I assure you, we will get back out there before they cut the cake."

"My people are outside," Alec pointed toward the window. "I'm being watched 24/7 by security, by the media….by everyone. I can't get away."

"That is why we are talking now," Jorge reminded him. "You're innocently enjoying a child's birthday party. Who could question your motivation?"

"I hope Miguel has a lot of parties coming up," Alec commented as he relaxed in his chair. "Cause I have a feeling I'm going to have a lot to discuss with you."

"Do tell."

"Let's start," Chase cut in and turned toward Alec. "Let's start with the indigenous community that was set on fire. Who wanted it done?"

Alec didn't reply at first but stared at Chase, his eyes eventually softened as he briefly looked away.

"It was a woman named Harriet-Siegel Noble and.."

"Wait, it was a woman?" Chase appeared surprised. "I thought…"

"Women, they are evil too," Jorge reminded him and watched Chase struggle with the news. "Do not assume that all girls, they are made with sugar and spice, as the nursery rhyme suggests."

"But a woman," Chase shook his head. "Wanted to kill these people. This community was made up mostly *of* women and children?"

Alec appeared hesitant to respond but eventually nodded.

"She believed that people would assume it was just another fire," Alec replied and glanced between the two men. "That no one would ever question it."

"But why?" Chase countered. "I don't understand."

"To send a message," Jorge reminded him. "So the others, they do not talk."

"She's since crossed the floor to join the opposition," Alec continued. "The plan was to make sure the truth got out and it brought down the government. She was working closely with one of the former prime minister's people, someone who apparently had an ax to grind"

"So, she used *that* community and killed those people to send a message?" Chase asked as a new pot of rage began to boil.

"Many of them were activist," Alec continued after some hesitation. "They were very vocal in the media about the lack of government support when it comes to issues like unsafe drinking water, missing indigenous women and children and environmental bills being killed. Other indigenous communities were starting to see that they also had a voice and were joining in."

"So this would shut them up," Chase added.

Alec nodded and looked away and Chase glanced toward Jorge.

"So tell me, Chase," He immediately picked up the conversation. "Do you have hesitations because it is a woman who made these decisions?"

"Are we sure?" Chase turned toward Alec.

"Yes," Alec spoke confidently and he shared a look with Chase. "I can assure you. No one is keeping secrets from me now."

"I'm not backing down," Chase replied. "Who is she? What do we know?"

"Well…" Alec stared but Jorge was already jumping in.

"I found her online," He glanced down at the screen, raised an eyebrow and turned his laptop around to show Chase. "She looks quite young. With a name like Harriet, I was expecting some old lady but this here, she looks young."

"In her late 30s," Alec responded.

"Single?" Jorge asked as he glanced at Chase.

"I believe so," Alec answered and his voice trailed off. "But I really don't know…she's not married."

"Close enough," Jorge replied as he shared a look with Chase. "This here, it should be easy for you, *amigo.*"

Chase appeared deep in thought but didn't respond other than to say he was going to rejoin the party, leaving Alec and Jorge alone in the office.

"So, this meeting, it must've been pretty explosive," Jorge commented with a grin on his face. "Your people, they talk now?"

"There are no more secrets," Alec insisted. "I was clear on the matter."

"I would hope they are smart enough to read between the lines, no?"

"I think they got the message," Alec replied and took a deep breath. "Look, I can't get into everything today. I'm still learning a lot myself but there's so much….*so much* that Canadians don't know. So much hidden information. I'm having meetings with different individuals, in private."

"But you must know some…"

"I learned a great deal already," Alec replied. "There's a lot of hidden meetings, affairs, death…"

"So me, I did not bring a new concept to your government," Jorge teased with a grin on his face as he leaned back in his chair, somewhat satisfied with himself.

"It doesn't appear so, no," Alec replied with some desperation in his voice. "This isn't the first secret mass murder that the government was behind and I suspect, it won't be the last."

"Ah yes," Jorge nodded. "And the homeless people…."

"They aren't the only ones," Alec offered with no further explanation. "But I think that problem has been…contained…"

"Yes, well me," Jorge replied and gestured toward himself. "I solve problems."

"I can't deny that."

"People," Jorge continued introspectively. "They talk about wanting friends in high places but they forget, it is often the friends in low places that are the most helpful in…certain situations."

"I need some help with something else," Alec spoke sheepishly. "It's a bit of a more….personal…sensitive nature."

"Oh, is this so?" Jorge couldn't help but demonstrate his power in Alec's moment of weakness. "Does this here involve an intern, a cigar…a stained dress or something of that nature?"

Although he was teasing Alec, under the assumption that their ideas of a 'sensitive nature' were perhaps vastly different, it quickly became clear by the look on the prime minister's face that perhaps he wasn't so far off track.

And that was the day that Jorge Hernandez knew he *owned* Alec Athas and the entire Canadian government.

This would be part of his legacy.

CHAPTER 12

"So he's getting sucked off every day at 3 p.m. and the taxpayer is paying for it?" Diego asked before his head fell back in laughter. "And he's trying to write it off as a 'meditation expense'? Are you fucking kidding me?"

"I am not kidding you, Diego," Jorge insisted as he watched his *hermano* gleefully absorb the information. "This here, it is our government. We're apparently paying for his daily stress release."

"Is *that* what he told you?" Diego asked as he leaned forward as if to invite more details. "That he's got some woman…or wait, it was a woman, wasn't it?"

"Oh Diego," Jorge shook his head and raised his eyebrows. "For a moment there, I see hope in your eyes but I am sorry to tell you that it *was* a woman that's crawling under his desk every day. The Greek God likes women, not men."

Diego shrugged and twisted his mouth up in disappointment.

"And this here," Jorge continued as he moved his chair ahead. "This will be our ticket to owning the government *and* Athas because we are to make sure it does not get out there, to the public."

"Why would it?" Diego asked. "As far as everyone knows, it's just meditation."

"He did not realize until after the fact that this woman was selected for a reason," Jorge replied. "Apparently one of his staff said she was quite well-known in the meditation world and he didn't question it. Turns out, she's popular in another world too. She comes to his office and when her meditation exercises aren't working…she decides to try a different method."

Diego's eyes widened as a grin returned to his face.

"So, it seems it was on purpose," Jorge continued. "Who knew that our nation's leader makes so many enemies within his own party."

"See this here, is the part that confuses me," Diego commented and tilted his head. "Why is his own party going against him."

"Because when a story like this breaks," Jorge spoke innocently. "It is only him that pays. No one looks at the details beyond the headlines and that is what his party is counting on. Also, Alec, he is often not doing what big corporations want so they sometimes give incentives to people within his own party to bring him down."

"Then he's got to get rid of those people."

"See this here, is a problem," Jorge said. "If he suddenly gets rid of another key staffer, there are a lot of questions asked. That person may talk and everything goes to shit."

"So no one's getting the bullet" Diego got right to the point.

"This time," Jorge answered. "I do not think we should kill. It would be too soon. It would look suspicious if Alec's team starts dropping dead too close together. No, for this one, I think blackmail."

"As in?"

"I must talk to Marco before he leaves," Jorge considered. "If some sensitive photos or information were to turn up on this key staffer's computer, I would think that Alec could hold this over his head and show *compassion* by keeping it under wraps. Especially if whatever is found could cause the police to become involved."

"A secret for a secret?" Diego nodded, his lips twisted with a look of satisfaction. "Good idea."

"Sometimes problems," Jorge continued. "They have simple answers. This one is easy."

"And Alec, you own him," Diego pointed out.

"I already owned him," Jorge insisted. "But now, I own him and the whole goddamn government. To a point, I always did but now, I got his balls on the line. The key is to find someone's vulnerable spot. And this here, it is his."

A quick message from Paige encouraged the two men to return to the party before they brought out Miguel's cake. Jorge found Marco and leaned in to let him know that he had a task for him.

"Yes, sir," He quickly agreed. "Just tell me what it is."

"We will discuss it later," Jorge replied. "But right now, I must make a speech."

Watching Miguel bouncing excitedly in his high chair as Paige carried in a large birthday cake with a toy from his favorite cartoon in the middle, Jorge couldn't help but smile. Beside him was Maria who was talking to Miguel with wide eyes as Paige moved the cake closer for the child. Everyone started to sing *Happy Birthday*. The room was full of joy as the family enjoyed a rare celebration together.

Watching his wife set the cake down, she proceeded to light the one, lone candle and Jorge moved closer to his family.

"I would like to thank everyone who has joined us for Miguel's first birthday," He spoke with warmth in his voice as he looked at the small group gathered around the table. Alec nervously glanced at his phone while on the opposite side of the room, Chase was clearly upset. Marco seemed lost in thought while he sat with his own family, who appeared excited to be there. Juliana and Clara were nearby, both beaming at the little boy. Jolene gushed over her godson while Diego was observing the others. His *familia* was as he expected.

"We have had some beautiful moments in the last year," Jorge continued while everyone listened. "And we've had some heartbreaks. I wish that our former associate, Jesús, he was with us today but I know, he is with us in spirit."

Sensing the despair in the room, Jorge felt it was necessary to increase the morale.

"We are family here," Jorge insisted. "Because family, it is not necessarily your blood relatives but the people who are there when you need them or, in a day such as this one, gather to celebrate a special occasion. This day last year, most of you met our son for the first time and shared in our joy. It is an experience like this one that bonds us and although Jolene and Diego are his godparents, I know that all of you would be there for Miguel if he ever needed you. For this, I thank you. *Gracias!*"

"I think it's time to cut the cake," Paige gently commented as Miguel leaned forward in his high chair as if trying to reach for the toy surrounded by blue frosting. "Or we're going to have a crying baby on our hands."

"Of course!" Jorge laughed and others joined in. "Maria, will you help your brother blow out the candle."

"I will!" Maria said and leaned forward to do so before kissing her brother. Everyone clapped.

Paige started to cut the cake, placing the first piece before Miguel, who immediately dug his hand in and proceeded to smear it on his face. He began to giggle causing a ripple of laughter throughout the room.

"I'll pass them out," Maria sang out as Paige continued to cut the cake.

"Maria," Jorge glanced towards Marco's kids. "Why don't you take the children outside on the patio? It is such a beautiful day."

"I can go with them," Marco's wife politely commented. "You have such a beautiful house, Mr. Hernandez."

"Thank you!" He gave her an infectious smile and gestured around him. "Please make yourself at home!"

After Marco's family and Maria went outside, the others enjoyed some cake and coffee. While everyone was all smiles outside, inside, the room was full of unease.

"Let us not think about work right now," He warned and glanced at his son, who was now covered in cake. "Miguel! You are supposed to eat the cake not wear it."

His son laughed as if it was a hilarious joke. Paige smiled as she reached for the toy in the center of the cake. Miguel plunked it in the middle of his cake and giggled.

"I guess that's the best we can hope for," She remarked.

"This is all my children's first birthdays," Marco announced with laughter in his voice. "Sir, they do enjoy making a mess."

"So does his father," Diego jumped in. "Just a different kind of mess." Everyone laughed.

"And it is much harder to clean," Jolene piped up and everyone laughed harder.

"The cake, *Señora* Hernandez," Juliana said as she pointed toward the blue icing on Miguel's face. "I can clean him."

"Juliana, you're off today," Paige reminded her. "He's fine. Besides, if you try to separate him from his new toy, he's going to cry."

"Never take a man's favorite toy away from him," Diego commented with raised eyebrows as he glanced at Alec. "Or all hell will break loose."

Jorge noted that Diego appeared gleeful and powerful, whereas Alec deflated.

"Well, you know," Jorge added. "Each man finds his pleasures in a different way."

Just then, Maria excitedly rushed back into the house.

"Chase, I'm about to sing a song for the children," She spoke with wide eyes. "You gotta come to watch!"

Distracted, Chase slowly took in the information and glanced toward Jorge. "Umm...yeah, sure."

Rising from his chair, he started toward the patio and Maria rushed ahead and grabbed his hand, walking him outside. Jorge grimaced and shared a look with Paige.

"My daughter, I do not like this crush she has on Chase," He complained after she closed the door. "And now, she wants to go to a co-ed school. Because this is what I need, my daughter surrounded by boys all day."

"Oh," Marco made a face. "I can understand, sir."

"Well, at least with Chase," Paige was quick to point out. "We know she's safe."

Jorge thought for a moment.

"This here, it reminds me of the issue we talked about earlier Alec," He commented, noting that Juliana and Clara moved away from their conversation and were drinking coffee in the living room, having their own discussion. "I am thinking that maybe this man, he will have......immoral photos in his government computer. Perhaps something that is illegal and shameful at the same time."

Alec perked up at the comment.

"This is what I was hoping you could help me with, Marco," Jorge continued. "Maybe something with children."

"Jorge," Paige made a face.

"Not *young* children," Jorge corrected his wife. "But slightly underaged, nothing too suggestive but suggestive enough that he will keep his fucking mouth shut. That is all we need."

"Blackmail?" Alec asked. "That would work."

"What is this here?" Jolene shook her head. "Why do I not know anything about this?"

"I'll tell you on the way home," Diego glanced at his sister then turned his attention back at Jorge. "It's an easy problem to fix."

"Don't worry Jolene," Paige muttered to the Colombian as she now tried to wipe her son's face with a paper towel. "I'm a bit lost too."

"I will fill you in on everything later, *mi amor.*"

Jorge noted that Alec turned white with the sudden realization that Paige would soon learn about his immoral behavior. Ahh! The prince has become a commoner.

"It is a small matter," Jorge brushed it aside. "Especially now that we know the woman who decided to set that indigenous community on fire."

Paige stopped cleaning her son's face. Miguel continued to play as his parent's shared a silent look.

CHAPTER 13

"You look like the cat that ate the canary," Paige observed as she climbed into bed beside Jorge. "Dare I ask?"

"Ah, Paige, you know me," He replied as he placed his phone on the nightstand and turned toward her. "There is never a moment wasted. It has been a beautiful day."

"Besides your son's birthday party, you mean?" She gently inquired. "There seemed to be a lot of meetings at the party. Jolene was getting suspicious."

"Suspicious or paranoid because she was not included?" Jorge asked as Paige yawned. "Knowing Jolene, most likely the latter."

"She doesn't feel you regard her the same way as the men," Paige reminded him. "Like it's an 'old boys' club and not inclusive."

"It is not that," Jorge insisted. "Chase, I had to talk to because I found out who decided to burn down the indigenous community. I wanted to have a private meeting to discuss it. Then later, Alec comes to me with his problems and then Diego popped in before I could get out of the office…."

"What is the deal with Alec?" She inquired. "There seemed some tension during the party. Do I want to know?"

Jorge thought for a moment. The idea of Paige knowing the immoral details of Alec's vulnerability certainly gave him some satisfaction but on second thought, it was best that he reveal nothing. He suspected Alec would assume Jorge told Paige everything and in a panic, reveal the story on his own.

"It is nothing, *mi amor,*" Jorge responded and stretched. "Just some more problems with his staff but nothing we cannot handle. There is a plan in place."

Leaning in, he kissed her before she could ask any more questions. His phone beeped, causing him to move away.

"This here, it better be good," He picked it up. "Ah, it is Marco. We have a meeting at the bar tomorrow morning. That man, he is worth his weight in gold."

"His family is nice," Paige commented as Jorge replaced his phone on the nightstand. "I'm glad you could help them with a house."

"He does a lot of work at home," Jorge shrugged. "He needed a nice place to do so, a private office. This allows him to do so."

"His wife thanked me multiple times during the party," Paige smiled. "She said that his income allows her to stay home with the children. If she's suspicious about why you do so much for Marco, she's not saying."

"She has a beautiful home," Jorge replied as he turned toward his wife. "This here is what she wanted. Why would she ask questions?"

"Why indeed," Paige replied. "So the meeting tomorrow, what's it about?"

"I believe Marco may have learned more information about this lady who gave orders to burn down the indigenous community last year. Chase is determined to seek justice on behalf of his people."

"He's been a passionate participant in his lessons too," Paige referred to the Line fighting being taught to him 3 nights a week. "The instructor has reported to me that he shows the same cold dissociation as someone in the marines."

"Ah, yes!" Jorge nodded. "These people are brainwashed to see others as the enemy and to kill, ask questions later. This here, it will be useful. I think Chase might become our strongest soldier yet."

"It's such a huge change from who he used to be," Paige reminded him.

"This is true," Jorge replied. "However, you must know that he is still uncomfortable with guns. But as I say to him, you do not need a gun to take care of a problem. You must be…creative."

It was that same creativity that would surprise Jorge the next morning when he joined Marco and Chase, who was already in a meeting when he arrived. Jorge saw this as a positive step. It showed that his army was becoming more independent which also meant it allowed him to step back. Although he wasn't quite ready to retire from the mayhem, Jorge did believe that it was time to start becoming more of an observer and less of an instigator.

"I see you started the meeting without me," Jorge announced upon walking into the empty bar. "Please tell me you're about to present me with some solutions. I'm still exhausted from Miguel's birthday party. My son last night, he was like ten Diego's hyper on coffee."

The two men laughed at Jorge's comment as he sat on a stool.

"Oh, sir, they can be exhausting," Marco replied. "There are days, I am more tired at home with my family than at work."

"This here, I can see," Jorge replied as Chase passed him a cup of coffee. "My son, he was like a roaring fire all day. You would think that a child's party would be relaxing and easy."

"Children, they are never easy, sir," Marco corrected him and Jorge noted Chase was also grinning. "At this age, you cannot turn away for a second."

"There is a reason why people have babies young," Jorge insisted as he stirred cream into his coffee. "This here, I am too old for. But Miguel, he is a blessing."

"My wife, she was very appreciative of your invitation yesterday," Marco continued to speak enthusiastically. "Her and the kids, they had a great time. Your daughter, Maria, she is good with children."

"She loves kids," Jorge replied. "I am happy everyone had fun."

Chase remained quiet and although he listened to their conversation with interest, it was almost as if he wasn't in the room at all. His eyes were vacant. If Jorge had an army, this would soon be his general.

"So Chase, tell me," Jorge seemed to break the trance. "Did you enjoy yourself yesterday? Maria was perhaps more excited you were there than over the party itself."

Chase grinned but didn't respond.

"Ok, so we must move on," Jorge decided to switch gears. "What is it we know today, Marco?"

"Well, sir, we know a few new things," He replied and reached for the iPad that sat beside him and started to tap the screen. "We know that everything is in place for Mr. Athas."

"Does he know?" Jorge asked.

"He soon will, sir," Marco explained as he showed Jorge some images involving teenaged girls. "This here, it is on the computer of Alec's employee, the man who has decided to blackmail him. Mr. Athas can easily take care of this problem today."

"Ah! *Perfecto!*" Jorge immediately grabbed his phone and sent Alec a message that referenced the birthday party. It wasn't about the birthday party. "This here, Marco, will resolve the situation Athas has found himself in."

"In reality," Chase cut in. "He *put* himself in that situation."

"Yes, but he is merely a man," Jorge said with a shrug after he saw that the message went through. "A man, he can be weak. We've all been there, am I right?"

Chase looked away.

"Now, moving on," Jorge rushed things along. "What else you got for me?"

"Sir, I have hacked this lady's email," Marco glanced at his screen and started to tap and slide his finger across the iPad. "This Harriet Siegel-Noble? We know that she lives and works out of Ottawa however, it does seem that she will be in the GTA next week for an event. We must find a way for Chase to meet her."

"I was reading some of her emails and it seems like she is meticulous about her schedule," Chase replied and glanced at Marco, who was nodding. "So we looked it up and found out the exact times I can cross paths with her."

Impressed, Jorge nodded.

"I'll try to work my magic," Chase continued and paused for a moment. "If that don't work, I have a plan B for the next day."

"No Plan B," Jorge shook his head. "Only plan A. Make it work."

Chase looked away and Marco glanced at his screen as if to avoid the awkwardness.

"Where will you be crossing paths?" Jorge decided to dig in even though he was only mildly interested, his thoughts elsewhere.

"At the gym," Chase replied almost as if it were a question. This lack of confidence concerned Jorge. "She goes every day. When in Toronto, there's one particular place she has a membership. From what I read in her Facebook messages, I suspect she's as much there to meet men as she is to get in shape."

"Is that so?" Jorge was suddenly interested again. "This here, it could be easy for you."

"I hope," Chase replied.

"No, you don't hope, you *know* so," Jorge insisted and noted Marco nodding his head. Chase didn't reply. At the end of the day, he had no horse in this race but Jorge would be there if needed. In a way, it was a test. His audition tape to join the club. The *real* club.

Back in his SUV, Jorge began to think of the things Chase wasn't considering. He had to be cautious about the details and it suddenly became obvious how he could kill two birds with one stone.

Glancing at his contacts, he selected a number.

"*Hola?*" Jolene's voice filled up the SUV as Jorge backed out of his parking space behind the club.

"Jolene, I need your help with something," Jorge jumped right in. "Go to the club and talk to Chase. We just had a meeting so ask him to fill you in. He mustn't make any errors."

"Ah, ok," Jolene spoke with a serious voice. "This I can do."

"And Jolene," Jorge quickly added. "Remember the devil is in the details. Make sure everything is covered."

"With you, the devil is everywhere," Jolene spoke in her husky tone before she started to laugh exaggeratedly.

"Make sure his plan is executed properly," Jorge replied as a grin crossed his lips. "I am counting on you."

She knew what that meant. Their conversation ended. It was up to her to make sure Chase didn't fuck up. He was still an amateur when it came to murder. The key was to make it easy for the police to write off quickly with little investigation. Something told Jorge that Chase's passion in this situation may work against him as much as it would work for him.

Stopped at a light, he hit another number. The phone rang.

"Hello," Diego's voice echoed through the car. "I got a problem that I need your help with."

"Diego, this here, is my line not yours," Jorge spoke bluntly. "I called you, remember?"

"I can't get my house!" Diego ignored him.

"What do you mean?" Jorge asked. "I thought you negotiated with the owner and he agreed to sell it to you?"

"He did and it's a done deal," Diego replied. "But now, it'll take forever to close the deal, for them to move their shit out…."

"Diego, you are so impatient," Jorge reminded him. "This gives you time to plan, *mi amigo.* You can decide on new furniture, maybe find a decorator….."

"I'm gay, I don't need no fucking decorator!" Diego complained. "I need my house!"

"Diego, relax," Jorge couldn't help but laugh. "This here, it will be soon. Meanwhile, plan the changes you wish to make, dream up a housewarming party….you know, pack up your stuff, figure out a way to get those God awful lime trees out of your condo without hurting anyone."

"They *are* getting big," Diego replied. "Can I bring them to your house for now? In case they get too big *to* move."

"Very well, Diego," Jorge shook his head. "*Hermano,* this is not why I call you today. I need your help."

"Oh?"

"Chase, he has something he must do," Jorge spoke carefully. "Can you drop by the bar and talk to him and Jolene about it. I want Jolene and Chase to take care of the details, I need you to….see any potential issues and perhaps help them…you know, clean up after the party…."

It was a code. There was no party. But there would definitely be a cleanup.

CHAPTER 14

"Politicians, they are puppets on a shelf, waiting to be bought," Jorge Hernandez announced in his usual abrupt tone, his dark eyes carefully monitoring each member of the group as they sat around the boardroom table. "They just got a different price tags."

Paige gave a haunting smile while the others hung to Jorge's every word and Chase merely observed, saying nothing. If he had learned one thing at an early age, it was that it was better to stay quiet. Saying too much as a child got him hit and as an adult, got him in awkward situations. It was better to remain silent.

"And Chase," Jorge's focus was suddenly on him. "About that lady, you know…"

"Harriet?" Chase asked and felt his strength temporarily weaken. "I'm taking care of it."

"Everything is planned?" Jorge asked with some doubt on his face. "You are sure?"

"Yes," Chase replied with certainty in his voice, if not his heart. "After what she did to that indigenous community, killing those people. I think she gets…what she gets."

He finished his sentence with such severity that it appeared to assure Jorge as he leaned back slightly, his head slowly nodding.

"Well, ok," Jorge appeared satisfied. "You are right to do so. This woman is a racist and a killer."

"Did you see some of the emails," Diego suddenly spoke up from the end of the table, lurching forward, his eyes bulging. "She wanted them dead because there were rumors they wanted to sue the government…"

"Ok, Diego," Jorge put his hand up as a grin crossed his lips. "We do not need to go over this again. The point here is that Chase, he must do what he must do. And as always, we support him."

"This lady, she is evil," Jolene spoke up loudly beside Chase. He could smell her perfume as she waved her arms around. "She do not care about those poor people…"

Chase didn't speak. It infuriated him to even think of an entire indigenous community dying as a result of pure malice. He hadn't realized the vile nature of politics. His naïvety continued to fade away.

"It was terrible," Paige spoke in a soft voice that appeared to spark something in Jorge, who automatically turned toward his wife and touched her arm.

"This here, we will take care of," Jorge insisted, focusing his attention on Marco. "The cameras?"

"They will be turned off, sir," He enthusiastically replied. "I have them set to turn off at the time stated."

"It's a busy gym," Chase added in. "Private showers. That's all I need."

He was in a trance for most of the meeting, his thoughts elsewhere. When it ended, Chase felt robotic as he left the room, merely focused on getting out of that room. Outside, he would finally be able to breathe again.

In a way, Harriet Siegel-Noble represented anyone who had ever hurt vulnerable people, exceeding her power in the evilest way possible. However, the fact that a woman could orchestrate the death of children, of other women was almost unimaginable to him. His distrust for the fairer sex had grown throughout his adult life, much to his disappointment. He wanted to believe that women were better people but they continually proved him wrong.

Once in his car, Chase glanced at his phone to see if either of his sons replied to his texts; they hadn't. When his ex-wife insisted that his elementary school level children needed smartphones, he thought it was ridiculous. The devices would become an overpriced toy. However, when she reminded him of the school shootings and other safety issues, he relented and bought them each one. Now they ignored his texts and calls.

Detachment never got easier. You just got used to the sting. It was that familiar feeling, like the morning after a boxing match when you woke up wondering if your head was about to explode. It wasn't comfortable. It wasn't easy. It became the new normal. It was familiar and there was something about familiarity that was comforting in a twisted way.

As he drove to the bar, Chase thought about the words he read in Harriet's emails. She was cold. Her pictures on Facebook told the story of a woman who was the life of the party, surrounded by friends, always smiling, having a good time. When he read the messages in her hacked account, Chase quickly discovered a woman who was willing to do anything to get ahead. She didn't care about anyone but herself.

Indians are just fucking animals, not people.

Those were the words that made Chase's blood boil in fury. She was attempting to justify killing an entire community by dehumanizing them. If they weren't real people in her eyes, she felt justified in allowing them to die in the fire. Although he didn't know anyone in that community, they were still *his* people. Chase hadn't spent much time with the indigenous side of the family as a child but as an adult, he recognized the signs of a community forgotten by society. He understood that there was a certain level of poverty that changed who you were and how you viewed the world. It wasn't easy to get out of that place. These people weren't given a chance.

It was only that evening when he headed to the gym that Chase began to have second thoughts. Was he any better if he killed her? Perhaps a threat would do? He had the information needed to hold it over her head… but could he? Chase knew he wasn't as powerful or intimidating as Jorge Hernandez and even mimicking him wouldn't create the same effect as that of a man who had killed many without as much as batting an eyelash. There was even a moment, as he walked into the gym and spotted the redhead across the room that Chase had a voice deep inside him suggest that this decision would define who he was as a person.

That voice quickly disappeared. There was something about the detached look in the beady blue eyes behind the glasses as he passed the bike she was on that said it all. She glanced at him with disdain on her face, perhaps recognizing that he was half-indigenous, something many others were never certain about. They would take stabs at his ethnicity, often confused because he looked caucasian and yet, there was something else there that they could never quite put their fingers on.

But she knew. It was the way her eyes slanted and her nose curled up that suggested that his original idea to seduce her was highly unlikely.

He quietly went to work, spending a brief amount of time on various machines in the room, each allowing him a different angle to watch her. Chase noted that she was chatting up a man on the next bike. Leaning over in such a way that displayed her cleavage, batting her eyelashes in a flirtatious manner, her intentions were less than pure.

It was when she rose from the bike and leaned in to speak to the man next to her, that Chase took notice. She walked toward the private showers in the back and after a minute, the man followed her. Chase glanced around the room to note everyone was in their own world. Watching their phones, most with their ears plugged to avoid everyone else, it suddenly hit him that these self-involved phone addicts were very much to his benefit. No one was paying attention. No one cared.

He headed in the same direction as Harriet and the man, catching them both walking into the private shower room together. The muffled sound of two people locked in a passionate moment was easy to hear. Fortunately, no one was around to notice Chase lurking outside. The noises became less and muffled as the water began to run. Harriet hardly attempted to hide evidence of her pleasure while Chase slid into the next room, the door ajar until he finally heard her door open. He pretended not to notice a man walking nude, holding his clothes, heading toward the main dressing room.

Chase carefully slid into her shower room, using his shirt sleeve to open the door. Glancing at the floor, he noted her clothes were still thrown in a pile. The shower was still on. Her glasses were on the sink. She was nearsighted. According to her prescription, she couldn't see her hand in front of her face. This would work.

Locking the door behind him, Chase removed his clothes and quietly walked toward the shower. He used a towel to open the door and quickly noted her back was to him. Glancing over her shoulder, he felt his heart race.

"I figured you'd be back," Harriet giggled in a girlish way that made his mind leap to her Facebook profile. She was the kind of woman who wanted stories to tell her friends on the sly. She thought this would be one of them. She thought wrong.

"I need a little extra attention today," She insisted as she lifted her arms in the air, subtly pushing out her ass as the water flowed down her lean body. Chase quietly approached, the warm water touched his skin. "It's been a stressful week."

Without saying a word, Chase wrapped his right arm around her neck, slowly allowing his hand to wander toward her breasts while his left hand slid around her waist and quickly moved down to caress her most vulnerable spot. She closed her eyes and began to moan, moving against his hand as her pleasure began to build, he squeezed her left breast and she let out an exaggerated gasp. He could feel her on the edge as her arms dropped to her sides and in one swift move, he entrapped them with his left arm while tightly wrapping his right arm around her throat.

"How did it feel to kill those people," He whispered calmly. Her eyes sprang opened and he tightened his grip, making it impossible to wiggle away. He knew he had the advantage physically. "If you make a sound, I will snap your fucking neck."

A soft moan came from the back of her throat, a whimper as tears formed in her eyes. They weren't for the community she had burnt to the ground though. They were for herself.

"How did it feel? You haven't answered me," Chase continued to whisper as the water ran down his body. He felt filthy and disgusting even touching this vile woman. "To kill those children?"

Her sobs became stronger now as she grew weak in his arms and his grip tightened so that she couldn't move. She gasped, struggling to breathe. Defenseless, he had originally feared that at this movement, he would have a change of heart. That when her life was literally in his hands, his views on Harriet Siegel-Noble would soften. But instead, he felt anger flowing through his veins, a power that caused his heart to pound with ferocity as if he were being reborn.

"How do you live with yourself?" Chase continued as she made one last-ditch attempt to get away but he was simply too strong so the fight was futile.

"Please," She whimpered.

"How do you think those kids felt, knowing they couldn't escape a burning house?" Chase continued. "Knowing they were going to die? How do you think that feels, you cold-hearted bitch?"

Feeling his anger building, he suddenly grew furious at the sight of her showing vulnerability, that she had the nerve to be scared in light of what she did to those defenseless people.

"How do you think it feels, knowing you're going to die?" He asked and without giving it a second thought, Chase tightened his grip around her neck until she finally was limb in his arms. He dropped her on the ground, staring at her for a moment before turning around and walking out.

CHAPTER 15

"I thought I'd feel bad," Chase spoke candidly with Jorge later that night. The two sat alone in his office, each with a drink in their hand. "I don't. I don't even worry about the police knocking down my door. I don't...I can't explain it but I feel nothing."

"But Chase, think for a moment," Jorge spoke thoughtfully, as he observed his student. "Why would you assume you would feel this way?"

Chase considered his question. It wasn't because he had viewed it when Jorge and the others killed. He had witnessed more than one murder courtesy of his associates. There was a silent period that followed, a few moments where everyone looked at the victim with their own, private thoughts but he had never seen remorse. No tears, no regrets, no second-guessing. Not even once.

"I guess...." Chase finally answered, taking a deep breath. "Television? I mean, I don't know why I thought I would feel bad.."

"Ah, yes, the media," Jorge replied with laughter in his voice. "They do love to tell us how we are to feel in every situation, am I correct? And when you do not, well then you feel guilty for being abnormal. This is something I learned long ago. The media, *amigo,* it lies. It lies about who we are, those Christian values, you know?"

Chase silently nodded. A chill ran through his spine and he attempted to shake it off.

"Now, I must ask," Jorge continued and sat forward in his chair. "Were you careful to remove fingerprints? Did anyone see anything?"

"I didn't hide that I was in the gym," Chase began. "As Diego and Jolene pointed out, I can't. But I also have no connection to this woman. No one saw us speaking. No one saw me come out of her stall. The cameras in the entire building were off. I left when others left, so it looked like maybe we were a group. I used a sleeve or towel to open or close the door to her stall."

Jorge nodded.

"People may have seen her with the other guy," Chase continued. "He followed her into the shower. It will be his…..DNA if any. Plus, how much gets washed away? Even if anything tracing me to her is found, once again, no cameras so maybe I had a shower before her. I assure you, no one was paying attention. Everyone was in their own world."

Satisfied, Jorge tilted his head to the side.

"I have no reason to think they can link this to me."

"If they did," Jorge was quick to jump in. "I assure you, my lawyers, they will get you out. There is absolutely no reason you'd be involved. But the police, they will take the easy road. This other man, that's the most logical solution and believe me, that's where the investigation stops."

He was right. The next morning, news of high power government official found dead in a shower hit the media. Jorge sent a cryptic message to Chase who merely replied that he was on his way to the club. Meanwhile, there were reports of one man being questioned but no leads.

"And life, it goes on," Jorge said to Paige as the news played in the next room. He watched her feeding their son and smiled. "At least, for some."

"He did good," Paige was slow to respond as she attempted to regain Miguel's attention, which was diverted more times than not. "I was a little concerned that maybe he'd change his mind…"

"I did not," Jorge insisted. "I saw the passion in his eyes, the hatred when he spoke of this woman. There is a point where a man cannot turn back. He crossed that line long before he entered that gym."

"Last day of school!" Maria loudly announced as she rushed into the room. "Well, before exams. And next year, *Papa*, remember I want to go to a co-ed school."

"I do recall you mentioning a few hundred times," Jorge spoke curtly. "Yes, Maria, we will discuss this later. Let us first just finish this school year. When will you receive a report card?"

"A week after exams," She shrugged and headed to the fridge, where she pulled out a container of yogurt and some strawberries. "And *Papa*, this summer I want to take a self-defense course or some martial arts thing. You know, like Chase is doing."

"Well, *bonita,* Chase he is doing some pretty intense fighting," Jorge chose his words carefully, glancing at Paige. "We will look into self-defense if you wish."

"No singing, dancing, acting?" Paige asked as she wiped some food off Miguel's forehead while the baby giggled. "I thought you mentioned dance class the other day?"

Jorge caught her eye and made a face.

"No," Maria replied as she grabbed a bowl from the cupboard. "Chase said I should learn to protect myself because there are a lot of dangerous people out there."

"Ummm....well, this is true," Jorge smirked. "You know that first hand."

He was referring, of course, to an incident when an armed man attempted to attack the family in their own home. It was something Paige decided was no longer a threat since they moved into a house with higher security but Jorge wasn't satisfied. The attacker was dead but Jorge was ready to take out others in his group. It was coming. It was coming soon.

"Yes, that crazy man last year!" Maria's eyes widened. "That's what Chase said. He's *so* sweet. Always worried about my safety."

"Yes, unlike us, your family?" Jorge spoke abruptly. "Like I do not do everything with your safety in mind, Maria. You know we all protect you, not just Chase."

"And that he's not the only one who's suggested self-defense classes, right?" Paige added and turned to her step-daughter in time to see her shrug.

"Yeah but-

"Yeah but *nothing,*" Jorge cut her off. "You had a self-defense class before and you dropped out. This will not be the case again. You stay until you're a black belt of...something or another. Got that?"

Maria appeared unaffected by his harsh tone and merely shrugged, joining them at the table. Miguel automatically turned his attention to the teenaged girl and placed his dirty hand on her arm.

"Miguel, stop touching me!" Maria pulled back. "You have gross baby food on your hands."

She grabbed a paper towel and her harsh tone caused Miguel to cry as he angrily attempted to reach for his sister again, even pulling himself up from the high chair.

"Well, that is my cue to head out," Jorge jumped up, rushing around the table, he kissed his wife quickly, followed by his two children. "Have a beautiful day at school today, Maria."

"Do we not get a 'beautiful day' too?" Paige asked.

Watching her attempt to hold her son down while he screamed, Jorge merely shrugged.

"Yes, well, please *try.*"

With that, he rushed out of the house and jumped into his SUV. He was barely on the road when his phone rang. It was Diego.

"He didn't even call me."

"Hello to you, Diego," Jorge spoke sarcastically.

"Good morning," Diego seemed reluctant. "Chase didn't even call me."

"Let us not talk about this much right now," Jorge reminded him. "Sometimes life, Diego, it gets in the way. People do not always need the help that we think."

"So…"

"All is well, Diego," Jorge continued. "I assure you."

"I gathered that," Diego cleared his throat. "I'm having my lime trees sent over to your house later today. Paige knows about it. She'll be there."

"How many of those lime trees will be cluttering my house, Diego?"

"A few."

"I see."

"Anyway, will you be by the office today?"

"Possibly," Jorge replied. "Right now, I am on my way to meet Makerson to discuss another interview."

"You mean *script* another interview," Diego spoke with humor in his voice.

"Diego, do you have anything else or is this all?" Jorge hurried him along.

"Yeah, I got something," Diego continued. "That guy was looking for you again."

"What guy?"

"The Mexican one? The guy that keeps dropping by the office, thinking he will see you?"

"Oh yes, that man…" Jorge shrugged. "I wonder if this here is something to be concerned about."

"I want to talk to him myself."

"Does he show up on the same days? Times?" Jorge wondered.

"Nah, it's hard to say when or if he'll return."

"It does sound as if he will," Jorge considered. "Next time, have the receptionist get his info."

"Can't," Diego replied. "She tried before. He won't give it."

"I wonder if this here is my cousin," Jorge asked. "He was asking me after Jesús death if I needed another person but at the time, I said no. I also don't know if I can trust him. Relative or not."

"Your family, didn't they turn against you after your brother died?" Diego asked. "I thought that's what you told me."

"A bit of an exaggeration," Jorge said and took a deep breath. "But not by much."

"I will get to the bottom of this," Diego insisted.

"Make sure you do, *amigo,*" Jorge said as he got closer to the café where he was to meet Makerson. "I gotta go. I'm almost there. We'll talk later today."

"*Adios.*"

The call ended. Jorge called home.

"Hello," Paige answered in her usual calm voice. It made it difficult to know when she was under stress. She hid it well.

"*Mi amor,* how are things?"

"Fine," She replied. "Miguel fell asleep watching cartoons and Juliana is here with him now. "I'm going to meditate."

"Perfect!" Jorge replied. "Solve everything on your meditation pillow."

She let out a small laugh that aroused him and he suddenly had a thought.

"Perhaps, you and me, we should get away sometimes soon," He said as he moved closer to the coffee shop. "Maybe, you know, a quiet afternoon away. Like we did in the past?"

"Maybe," She replied. "I'm expecting a call from Alec later but after that.."

"What does Alec want?" Jorge asked and felt his desires drain slightly.

"I don't know," She admitted. "But he said he had something to talk to me about. He wasn't clear."

Jorge suddenly realized what he wanted to talk about. Athas was so transparent. All he had to do was sit back and watch.

CHAPTER 16

"Another busy news day," Jorge commented as he sat across from Makerson. The editor of *Toronto AM* knew to sit away from others when they met in public and to choose his words carefully. He was as much part of the group as the others. Proving his loyalty, again and again, Makerson was living quite comfortably in his new condo.

"Nothing ever stops in this city," Makerson replied as he set his phone aside, quickly glancing at a message. "Hey, I got some news."

"What's that?"

"A national news channel has asked me to join one of their regular panels discussing politics and events taking place in the city."

"Very nice," Jorge replied while catching the eye of the waiter to ask for a coffee before returning his attention to Makerson. "So this here, it will help the status of your paper."

"That's the goal."

"I'm impressed," Jorge replied as the waiter returned with his coffee. After asking if he wanted anything else, he slipped away. "Your star, it continues to rise."

"I have you to thank for that," Makerson insisted as he turned off his phone. "You helped me get here."

"Well, I have always been supportive of young talent," Jorge replied as he poured cream into his coffee. "I hear that a young lady had an unfortunate accident in the shower yesterday."

"I hear that too."

"I also hear that she had something to do with the fires in that indigenous community last year."

Makerson appeared surprised.

"Let's see if you can connect the dots on this one."

"Well, she was part of the government…."

"Yes, she was."

"She was in the news a lot last year when the fires happened."

"This is true."

"Why do I feel like there's a huge distance between the dots that I'm supposed to connect?"

"This lady," Jorge began and glanced around quickly before he continued. "She was behind the indigenous community burning to the ground last year."

"She knew about it?" Makerson attempted to understand. "She was one of the people who didn't send people to help?"

"Ah! You Canadians," Jorge leaned back in his seat. "Always wanting to see the best in people."

"That's the best?" Makerson replied with a grin. "If that's the best then…"

Jorge watched as the grin slid from his face.

"Wait…I think I remember something about that community wanting to meet with the prime minister to talk about some environmental issues…."

Jorge raised an eyebrow.

"I hope you're not telling me what I think you're telling me," Makerson finally replied.

"That lady," Jorge said as he loosened his tie. "She held the match."

Makerson looked appalled.

"Are you…..are you serious?"

Jorge nodded.

"Do you have proof?"

"Now that there," Jorge thought for a moment. "It may be a little more difficult. But that lady, she was no saint."

"And this comes from the top?"

Jorge didn't reply but raised his eyebrows.

"Can someone leak documents…"

"There are emails."

"I can work with emails."

"I will see what I can do."

"It's about timing though," Makerson thought out loud. "She has to be buried before we dig her up again."

"I want you to dig her up," Jorge replied and leaned forward. "Just to bury the cunt again."

"Wow," Makerson appeared to be processing it. "Unbelievable."

"Stick with me," Jorge replied. "Nothing will be unbelievable soon."

"I'm seeing that."

"So our interview this week…"

"Yes, I want to do it in such a way that we discuss you helping supply the CBD oil to rehab facilities," Makerson suggested. "Also, we should talk about the edibles you're planning to launch with that french bakery."

"We're working on it," Jorge replied. "I should say, my people, are working on it. I don't got time for the details but they're on board."

"I'm hearing the future is a lot about medicinal," Makerson commented. "Big Pharma won't like that."

"Well, they got their fake pot," Jorge reminded him. "But it's not the same."

"They would love to take over your company."

"Over my dead fucking body," Jorge replied. "But between medicinal and edibles, we got the market. Think about it, we have the sick people, the people wanting to relax, have fun and for those who want something extra in their French pastries, we got that covered too."

"You're way ahead of the others," Makerson replied. "I mean, other companies are springing up…"

"And they can do so but I will beat them again and again," Jorge replied as he reached for his coffee. "This here is the nature of business. That's why I got started right off the bat. It's about timing and strategy."

"Should we talk about Big Pharma in the interview?"

"We should talk about how their product is substandard," Jorge suggested. "I mean, we boast being natural."

"There's a young director," Makerson began. "I heard he wants to do a documentary on the benefits of pot and he's strongly opposed to Big Pharma. I guess he used to work for them and he left on bad terms. You might want to consider financing his project."

"I might do that."

"I'll get his name for you to look into it," Makerson said as he reached for his phone and turned it on. "I heard someone suggested you, some guy you know? I forget who it was but anyway, the director wasn't sure how to contact you."

"I will consider it," Jorge nodded and thought for a moment. "I could make this work for me too."

"I'll keep you posted."

Their coffee date ended shortly after with the last details put together for the upcoming live stream interview. Each time they did one, the audience grew as did the response. However, the idea of being involved in a film intrigued Jorge. He decided to call home to mention it to his wife.

"I like the idea," Paige spoke calmly. "But make sure we can trust this guy."

"Oh, *mi amor,* you know me," Jorge replied as he drove toward the office. "I leave no stone unturned."

"Even if it doesn't work out," Her voice echoed through the SUV. "Doing this kind of film would be a good idea. These documentaries and series are very popular."

"This is what I'm thinking," Jorge said as he sat in traffic. "This here would give me a new audience."

"Listen," Paige suddenly shifted gears. "I had an interesting conversation with Alec today."

"Is this so?"

"He seemed to think I would know something about a 'meditation' experience he had," Paige replied. "Of course, I said I was all for it until I started to understand that we had a very different interpretation of what 'meditation' is."

Jorge laughed.

"Why didn't you tell me about this….situation?" Paige asked. "I thought he was being serious, at first."

"I think he did too," Jorge replied as he moved through traffic. "But the lady he was sent, she liked to try…other methods."

"Yeah, that's not meditation," Paige spoke smoothly. "He seemed horrified to have to confess it to me."

"I bet."

"I have a funny feeling you didn't mention it to me on purpose."

"*Mi amor,* it must've slipped my mind," Jorge spoke candidly with laughter in his voice. "it was the day of Miguel's party.…I must've forgot."

"I somehow don't believe that," Paige giggled.

"But at least you know what your tax dollars are paying for now," Jorge commented. "The situation, it has been handled."

She remained silent. He would explain more when he got home.

"Where are you going now?"

"The office," Jorge replied. "I haven't been there much lately. It is nice to pop in from time to time. There is probably something Diego wants me to review or sign. By the way, did his lime trees show up yet?"

"You mean his lime forest?" Paige corrected him. "Yes, they did."

"Ughh.."

"But they do have some nice limes," Paige insisted. "And Miguel is enjoying the trees. He's using them to pull himself up and he keeps smelling the limes for some reason."

Jorge noticed another call coming in.

"Paige, I must go," Jorge said as he stopped in traffic again. "It is Diego."

"I have to go anyway," She replied. "Miguel is trying to pick the leaves off the lime trees…"

Jorge ended the call and hit the button to start another.

"*Hola!*"

"That guy, he's here!" Diego insisted. "The one who keeps trying to see you."

"I'm already on my way," Jorge replied. "Keep him there. I don't care how don't let him leave."

"This man will not be going anywhere," Diego assured him. "That I promise."

CHAPTER 17

"He's in my office," Diego said as soon as they met at the door, barely giving Jorge time to notice the receptionist's adoring smile. Muttering a quick hello, he wanted to appear natural as the two men headed down the hallway. "I didn't think the conference room would be such a good idea."

The man who waited sat slumped in a chair wearing casual clothing, badly worn running shoes and he held a dirty baseball cap in his cracked hands. There was an unmistakable odor that filled the room and immediately looking in his eyes, Jorge recognized a broken man.

"Hola, Señor Hernandez," He quickly rose from his chair and extended his hand. Jorge took it even though he noticed Diego cringing as he did. "Please, thank you for seeing me."

"Diego," Jorge let go of the man's hand and turned toward his wary associate. "Can you get this man some coffee, maybe something to eat from our break room?"

Without saying anything, Diego squinted, twisted his lips skeptically and nodded before leaving the room. He closed the door behind him.

"Please, sit down," Jorge pointed toward the chair and made his way behind Diego's desk. "I am told you have attempted to see me many time as well as perhaps call?"

"Sí, Señor Hernandez," He replied and hesitated as Diego rushed back in the room carrying coffee and some donuts on a plate. "I have."

"Diego," Jorge said as he sat the food in front of the stranger. "I will be borrowing your office for a few minutes."

"Sure," Diego replied skeptically. "I checked him. He's got no weapons."

The stranger appeared nervous under Diego's dark glare.

"This here, it is fine," Jorge nodded and watched Diego leave, closing the door behind him.

"I mean you no harm," The man quickly raised his hands in the air. "I just was wishing to speak to you."

"Please," Jorge gestured toward the food and watched the man grab a donut, taking a massive bite. "First, let's start with who you are and why you are here."

The stranger quickly chewed and swallowed the piece of donut.

"As I told your associate, my name is Enrique Mata Blanco," He replied. "My family and I are here from Mexico. We had to leave in a hurry. That is why…."

Enrique pointed toward his clothes shamefully.

"So what made you leave in a hurry?" Jorge asked with interest as he leaned back in the chair.

"Mr. Hernandez," Enrique spoke slowly. "I am the man who informed your associate Jesús about the people who kidnaps your mother? I am here because of someone else, they know that it was me…"

Jorge nodded. He thought back to when his mother was kidnapped by a relative as a way to extort money. Jesús investigated and once he learned the culprit, Jorge's cousin and those who helped experienced a brutal death that was as much about sending a message as it was ending their lives.

"My family and I, we are in danger," Enrique continued. "We had to leave because this man, he wanted to kill us. I knew Jesús, he was now living in Toronto and thought I could find him. Perhaps, he would help us."

"Jesús is dead," Jorge commented flatly even though a ripple of emotions filled his chest.

"I did learn that after arriving and I am sorry for this loss," Enrique continued. "I did not know what else to do so I hoped I could talk to you about this matter."

"At the time, did we not take care of all of the men?" Jorge thought back. "Then give you money to reestablish yourself?"

"Yes, and you were quite generous and I do thank you," Enrique looked down in shame. "This man….I did not give his name because, at the time, I thought he did not participate in the kidnapping but just knew about it. I have since learned otherwise but unfortunately, he has since also learned that I was responsible for telling…"

Jorge listened in silence.

"Always, we look over our shoulder," Enrique continued as he took a drink of his coffee. "I am so scared for my children. I know that telling the truth was the right thing but now, I feel I lost so much."

"How do I know this is true?" Jorge asked evenly. "I was never told the name of the informant. You could be anybody."

"I can prove it," Enrique assured him. "I know Jesús, he is no longer here but the men that worked with him to learn the kidnappers, they are very much alive in Mexico. If you speak with any, they will tell you."

Jorge nodded.

"I do not want charity," Enrique continued. "This is not what I ask. I will work for you. I can do whatever you need."

"Is that right?"

"Yes, Mr. Hernandez," He nodded vigorously. "I am not afraid of hard work."

"Enrique, what do you know about me?" Jorge asked as he watched him take another massive bite of a donut.

"I know of you, sir…" He appeared to pick his words carefully. "You are a very powerful man. Both here and in Mexico."

"And yet, you felt comfortable coming here and asking to see me," Jorge asked.

"I would not say comfortable," Enrique shook his head. "But we must do what is needed, what is right for our family."

Jorge thought about his words.

"And your family is important."

"My family, it is my life," Enrique spoke emotionally, his eyes downcast, he took another drink of coffee. "I take the risk of coming here today to see you because I did not know what else to do."

"How long have you been in Toronto?"

"Three weeks….close to a month."

Jorge nodded.

"*Por favor*....please," Enrique begged, his face showing the signs of exhaustion. "I will do anything."

Jorge thought for a moment. A knock at the door interrupted their conversation. It was Diego.

"Yes?" Jorge asked.

"I need to speak to you," He gestured indicating the hallway.

"If you will excuse me," Jorge said and rose from his chair. He noted the man reached for the second donut and nodded.

In the hallway, Diego closed the door and wasted no time to speak.

"It's him," He muttered.

"Him?"

"He's who he said he is," Diego confirmed. "He told me this whole story before you arrived and it's true. I checked with some of the associates in Mexico, they gave me a name, description, me and Marco did some detective work on the computer and it's him."

"He is telling the truth?"

"Rumor has it, there's a hit on him in Mexico," Diego confirmed. "And his family. They left their home, left everything months ago."

"His bank account?"

"Empty."

Jorge nodded and returned to the office. He noted Enrique had finished both his food and coffee.

"Diego, he has informed me that you are being honest," Jorge said and sat down next to Enrique. "Where is your family now?"

"At the mall," He replied and hurried to explain. "We were in a homeless shelter and had to leave during the day."

"I will contact my wife," Jorge thought quickly. "We will find you a place to stay."

"I will pay you back," Enrique assured him as he sat up straighter. "Tell me what you need me to do."

"Today, I need you to find a place for your family," Jorge suggested. "It will be temporary until we find you a home. Then, you will work for me. I am not sure what I will have you do yet but whatever I ask…"

"I will do."

"Anything?" Jorge asked.

The man nodded vigorously.

Jorge reached for his phone and text his wife.

Paige, can you come to the office? I have something I need help with.

Sure. On my way.

"Enrique, tell me," Jorge asked with interest. "How old are your children."

"My daughter, she is 13 and my son, he is 10."

Jorge nodded and thought for a moment.

"Do you have any children?" Enrique spoke cautiously. "If I am permitted to ask."

"Two," Jorge replied, noting the skepticism in his voice. "My daughter, she is about to turn 13. My son, he just turned 1."

Enrique reached in his pocket and pulled out a phone. He hit some buttons and turned it toward Jorge. It displayed a family photo. Jorge noted the phone was also out of service. He looked up and was about to say something when he noted the tears in the man's eyes.

CHAPTER 18

"So much for my fantasy of escaping to a hotel," Jorge commented as he climbed into bed beside his wife. He watched her place her phone on the nightstand and turn toward him. "This day, it did not go as I expected, *mi amor.*"

"No, but you did a good thing," She gently reminded him as she leaned in to touch his arm. "Those people needed your help and you came through for them."

"No, Paige, it was you that came through," He reminded her as he moved in to give her a quick kiss. "You found them a place for tonight and are helping them find an apartment. Me? I just talk to the man."

"But you didn't have to."

"At the time, he told Jesús the truth when he asked," Jorge said and took a deep breath. "He would tell me today, if he was here, to help this man. He would remind me of what he put at risk to help us."

"So, what happened that he even got involved?"

"This man, he knew my cousin," Jorge replied. "They tried to recruit him to help them but he says no. He did not want to get involved in kidnapping even though the money, would be good. When Jesús later found him, asked him questions, he was reluctant to talk out of fear. Jesús offered him money and assurance he would be safe."

"Sounds like a hellish few months," Paige muttered. "When I spoke to Enrique's wife this afternoon, she was terrified. In Mexico, she lived in fear and in Canada, she was unsure if approaching you was a good idea. After all, it was your cousin that was involved and he snitched on."

"It was my cousin who extorted over a million dollars from me," Jorge reminded her and shook his head. "No, to me, that is not my family. They can burn in hell for all I care. Even before this here happened, many were jealous of my wealth. They turned against me when my brother died and in their minds, I was supposed to fail in life so when I found success, it made them angry."

"Whatever happened to your cousin?" Paige paused for a moment. "You know, the one who's dirt bike…."

"Who's dirt bike I used without permission and killed my brother," Jorge finished her sentence.

"You know that's not what I was going to say."

"I know, *mi amor,* I know," Jorge replied solemnly. "But this here, it is true. And honestly, he was part of a cartel. That is why he could afford the dirt bike. He was murdered years ago. Another injustice, as far as my family was concerned. He joins a cartel to help his family and dies. I join a cartel because I'm the devil and I prosper. You have no idea of the jealousy in my family."

"I think it was wrong they turned their backs on you after your brother died," Paige commented. "You were a kid."

"Family, Paige, it is not what you are born into but who shows you loyalty," Jorge spoke warmly. "You know this is my feeling. That is the reason I was happy to help Enrique today. I believe me showing him loyalty will only make him more loyal to me. He will do anything for me now. I could see that in his eyes."

"What are your plans?"

"I'm not sure but for now, he will work with Chase at the bar," Jorge spoke thoughtfully. "This here, it will be a test for both. For Chase, he will keep an eye on him and decide on his character, his strengths and what he foresees him doing in the future. For Enrique, it is an opportunity to prove his loyalty, his work ethic, these things. I think this will be a good thing."

"His wife wants to work too."

"Maybe with Jolene at the warehouse," Jorge replied. "Maybe someday, we will have the family over. His daughter is Maria's age. It would be nice if she had a Mexican friend. I think she is getting her attitude from her white girlfriends."

"Really?" Paige appeared humored as she raised an eyebrow.

"You, Paige, you are different," Jorge said and winked at her as he moved closer. "But white girls her age, they have a lot of attitude."

"You don't think Maria had an attitude before she moved to Canada?"

"Yes, but it was different," Jorge thought back.

"Wait till you get her into a co-ed school," Paige reminded him. "White *girls* will be the least of your problems."

"Oh, *mi amor,* please let us not talk about that," Jorge took a deep breath and closed his eyes as he reached under the covers. "Let us talk about something more pleasurable than this."

The topic would come up again the following morning when Jorge was having breakfast. He was surprised to see Maria wander downstairs in her robe, her hair disheveled with big, pink slippers on her feet.

"You are up early this morning, *bonita,* you do know it is the weekend?"

"I heard Miguel cry and smelled the coffee," She gestured toward the counter. "I need my caffeine."

"You know, Maria, you are a little young to start relying on coffee to wake up," Jorge reminded her as he started to shut off his iPad. "You're 12 going on 20."

"You say that like it's a bad thing," Maria commented as she poured a coffee.

"It is not a good thing," Jorge reaffirmed, wishing Paige was there to back him up but he could hear her upstairs with Miguel. "This summer, you are not lounging around the house. I expect you to help out Juliana and Paige with the baby, cleaning the house…I want you to start doing your laundry…"

"*Papa,* I *won't be* lounging around the house," Maria corrected him as she put in multiple spoonfuls of sugar in her coffee, causing Jorge to cringe. "I plan to take self-defense or whatever Chase thinks is best. We're going to discuss it later today and I want to decide on what school to go to in the fall…"

"*You're* deciding this?" Jorge spoke gruffly. "Do you plan to pay for it as well?"

"I'm the one going so I should help make the decision," Maria insisted.

"I cannot disagree with you on that point," Jorge replied. "Ok, you look at the schools and come to me with solid reasons why we should go with a specific one."

"I know," Maria said with attitude in her voice as she wandered over to the table with her coffee in hand. "You think I'm so dumb but I'm not."

"Maria, I never say you are dumb," Jorge commented as he pushed the iPad aside. "I worry about you. I see these young people who are clueless, who get into the world and cannot do the simplest thing. I do not want you to become one of these people. I want you to be smart, to be strong and be able to look after yourself and make good decisions. Better decisions than what I made when I was young."

A look of understanding crossed Maria's face and she nodded.

"*Papa,* I will be fine," She insisted. "You have to let me try to figure things out for myself."

Jorge considered her words and nodded.

"You are right, Maria," Jorge said as his phone beeped. "I do."

"Who is texting you this early?"

"Maria, people are always texting me at all hours of the day and night," Jorge reminded her. "This here is not that early."

Glancing at his phone, it was a message from Makerson, asking when he wanted to do the interview. He also discovered a message from Enrique, thanking him again for his help. He sent along a photo of the family together having breakfast at the hotel he paid for them to stay in. He looked like a different man once cleaned up and with a new sense of hope.

"Maria, there is a family from Mexico that I am helping," Jorge commented as he began to rise from his chair. "They have a daughter, she is your age. I would like to introduce you two some time. I think it would be nice for her to make a friend."

"Ah, Mexican girls, they are so…" Maria rolled her eyes.

"I hate to tell you this but you *are* a Mexican girl," Jorge teased as he leaned in and kissed her on the forehead while reaching for his iPad. "I do not care how long you live in Canada, you're still Mexican in here."

Jorge touched his chest as he spoke, patting his tie.

"I know, *Papa.*"

"Do not forget where you come from," Jorge commented as he rushed toward the door. "Give Paige and Miguel a kiss for me."

Outside, he jumped in his SUV and pulled on the street. It was still early, so the traffic wouldn't be too bad. Hitting a button, he called Makerson.

"Good morning, Jorge."

"Good morning, I see you want to know when to do the interview."

"Yeah, I can fit it in anytime today," Makerson replied. "Unless an emergency comes up."

"I will be in touch a bit later," Jorge replied. "I am thinking this morning but I have to check on a few things first."

"Sounds good and by the way," Makerson continued. "Thanks for the tip. I'm in the process of breaking the story in the next few days."

"*Perfecto.*"

"I'll make sure it reminds people it took place before Athas was prime minister," Makerson continued. "That the idea was from this Harriet chick."

"You are the word man," Jorge reminded him. "I do believe you can spin it the right way."

"Always do."

Jorge ended the call and decided on a whim to head to the bar and not the office. He would visit with Chase to discuss Enrique but also check how things were going since the gym murder.

He wasn't prepared for what he found.

CHAPTER 19

"Why is there a dead man on the floor?" Jorge asked Chase upon arriving at the *Princesa Maria* and discovering a middle-aged man on the ground. He attempted to move him with his shoe but then decided against it. "I would be happy to find almost any other kind of surprise this early in the morning. A naked girl running through here? An orgy? You shooting a porn? But not so much a dead man, you know?"

Jorge noted that Chase cringed at the reference to shooting porn but quickly contained himself.

"He's not dead," Chase spoke in his usual wide-eyed innocent way. "I just knocked him out."

Jorge hesitated for a moment, glancing down at the man again and then gave Chase a humored look.

"Chase, I assure you, I know what a dead man looks like," Jorge insisted with laughter in his voice. "This man here, he's fucking dead."

"No, I did this thing so he'd briefly lose consciousness," Chase said as he knelt on the floor to check the man. "I got him from behind and..."

"I must be careful to not arrive unannounced in the future," Jorge cut him off. "Or I might be a dead man on the floor too."

"He's not..." Chase's voice trailed off as he attempted to find a pulse on the man. "He can't be..."

"Chase," Jorge knelt beside him and put a hand over the man's nose. "This man here, I'm telling you, he's fucking dead."

A look of horror crossed Chase's face as he hurriedly attempted to find a pulse, heartbeat, some signs of life but to no avail. He sat down on the floor, his mouth fell open.

"Look, these things, they happen," Jorge suddenly felt the need to reassure him as he reached for his phone. "We will take care of it."

"Oh fuck!" Chase appeared shocked as he stared at the man.

"I will get Diego over here," Jorge said as he reached for his phone. "Paige, Jolene….and, you know what….I'm gonna get the new guy."

"New guy?" Chase continued to stare at the man.

"Long story, *amigo,* but this man helped me in Mexico," Jorge replied as he tapped his phone. "In the meantime, you might want to check our friend for some ID or something. Hopefully, he wasn't here to give you the good news of the Lord and you snapped his fucking neck."

"Oh fuck!" Chase said as he closed his eyes and ran a hand over his face. "How the fuck did I do this?"

"You do not know your own strength," Jorge continued to tease as he stared at his phone. "Everyone is on their way. "Diego is going to pick up the new guy and Jolene, Paige, they will be here soon."

"New guy?" Chase repeated his earlier question as he searched the man's pockets.

Jorge opened his mouth to reply but decided that a sarcastic remark probably wasn't fair at that particular moment.

"What you find?" Jorge asked. "You got anything?"

"No," Chase shook his head. "There's a free drink card in his pocket and a gun but that's about it."

"The card is from Mexico," Jorge nodded toward the man. "So's this one."

"I came in and…"

"How about we get away from the corpse and have a drink?" Jorge suggested as he rose from the floor and watched Chase do the same. "This here, it's over. We cannot make him alive again so let us have a drink and calm down."

The two men headed to the bar.

"So, let us talk about what happened here this morning," Jorge asked as he gestured for Chase to sit down while he went behind the bar to reach for a bottle of tequila. "This man showed up at the door?"

"He was here when I arrived."

"Didn't you have the alarm on?"

"I wasn't here last night," Chase was in a daze. "I text the guy from last night and he said he thinks he forgot to turn it on."

"Or was told not to," Jorge suggested as he poured them each a shot. He glanced around the bar. "You got any limes?"

"Nah, I get the supplies later today," Chase replied.

"Too bad I didn't know," Jorge rolled his eyes. "I got *five* of Diego's fucking lime trees in my house."

"Really?" Chase seemed to suddenly return to earth. "He still has those?"

"He got them at my house until he can move next door," Jorge shook his head. "Miguel may not let him part with them. He has an odd fascination with those fucking trees. He tried to eat a lime yesterday, peel and all."

"Wow." Chase seemed to be in a daze.

"I'm in lime tree hell," Jorge replied as he glanced at his phone again. "Let's do a shot and talk about how we got a dead man on the floor."

Chase, who usually avoided liquor, seemed more than grateful to knock back the powerful shot. Jorge did the same while watching him carefully.

"Did you check to see if anyone else was here?" Jorge asked and glanced around. "Maybe in the office or hiding?"

"No, I mean, I checked the doors but no…you arrived and then…"

"That is the first thing you should do, *amigo*," Jorge said as he glanced around and reached for his gun. "Although, I sense he was alone. Do you got a gun?"

"No."

"That's about to change," Jorge insisted even though he knew how Chase felt about rifles…and why. "You need something here if people show up at your door. I don't gotta remind you that it is not the first time."

Chase reluctantly nodded.

"And we will have Jolene or Paige teach you how to shoot," Jorge continued as he walked out from behind the bar. "I'm gonna look through to make sure we are alone. Stay alert."

Jorge slowly made his way through the building with a gun in hand. He checked the office again, the washrooms, the VIP room, and staff areas. When satisfied, he returned to the main bar to find Chase pouring himself another shot just as his phone beeped.

"Jolene is here."

Jorge went to the door and let her in.

"*Hola,* what is the…" She began to speak as her eyes glanced past Jorge to the dead man on the floor. "Who you kill so early?"

"This here, it wasn't me," Jorge replied as he locked the door behind her and Jolene moved closer to inspect the man. "That was Chase."

"Chase? You kill?" Jolene appeared shocked.

"You got a short memory," Jorge reminded her. "Remember the woman from a few days ago."

"I know…but, this was so fast after that day," Jolene appeared confused. "You kill someone else already? What happened?"

"I tried this move that I thought was going to knock him out temporarily.."

"I hope you never get the idea to knock me out temporarily," Jolene retorted.

"It was a mistake," Jorge cut in. "This here, it happens. If he didn't want to get killed, he shouldn't break in here."

"He broke in?" Jolene repeated. "But how, the lock, it looks fine."

The two men exchanged looks.

"Back door?" Jorge asked.

"It, fire exits, all fine," Chase shook his head. "That's the first thing I checked after…"

"Ok, so this man, he does not have a key on him," Jorge said as he pointed toward the floor. "He did not break in. How did he get in here? Change the locks today."

Chase nodded vigorously. Jorge got another beep on his phone.

"Paige, she is here….."

Jorge walked toward the door to let her in while Jolene continued to talk to Chase.

"Hi," Paige entered the room and glanced toward the man on the floor and without batting an eyelash, she continued. "Who's the guy?"

"*Mi amor,*" Jorge leaned in to kiss her. "This is what we are trying to figure out and how he got in."

"The door looks fine."

"That is what concerns us."

"We might want to get Clara in to check for devices," She muttered.

"Oh shit!" Jorge hadn't even thought of that. "I will message her right away."

"I'll check around the bar and the office until she does," Paige replied and went to work as she chatted with the others.

Jorge messaged Clara and then his phone beeped. Diego and Enrique were outside. He went to let them in.

"I got your…." Diego stopped in his tracks when he saw the man on the floor. Enrique followed behind and seemed to take a minute to realize what was going on as Jorge closed and locked the door. "What the fuck happened here? A little early to start slaughtering people, isn't it, Hernandez?"

"It was Chase," Jorge quickly replied and noted the shocked look on Enrique's face. "The man was here when he arrived. We are trying to figure out why."

"So you killed him?" Diego turned toward Chase then shrugged. "Ah, probably better safe than sorry."

"This man, I know him," Enrique was quick to jump in, grabbing everyone's attention. "He is the man who knew that I snitched about the kidnapping, Mr. Hernandez. It was he who wanted to kill me."

"Are you sure?" Jorge was intrigued.

"Yes, it is my brother-in-law," Enrique replied.

CHAPTER 20

"So this here was your first day," Jorge remarked to Enrique in the privacy of Chase's office. The two men were alone while the others took care of some final details before opening the bar. This was after disposing of the body, having the locks changed and checking the cameras to see how Enrique's brother-in-law got in. "We work fast and often under stressful circumstances. This is not a 9-5 job and as you saw today, you may get your hands dirty."

Enrique nodded in silence.

"Now, I gotta know," Jorge continued. "Your brother-in-law, why the fuck was he here waiting for Chase this morning?"

"I believe he was here to kill me," Enrique insisted as he sat up straighter, his eyes widened. "This is the man I spoke to you about. It was him who first approached me about helping your cousin and the others. He knew that I struggle with money and since we are family....he feel that I would say yes."

"And when you said no?"

"He was not happy," Enrique shook his head. "I did not tell my wife. I knew this would bring her shame and I was scared she would confront him and put us in danger."

"So you said nothing?"

"To no one, no," Enrique said and took a deep breath. "Until Jesús, he found me and put a gun to my head. He ask me what I knew."

"So am I to believe you only told him the truth because he put a gun to your head?"

"Mr. Hernandez, you must understand something," Enrique replied nervously. "I was scared for me and my family. I did not want to get involved one way or another. But when he ask, I tell him the truth."

"And what happened?"

"He take the gun away," Enrique said and paused for a moment. "He asked me to tell everything, so I did. I tell him the truth and made him promise that he not hurt my family."

"So, my cousin, your brother-in-law," Jorge thought for a moment. "Are there more?"

"They are all dead."

Jorge nodded.

"My brother-in-law, I did not tell his name because he was family," Enrique said as he lowered his eyes. "This, I now regret because he figured out I was the snitch and he come after me instead."

"And your wife, she did not know?"

"No," Enrique assured him. "I told her to not contact family because we were in danger. I suspect she did not listen. She did not know it was her brother that wanted to kill us."

Jorge considered the information.

"Would he tell anyone else he's here?"

"No," Enrique shook his head. "He would not want anyone to know how he got this money. See, my wife, she would tell him that I was working at the bar. He would come here to find me."

"But to come and stay all night?" Jorge asked.

"My wife, she knew I was working in the morning so he would be waiting," Enrique reminded him. "She was not aware that I first had to go to the office with Diego."

Jorge nodded. "So, you think your wife called him and said where you were, that you had a job…."

"Yes," Enrique nodded. "I know my brother-in-law. He would hope to find me first thing, kill me and no one would ever find out his truth.

He was extremely paranoid. This would assure him he would never be found out."

Jorge thought about it for a moment before continuing.

"And we know he paid off the night manager," Jorge continued calmly, even though he hadn't been so calm earlier that day when confronting the man in question. "To leave him here all night."

Enrique appeared nervous.

"In this company," Jorge gestured around, his eyes watching Enrique carefully. "We don't give second chances. I don't fuck around with these people."

"You did scream a lot, Mr. Hernandez," Enrique referred to the meeting that took place earlier that day. "I could hear it through the door. That man, he was crying when he left this office."

"He was lucky to leave the office at all," Jorge spoke sternly with an intensity in his eyes. "Because I could have easily removed two corpses today

Enrique nodded in understanding.

"Now," Jorge continued and leaned forward on the desk. "We must move on. I do not believe in sitting in the past. This here, it is finished. If you are certain there are no other men that will be coming for you that I should know about…maybe another relative you are trying to protect?"

"He and I, we were the last that knew anything about it," Enrique assured him with worry in his eyes. "My wife, she knows nothing other than we were in danger. I refused to tell her why for her safety."

"And you're gonna keep it that way," Jorge insisted. "No guilty confessions to her or it may be your last."

Enrique nodded.

"You did not see her brother this morning," Jorge reminded him as the man shook his head no. "You did not see *anything* this morning. If you want to work for me, this is how it goes."

"I understand, sir," Enrique replied. "I do not want to cause trouble, sir."

Jorge studied him carefully.

"When I say I wanted to work for you," Enrique continued. "I will do anything you need. Just help me stay here and protect my family, that is all I ask."

"Are you sure," Jorge wondered. "Now that this man is out of the way, you could go back to Mexico."

"Now that I am here," Enrique confessed. "I want to stay. My wife, she would move back but it is better for us here."

Jorge nodded.

"Mexico, there are so many dangers," He continued. "I want better for my family."

"Ok," Jorge pushed. "So, you did not see your brother-in-law. You know nothing. If your wife freaks out that she cannot find him…"

"I know nothing, Mr. Hernandez."

"Then, in this case," Jorge continued as he relaxed. "You have a new job as night manager since our last one, he did not do so well. Can you do this?"

"*Si,*" Enrique nodded vigorously. "Whatever you wish."

"Chase will train you," Jorge continued. "There will be other things from time to time but let us start there."

"Thank you."

Without responding, Jorge rose from the chair and headed toward the door. Enrique followed him. They joined the others, who sat around the bar.

"Fuck!" Diego automatically spoke up. "It's barely lunchtime and I'm already exhausted."

"Diego, you will be fine," Jorge insisted and glanced as all eyes turned in Chase's direction and gestured toward Enrique. "This here is your new night manager."

Chase nodded while the others listened.

"We have discussed everything," Jorge continued. "This man from this morning, he was the last one involved in my mother's kidnapping. We believe he came here to kill Enrique since he was the only person left who knew the truth."

"He caught me by surprise instead," Chase replied. "When the alarm wasn't on, I knew something was up."

"Where was he?"

"Near the VIP room," Chase replied. "I snuck up behind him."

"And killed him."

"I thought I...," Chase spoke toward Jorge. "I thought he was unconscious. I was about to contact you to come here..."

"Sounds like you got your moves mixed up," Paige offered. "You might want to sort that out before trying it again."

Jolene let out a loud, abrupt laugh that caused Diego to jump.

"Jesus Christ, Jolene," Diego snapped. "It's been a long day, we don't need any loud, unexpected noises around here."

"That is my laugh," Jolene barked back. "You don't like, you can leave!"

"Ok, this here," Jorge cut in. "I am not here to referee you two."

Both clamped their mouths shut but glared at one another.

"As I was saying," Jorge continued. "We will make Enrique our night manager. I want him to pay close attention to the people who are here. If anything stands out, he must let us know. I am confident that Chase, you can teach him this."

The bar manager nodded.

"Today's episode, it shows we must be vigilant," Jorge continued as he looked into each of their faces before ending with Enrique. "And you, your former life, it is over. You are no longer the man you were in Mexico. Here, in Canada, you work for me and I do not have to tell you what that means."

Enrique shook his head as the others watched him.

"Of course, your life, it is forever changed," Jorge insisted with a shrug. "But, you must also know that here, you have us. And we are *familia*. And no one and nothing gets in our way. That I can assure you."

"I do appreciate this, Mr. Hernandez," Enrique replied. "I will repay you in any way I can."

"Just do your work," Jorge answered. "Whatever we ask, you do. And do not ever tell your wife or anyone what happened to your brother-in-law. This here, it stays between us all."

"I will not, sir."

"Were you close?" Jolene asked. "Your brother-in-law, were you close?"

"No," Enrique replied, his eyes softened when met with Jolene's. "This man, he has caused me a great deal of trouble but my wife, she makes excuses for him."

"Not anymore," Diego muttered.

The laughter stared with Paige. Enrique was the last but seemed to laugh the most. It was telling.

"But why now?" Diego's voice boomed through the room. "Why not months ago, when Jesús caught the others?"

"My brother in law, he went in hiding until recently."

"He did not give his name at first," Jorge answered for him. "Family. This here, I can understand but the man, he turned against him."

"I was the only person who knew his secret," Enrique continued to explain. "We met and talked about the situation and I knew, there was something in his eyes that tell me, I could no longer trust him."

Enrique's eyes met with Jolene's and she showed sympathy while Diego continued to appear skeptical. Jorge noted everyone's reactions.

"He was paranoid that he was being watched," Enrique continued and turned toward Jorge. "He was scared your people, they would find him. This was even though I promised that I did not tell his name. He didn't trust me."

Jorge nodded.

"I told my wife we were in danger but didn't tell her who we were in danger from," Enrique explained to the others.

"Maybe, if you had told her the truth…" Jolene spoke up.

"No, you do not understand, my wife," Enrique shook his head. "She would choose her family over me. This is how she is."

Jorge glanced at Paige and they shared a look.

CHAPTER 21

"Say what you want," Jorge spoke in his usual abrupt manner in response to Diego's question. He noted a horrified expression on Jolene's face, while his wife merely grinned. "They have not called since, those telemarketers."

"If I phone somewhere," Jolene spoke up in her loud voice. "And they threaten to find me and slit my throat, I may not call back either."

"I only said I would find them and slit their fucking throat *if* they called *again*," Jorge corrected her with an amused shrug as he leaned forward on his desk. "This here, it gave her the option...no, *opportunity* to remove my phone number from her list."

"I am sure it was removed," Jolene insisted as her eyes widened.

"Yeah, right after they called the police...." Diego said and rolled his eyes. "Because that's what we need at the door."

"Most of these call centers are illegal in the first place," Paige gently corrected him. "They won't call anyone."

Diego considered her words, twisting his lips together, he gave a reluctant shrug.

"Me, do you think I worry about such things?" Jorge retorted with a smooth grin. "Now, let us get back on topic before this morning is over."

"So, you hired this Enrique guy," Diego automatically jumped in. "Do we even trust him? I dunno."

"You said his story checked out, didn't you?" Paige turned toward Diego. "In Mexico?"

"Yeah, it does," Diego replied in a gentler tone. "But still, Paige, we also thought we could trust Michael."

The mere mention of Diego's former boyfriend caused Paige to give him a compassionate smile. The truth about their former associate had been a rude awakening however, it was quickly managed.

"Diego, not everyone is Michael," Jorge reminded him. "However, I do believe he is telling the truth."

"It don't mean we can trust him," Diego insisted. "It's one thing to take him on as an employee, quite another to have him privy to our secrets."

"Yes, but Diego, you must remember," Jorge said as he took a deep breath. "Knowing the secret about his dead brother-in-law, it also lets him know what will happen to him if he betrays us."

"I think he knows," Jolene spoke with compassion in her voice. "We talk some and he seems nervous."

Diego shot her a dirty look.

"What? I cannot talk to someone?" She automatically snapped at her brother.

"Anyway," Jorge cut in before they could launch into an argument. "We are here today to discuss what to do about a few things."

"What you want?" Diego asked abruptly as he moved to the edge of his chair.

"Relax, Diego," Jorge said as he put his hand up indicating for him to stop. "That is my first instruction. The second is that I wish for you to travel to Mexico and meet with some of my associates there. I have spoken to them about Enrique but I would feel better if you went to do a little more snooping around. I want to make sure there is no one else that knows anything and if there is, that they keep quiet."

"Enrique, he said no," Jolene said with wide eyes.

"What if he is afraid to talk?" Jorge replied with a shrug. "Or even more likely, what if he, himself, does not know. Maybe he feels there is no one else but there is."

"Fair enough," Diego twisted his lips together and squinted his eyes as he nodded. "I can do that."

"Keep it quiet though, Diego," Jorge continued. "I do not want anyone else to know you are going. It does not leave this room."

Noting that Jolene nodded in agreement, Jorge didn't have to look at his wife to see her reaction. They had already discussed this before the meeting.

"And me?" Jolene piped up. "What do you want from me?"

"I have two things for you," Jorge replied with some consideration. "First, you seem cozy with Enrique, so I want you to befriend him and see what you can find out. I suspect he's clean but he might let something more slip to you than me."

"I will do."

"Make it casual though," Jorge insisted. "You drop by the bar and chat with him, that kind of thing."

"I can do."

"Now, there's something else too," Jorge said and hesitated for a moment. He glanced toward Diego and back at Jolene. "This here, it is perhaps something we all need to work on."

"I don't think we need to work on it at all," Paige quietly added. "I think that we need to let sleeping dogs lie."

"What?" Diego asked with concern on his face. "What's going on?"

"I want to get revenge against those who were involved in Jesús murder," Jorge replied. "I know that the man who killed him, yes he is dead but I want to know if there are others that worked with him."

"If we keep killing their people," Paige reminded him. "They're going to kill ours."

"We kill that guy and his brother and they kill Jesús," Jolene reasoned. "Perhaps, this is it."

"I'm not sure," Jorge admitted. "Look, it was not just that they kill Jesús. They wanted to kill us all including my children. He arrived at my house ready to kill me, Paige, the kids….this here, I cannot leave alone. I must learn who was behind that."

Everyone fell silent. It had been a horrible chapter in their lives. Burying one of their closest friends, a family member at heart, had been very difficult. Not only had their *hermano* been taken away but it reminded them of the fragility of their own lives, especially in light of their common enemies and dark pasts.

"I agree," Diego replied and glanced at Paige nervously. "We don't need anyone jumping out of the shadows."

"And that is exactly why we must investigate," Jorge insisted. "I also want Marco to do some research on these people. At the time, Paige asked me to leave it alone and not stir the pot but now, I feel we must look into it. At this point, my goal is to have these loose ends tied. I do not want to worry about someone coming out of the shadows."

"Me, I am growing tired of this," Jorge continued. "I am often thinking of retiring."

"What?" Diego's eyes widened. "You want to get out of…all of this?"

"I will still be an owner of my company, Diego," Jorge replied with a shrug. "I am tired and want to spend time with my family. I have succeeded in my goals. I am rich. I am powerful. I have everything I want. Now, my last goal is to have peace. To watch my children grow. To teach Miguel to be a man. To make sure my daughter doesn't turn into a Gucci bag wearing elitist. To spend time with my wife. I have both of you and Chase to run my empire."

Diego appeared saddened by this news.

"It's time," Paige quietly commented. "We want a peaceful, normal life."

Jorge eagerly nodded.

"I do not understand," Jolene spoke up. "What would change?"

"Diego, he would be the CEO," Jorge replied and pointed toward his best friend, who appeared less than enthused. "He would take care of things and I will merely be an advisor. This here will make me less of a target. I know Diego can deal with Big Pharma, the media and the day to day bullshit."

"But the media, they love you," Diego reminded him. "That interview you had with Makerson…"

"I know but Diego, this here, I do not want anymore," Jorge replied and took a deep breath. "I am a lucky man, you know. I have lived through the most dangerous profession in the world and made it to middle-age. Do you know how rare that is? Do you know how many men I've seen die? Or run from the police? And yet, I am here. How many other narcos can I say this about?"

No one replied as the news settled in.

"But you've said this before," Diego reminded him.

"I know and I meant it before too," Jorge replied and glanced at his wife. "But life, it got in the way. My ego, with the election, it got in the way. It is time I stop getting in my way and retire."

"It's time," Paige said.

"And Chase, he is proving himself to me again and again," Jorge continued. "He has come a long way from those days in that shitty little office in Alberta."

Jolene and Jorge exchanged looks and she giggled.

"He was so naïve," Jolene spoke with emotion in her voice. "I remember the time, that woman, she OD at one of the sex parties we used to host. He run with her to the car, take her to hospital….come back, he look so scared."

Everyone laughed.

"He had no idea that we sell drugs at those parties," Jolene spoke reflectively. "He believe whatever I say."

"That's what we needed then," Diego reminded her. "He was perfect."

"I saw his potential," Jorge remembered. "I saw it from the beginning. I saw his loyalty."

"But do you see the same in Enrique?" Diego asked.

"Fear and desperation but that is not bad," Jorge said and glanced at the clock than at Paige. "'Ah! We must go. We are going to check out a new, potential school for Maria."

The four headed toward the door but it was only after Diego and Jolene left that Paige turned to Jorge.

"So what's my assignment?"

"*Mi amor,* you and me," Jorge leaned forward and pulled her into his arms. "We will be taking a weekend together in a hotel. Away from all of this. That is your only assignment."

CHAPTER 22

"Maria, you are to stay here and go wipe that shit off your face," Jorge's voice grew louder as he felt the anger rise inside him. Faced with a defiant daughter, he felt his frustrations quickly mounting. "The meeting we had at the school was for parents only and now, me and Paige, we are going away for the weekend. This is not news. We told you this earlier in the week."

"First, you don't let me go to the meeting and now I can't come with you to the hotel!" Maria complained in a voice that dragged out into a moan. "I need a break from Miguel's crying."

"Oh, is that right?" Jorge shot back. "Well, Paige and me, we need a break from both of you. We are going to the hotel for some peace and quiet, something we do not get a lot of here."

"That's what I'm saying," Maria automatically pointed toward Paige, who was comforting a fussy baby. "I need a break from him too."

"Maria," Paige jumped in, her face flustered. "Miguel is getting his teeth, that's why he's crying. Can you please try to understand?"

"You guys are leaving," Maria complained. "Why can't I? You can get me a room next to yours and I can watch TV and go online…."

"No, *Princesa,* this here, it is not happening," Jorge insisted and met her eye to eye. "Now, go upstairs and take that makeup off your face."

"I can wear makeup if I want!" Maria shot back. "I'm a teenager."

"You're *12*," Jorge pointed out. "You turn into a teenager this summer and still, I think you are too young for makeup."

"Maria," Paige cut in as she continued to comfort Miguel. "Let's try to compromise here. I think *some* makeup is fine," She glanced toward Jorge who wasn't convinced. "But right now, you have *way* too much on. Makeup should enhance your natural beauty not…"

"Not look like a clown," Jorge cut her off. "Maria, I do not know what possessed you to put on this makeup but it's terrible."

"I was watching a celebrity tutorial on YouTube where one of the…"

"Take it off!" Jorge cut her off again. "And stop trying to be like those idiots. Do you know what those people are, Maria? Do you want to know?"

"Jorge," Paige gave him a warning glance.

"No, Paige, she must hear the truth," Jorge insisted and returned his attention to Maria. "These celebrities with all their makeup, who talk like morons and are half-naked in photos, do you know what they are Maria? They are classless *putas*. And you are better than that. So go upstairs, take that fucking makeup off your face and think about what I said."

Maria seemed to grow smaller as her big, brown eyes filled with tears and she ran upstairs.

"Jorge, you need to calm down," Paige muttered as she passed him the baby. "This isn't going to get easier with her."

With that, his wife followed Maria upstairs while Miguel started to fall asleep in his arms.

"Miguel, please tell me that you will be an easier teenager than your sister," Jorge said as he ran a hand over his son's soft hair, kissing him on the top of his head. "Boys, they have to be easier."

His phone beeped and Jorge struggled to get it out of his pocket while holding Miguel in the other arm. Checking the message quickly, a grin crossed his lips. Everything was falling into place.

Juliana came downstairs to get the baby just as Paige made her way back downstairs.

"Maybe we should go another weekend…."

"No! Absolutely not," Jorge insisted. "Maria must learn that the world, it does not center on her. She will be fine."

"She seems to have a lot of problems," Paige said as she walked into the kitchen with Jorge following behind. "It's like she can't decide if she's a kid or an adult and she doesn't understand how to make that transition. I can't make her understand that there's no rush. I think kids today are sent mixed messages."

"Well, me, I will send her a strong message," Jorge said as he sat on the stool while Paige made some coffee. "That there, it was way too much makeup. I do not want my daughter walking around like that."

"I agree but some," Paige hesitated with the coffee pot in hand. "Some is ok."

"But Paige here is the thing," Jorge turned toward her as she poured the water into the machine. "It will be one thing after another. It will be boys, dates, you name it. I feel that this here is too much for me. Why does she want to grow up so fast?"

"We can only take one thing at a time," Paige replied as she turned on the coffee maker. "I managed to make her see what she had on was too much. She's calmed down. I told her that we're concerned she doesn't see her value as a person. I don't know. Maybe I said the wrong thing, I'm not sure."

"No, Paige, you always say the right thing," Jorge said and they shared a smile. "It is me that says the wrong thing."

"With teenagers, everything feels like the wrong thing."

"This here, it is true," Jorge commented and remembered his message from earlier. "Oh yes, Diego has his flight booked for tomorrow and Jolene is planning to hang around the bar and talk to Enrique tonight."

"Is that a good idea?" Paige pointed out. "I was thinking about it earlier and with her drinking issues…"

"She is only drinking non-alcoholic drinks," Jorge replied. "I discuss this with her already."

"I hope you're right," Paige replied as she leaned against the counter. "I just don't want to put her in a situation where…."

"Paige, it is ok," Jorge said as he gestured for her to come and sit beside him. "I told her she is on the clock so it is important she not drink. I want her head clear."

"So everything is falling into place?"

"Perfectly, yes," Jorge spoke gently as his wife sat beside him. "She will warm up to this man and he will feel comfortable confessing to her."

"How warm do you want things to get?" Paige countered as the two made eye contact.

"As warm as necessary," Jorge murmured. "Me, I don't care. As long as he feels safe with her to tell any secrets and this will also preoccupy Jolene."

"Not to mention she will put the fear of God in him," Paige reminded him. "If your name comes up, she might mention how dangerous you are. Remember, you did have a gun to her head once."

"Ah yes, *mi amor,* do not think that I didn't also consider this," Jorge winked at her. "She will tell him that I almost killed her for disloyalty and I believe this is exactly what he needs to know now. This will remind him of his place in our group. And Paige, people must know their place."

"No disagreement here," Paige said as she leaned in and kissed him.

"So, everything is settled?"

"Oh, one more thing, Maria asked about the school we went to see today," Paige continued with some hesitation. "I told her that we aren't sure yet. She keeps insisting on a co-ed school."

"Oh fuck," Jorge rolled his eyes. "Paige, I do not like this idea."

"I think we have to do it," She replied with a shrug. "When we looked at the other schools…"

"I know, this one from today, it is the best one so far," Jorge agreed and glanced across the room for a moment. "I do not know the answer."

"How about we sleep on it," Paige suggested with a shrug.

"Oh Paige," Jorge leaned in as he placed his hand on her thigh. "I do not believe we will be doing much sleeping this weekend."

"I look forward to that," Paige commented as Jorge moved in to kiss her with more intensity. This ended abruptly when Miguel started to cry again.

"I should go upstairs," She spoke with an apologetic look in her eyes. "He needs me."

"I need you too," Jorge reminded her. "And Juliana, she is upstairs."

"I know but we'll be gone all weekend…"

"Fair enough," Jorge said as he squeezed her thigh one more time before Paige rose from the stool and headed upstairs.

It was when he stood up to get some coffee that he felt it. An unexpected pain in his chest caused him to halt as if moving would somehow cause him to lose control over his body. Closing his eyes, fear spread through his soul. What if this meant something? This wasn't the first time.

It was this rare moment of vulnerability that reminded him that he was human. There were times when Jorge doubted this fact. It was only when looking into the eyes of his children or wife that he saw reflections of his humanity. When he yelled at Maria earlier that day, he recognized her fear and was momentarily back to his childhood. He didn't want to be like his father but was he?

Taking a deep breath, a cold sweat seemed to swallow up his anxiety and flush it out of his body. He glanced toward the stairs. Without even thinking, Jorge automatically made his way to Maria's room. He stood outside her door for a few minutes before finally knocking.

"Come in," His daughter's voice suddenly sounded so young, as if she were merely a child again. It filled him with shame.

"Maria," He opened the door to see her sitting on her bed. The makeup from earlier was gone. "I would like to talk to you."

She didn't reply but nodded as he sat in the chair across from her bed.

"Maria, today, I should not have yelled at you," Jorge admitted. "It was not right of me to do so but you must understand, the makeup you had on, it was too much."

"I know, Papa."

"I do not want to be critical of you," He continued. "But it is my job to take care of you and to make you into a respectable, responsible adult. I cannot send you into the world with a face full of makeup. People, they misunderstand this."

"I know," Maria spoke shamefully. "Paige told me that it over-sexualized me and that it sends the wrong message to creepy, old men."

Jorge cringed at this comment even though he agreed.

"Yes, Maria, Paige is right," Jorge agreed. "This, it does worry me."

"But Papa, I can look after myself," Maria seemed to gather her confidence again.

"I know, Maria," Jorge replied, choosing his words carefully. "I do understand. But still…"

"It's too much makeup," Maria replied and nodded. "I understand."

Jorge paused for a moment, thinking of the chest pains he had experienced.

"Maria, I try to do what is best for you," He insisted. "I do not always do well but my intentions are good. I promise you that."

His daughter looked at him with wide eyes but didn't say anything.

"This here, raising children, it is not easy," He confessed. "As you know, my parents, they failed me. I do not want to fail you."

Maria looked stunned as her father rose from the chair, crossed the room and kissed her on the top of the head before leaving.

CHAPTER 23

"No crying babies, no loud music…" Jorge collapsed on the bed and momentarily closed his eyes as he loosened his tie. Opening his eyes again, he observed Paige as she took in the bedroom of their hotel suite. She was wearing a summer dress that hugged her curves beautifully. "This here, it is heaven to me. These days, there is no greater aphrodisiac than quiet. It is beautiful, *mi amor.*"

"This suite looks familiar," Paige commented as she moved closer to the bed. "Isn't this the same one…"

"The very same," Jorge stared at her as his memory traveled back to the unconventional way they met. A gentle vibration ran through his body as his mind returned to the intense pleasure of that night. "It was in this bed where I woke up to the sound of someone in my suite and then later….why don't you come here *mi amor,* so I can remind you?"

"I have a better idea," Paige spoke smoothly, her voice thick with insinuation. "I've been working on a little something for you."

"You've been working on something?" Jorge prompted up on his elbows. "Now this here, I got to see."

Paige grinned as she reached into her purse to pull out her phone. Sitting the bag and phone on a nearby table, she gently tapped a button before returning her attention to Jorge. He could hear a dark, sexy song start to play, taking him back to the 90s and a time when music wrote the soundtrack of his life. And yet, he was very much in the present when he watched his wife move to the hypnotic beat, dancing with a seductiveness that made his heart beat faster.

At first, it was simply the way she moved her hips to the beat, slowly running her hands over her dress, the material so thin that he swore he could almost see through it. However, it was when the music picked up that he sensed her deep connection to the song that went beyond the hypnotic beat. It was as if the lyrics ran through her veins and connected with her soul, reminding him that no one else was quite like Paige Hernandez.

He sat up, watching intently, his body aroused, as she started to slowly pull on the material of her dress, her fingers gliding up her naked skin as she lifted the skirt up over her hips to reveal a pair of pretty, almost translucent panties with tiny flowers on them. They were expensive. He had bought them for her as a surprise gift.

She slowly pulled the dress over her torso as she continued to dance with ease until the material was gathered together at her breasts, when she made one swift move, lifting the dress and tossing it aside. Wearing a matching bra with a thin, delicate string that tied together in the front, Jorge suddenly had the urge to untie it but she seemed to move away when he reached out as if to tease him. She instead turned around, continuing to dance with her back to him.

Feeling himself growing warm, Jorge started to unbutton his shirt as she turned back in time to see him tossing his tie aside and unzipping his pants, which were quickly growing restrictive. He watched with anticipation as she moved to the edge of the bed, his eyes widened and heart raced as he lurched forward. He grabbed her head with both hands, his lips aggressively met with hers as she shared his passion with a hunger that only made him want her more as she got on the bed.

A sound that rose from the back of her throat alerted something inside of him that caused Jorge to instinctively reach out and pull her body closer to his own. She worked quickly to remove his clothes as they kissed with a desire that was stronger than it had been in months. It reminded him of their first night together a few years earlier. There had been a connection from the moment he looked in her eyes, a powerful, animal-like lust that set afire throughout his body in a way no other woman had before. It was addictive, more intense than anything he had ever experienced.

It still was.

He devoured her; touching, tasting every inch of her body, his tongue, his lips, his teeth, Jorge had no limits. Watching her experience such intense pleasures only increased his desires until he was unable to stand it any longer. He took her from behind, spreading her legs, Jorge entered her causing a pleasurable cry that was only drowned out when he heard an unexpected, loud gasp escape his lips. He had never let go like that; a pleasure so carnal, somewhere between the world of fierce satisfaction and a combination of intense sadness and love. It frightened him.

It was only afterward as they lay in bed that Paige caught something in his eye that Jorge attempted to hide it but it was too late.

"There's something wrong," She said in a gentle tone with no judgment. "I feel it."

"No, Paige, there is nothing wrong," He attempted to lighten the mood. "Everything right now, it is perfect. I feel as if I'm floating on a cloud. It is beautiful."

"Your eyes though," She rose slightly, leaning on her arm. "I can see it."

"Paige, I assure you, I am fine," Jorge continued to insist. "This here, you and me, it was….you know, very intense. I had not expected whatever…emotion, I do not know the word but it was powerful. Maybe we make another baby?"

"No!" Paige answered quickly even though she knew he was teasing her. "That is the last thing we need."

"Ah! But a houseful of babies," Jorge continued to joke. "We could start a gang to carry the family name."

"I don't think that's necessary."

Jorge turned toward Paige as she snuggled up to him.

"Remember that night when we met?" Jorge decided to change the topic. "Under any other circumstances, I would've killed someone who broke into my room like that."

"I know."

"Under any other circumstances," Jorge continued. "You probably would've killed me even if you knew it was a mistake."

"I know."

"Then, why did you not?" He asked. "I am curious."

"I…" Paige replied and appeared troubled by the question. "Something told me not to, my instincts. And you were talking about your daughter…"

"But many people would say that to play on sympathies," Jorge reminded her.

"And it wouldn't have worked," Paige replied as she ran a hand through his hair. "But with you, something told me to wait and then I phoned my contact and was told who you were."

"And that was?"

"A powerful narco," Paige replied with a grin on her face. "Someone to not fuck around with."

"Is that so?"

"Specifically, I was told 'either fuck him or kill him but make sure you do one of those things'," Paige grinned. "Not that I stayed the night because of that but when I think back now, it's kind of funny."

"I think I have played that game before," Jorge went along with it. "I think it's would you rather fuck, kill or marry?"

"I did two of those things."

"I am quite relieved those were the two you chose," Jorge teased. "Those two, they are my favorites."

They both laughed.

"Does this boss know we eventually married?"

"I don't know," Paige replied. "I try to separate my personal and professional life. I stated that I wanted to retire as an assassin."

"And that was fine?"

"I get a call sometimes," Paige replied. "But I think it's not like being a narco. You aren't tied to it. If anything, they miss my professionalism."

"Ah yes, the new generation of slackers," Jorge piped up and took a deep breath.

"They aren't all slackers," Paige reminded him. "But there's a different attitude that we didn't have."

"Hmm….yes, what is in it for me," Jorge said. "Loyalty, it is dead."

"Are you really retiring from the business?" Paige asked as she batted her long, beautiful lashes. "You aren't just saying that again?"

"I always mean it when I say it but sometimes, it does not work," Jorge replied. "I do not wish to do this anymore. I want to live my life, whatever is left of it, in peace with my family.."

"What do you mean, what's left of it?" Paige cut him off, "You're only in your 40s."

"*Mi amor,* I hate to tell you but we are middle-aged," Jorge reminded her. "It is going to move quickly from here."

"That's so depressing."

"No, depressing is that many of us won't make it to old age."

"That's *extremely* depressing," Paige looked troubled.

"Paige, this here, it is a reality," He continued even though a dark cloud seemed to move over their bed. "We must be realistic. That is why I want to move away from the business. I want to focus on my family. I am tired of taking care of problems. We must make sure that Chase, Diego, all of them, they are ready."

"You think you're going to die, don't you?"

Paige's question caught him off guard. He turned in time to see her eyes fill with tears.

"No, Paige, do not cry," Jorge leaned forward and kissed her forehead. "Do not worry about such things. I have lived through so much, even a potential murder from one of the best assassins in the world, I will be fine."

Paige laughed through her tears but suddenly stopped and shook her head.

"This here, this is why I want to retire," Jorge continued as he pulled her close. "I want to focus on what is important. I will still be a part of the company and call the shots but from a distance. Out of the spotlight."

"Can you imagine if you had stayed in politics?"

"No, *mi amor,* I cannot," Jorge spoke frankly. "When I talk to Alec about this, I shake my head. I could not do this job, Paige. There is too much red tape, too much double talk, too much trying to put out fires. Me, I have enough fires to put out in my life without doing the same for a country. And no matter what he does, he is criticized. This here, it would piss me off."

"It was beautiful though," Paige reminded him. "All the support you had. People believed in you."

"People believe in whoever reminds them of themselves," Jorge said. "My directness, it represented the directness they aren't allowed to express in their own lives. We choose our leaders because we think they are like us and when they start to fail in our eyes, we grow angry and turn against them."

"Its human nature," Paige reminded him. "We put people on a pedestal only to rip them down."

"Yes, this is true," Jorge said just as his phone beeped. "I am sorry, Paige, but I must check this."

She seemed unconcerned as he reached for his phone.

"Ah, it is Maria," Jorge said with a grin and turned the phone toward Paige.

They shared a smile.

CHAPTER 24

"They loved it, Miguel!" Maria exclaimed, turning to her baby brother who sat against the propped up pillow on her bed. He stared at his sister with amazement in his eyes. "Look at us. Isn't this the best picture *ever*?"

Leaning closer, she attempted to show him the image on her phone but instead, the distracted 1-year-old reached for her shiny necklace. Maria noticed and moved away.

"No, Miguel, you will break it," She reminded him.

Crestfallen, his face crumbled and although she expected him to cry, he instead started to giggle.

"Miguel, you laugh a lot," Maria grinned as she tapped a message on her phone and sent it off. "When you're a happy baby, you're a *really* happy but when you're upset, you're a little asshole."

The baby continued to laugh as if his sister had said the most hilarious thing and she couldn't help but join him. His mood was infectious.

"I can't wait until you can talk," Maria continued as she set her phone aside. "But I guess it's good that you can listen. I don't have many people who listen to me."

Her last words were melancholic. She turned to see her baby brother watch her with interest as his eyelids began to droop. His little body slumped over and Maria's heart filled with love as she leaned over and gently laid him on his side. He fell asleep immediately.

Returning her attention to her buzzing phone, she found another message from her *Papa*.

I love how you are holding Miguel's hand in the photo. It shows you are close, that your loyalty is strong. I am very proud of you both, Bonita.

She smiled. Maria loved holding hands. It gave her a sense of comfort, of safety but now that she was getting older, it was different. It was cute to hold hands when you were a kid. It implied something completely different when you were a teenager. You were only supposed to hold hands with a boyfriend and everything else was weird. She missed it.

Maria took a picture of Miguel sleeping and sent it to her *padre*. On impulse, she also sent it to Diego, Jolene, and Chase.

Ah! The baby! He is so handsome.

That one was from Jolene.

He looks like his Godfather.

This was from Diego.

You're taking good care of him.

This was from her *papa*.

Then silence.

It wasn't that Chase never texted her back anymore it was that he didn't do it as often. She knew why. He knew about her crush on him and wanted to get her to leave him alone. That's how boys were. They pretended you were invisible when they didn't like you back.

Too bad she wasn't invisible to other people who didn't like her.

Maria flipped through her messages and found one from a former classmate, a white girl named Briana.

FYI, everyone is saying you're not coming back to our school because you were kicked out. You Mexicans are dirty. You should stay in your own country.

Maria wiped away a tear as she read the series of messages. At least it wasn't as bad as it had been when her father was in politics. Some kids admired her back then but others were vicious. They made fun of how her father talked, his accent and his poor English. Some implied he was a narco, a crazy man who had no right to run their pristine country. One girl even suggested that being the Canadian prime minister was a job for a 'white man' and no one else.

Not that he cared. Nothing bothered him. When their neighbor attempted to cause problems for them, he didn't sit and cry like her. He managed to get the lady to move. Maria remembered him confronting her on more than one occasion while Paige cringed.

"This won't end well…"

That was what she said. At the time, Maria had simply assumed that she meant her father would be an asshole to the neighbor lady but then again, she *had* disappeared shortly after. Thinking about this fact and returning to her former classmate's message, Maria felt fury run through her veins and hit reply.

Burn in hell, bitch.

Satisfied, she hit send.

It was confusing sometimes. When Maria didn't retaliate, she felt like shit but when she fought back, she got in trouble. Like the time she brought a knife to her school in Mexico. The other kids could bully her but she wasn't allowed to protect herself? Going to teachers and principal was a waste of time. They didn't listen. They didn't care. It was the same in Canada.

She could tell her father but he would get upset. It was easier to not say anything.

But then again…

Fuck you, Maria.

Fuck you, you dirty white cunt.

Maria finally blocked her. Why hadn't she done that before? Probably because it didn't matter. These girls had too much time on their hands and created fake accounts and hounded her that way. It never ended.

She glanced at Miguel sleeping peacefully. If kids ever bullied him, she would hurt them. She felt the same protectiveness that Maria assumed her father felt for her. It filled her with pride. She was lucky to have her family.

She went on Facebook to see if anything new was on Chase's page. It was private so few people could see it. His profile picture was of boxing gloves with no background image. He didn't even have his real name. Just Chase Carl. Maybe that was his middle name?

He hadn't updated anything in weeks.

Sighing heavily, she was bored. Maybe, Maria considered, this was why other kids bullied. She used to spend her days dancing and singing but since her terrible audition experiences the previous summer, she had lost interest. Some of the snobby bitches in her school found acting work.

The pretty blonde girls, the white girls mostly because that's what the directors wanted.

Too bad Paige wasn't her real mother. If she were, maybe Maria would've had lighter skin or blue eyes or blonde hair. Even her father treated her like a queen, unlike her biological mother, whom he hated. Then again, she hadn't been a good mother. This was something Maria hadn't realized until Paige came into their lives because she was nurturing and caring.

Then again, all her *familia* took good care of her. Jolene and Diego would do anything for her. Jesús had been the same.

She missed him. After he died, Maria started to have nightmares that someone murdered her father. If anyone killed her father, she would kill them. It didn't matter if she was only 12, she would find a way to do it. In Mexico, it was not unusual for kids her age to murder. Many were part of cartels. She often wondered how old her father was when he started but he refused to talk about it.

Chase was her family too but she loved him in a different way. She would be his girlfriend someday. Of course, she was too young now. He saw her as just a kid but one day, when she was older, Maria wanted him to fall in love with her. Just like her father had made Paige fall in love with him.

On a whim, she sent Chase an image of the message sent to her from the girl at school. People encouraged you to tell someone if you were bullied. She would tell him.

Who sent this to you?

A girl at school. Well, my old school. Papa is putting me in a different one in the fall.

Maria, you should tell your parents.

They are away for the weekend plus, you know Papa, he will go crazy.

When did this start?

Maria felt her heart drop. When had the bullying started? Good question.

It has been like…. always.

There was no reply for a few minutes.

Maria, have you told anyone this?

No. It won't help anyway.

We should talk about this.

Excited, she jumped up from the bed and thought about what she would wear. However, when the phone rang, she quickly realized he meant a phone conversation and not meet in person. Her heart dropped.

"Hello?"

"Maria, so you haven't been telling your parents about this?"

"Not really."

"And it's been going on for a while?"

"Since Mexico."

There was a long silence.

"I had to tell *Papa* a few times when I got in trouble at school," She relented. "But that's it."

"Maria, you don't have to put up with this."

She loved how he said her name. It sounded powerful. Like superhero powerful.

"I know."

"You're starting at a new school?"

"Yes."

"Is there a lot of them....bothering you?"

"Some. I blocked that girl."

"Good! Keep doing that and report them."

"But they start rumors about me even though I'm not there."

"And you don't tell teachers?"

"Sometimes but it only makes it worse if they talk to them."

Chase hesitated for a moment.

"You're taking those self-defense classes I told you about?"

"Yes, of course," Maria exclaimed. "I go twice a week."

"Keep that up," He insisted. "Maria, you need to learn how to protect yourself but you also have to stand up to these kids."

"I know."

"These assholes," Chase continued. "Maria, they'll always be there. I deal with them as an adult. Part of growing up is learning what to do when someone tries to cross a line. Trust me, I didn't learn that fast enough and I wish I had."

"Did anyone ever bully you?"

"Yes," Chase replied. "My mother was abusive when I was growing up. My ex-wife, she was controlling too."

"I remember you telling me," Maria spoke quietly. "Do you think how your mother treated you made you marry a woman who was also controlling?"

Chase paused for a moment.

"I suppose, yes," He gently agreed. "But Maria, this is a struggle we all have. It could be a family member, a coworker, or in your case, a classmate."

"Chase, my father is a very powerful man," Maria said as she walked across the room and looked outside. "Paige, she is powerful too. It seems like...weird that I'm not like them. Does that mean I'm like my biological mother? She was spineless."

"Maria, you are *not* spineless," Chase insisted and began to laugh. "Far from it!"

"But why are these kids bothering me then?"

"You want the truth?" Chase asked and then continued before she could answer. "Because they're spoiled brats, that's why."

Maria began to giggle.

"I deal with them here at the bar too," He added. "Look, Maria, I gotta go but remember this, you're more powerful than you realize."

She didn't reply.

"When I started working out," Chase continued. "I got big fast. Lots of muscle. People began to comment on it and I felt awkward, so I tried to make myself seem smaller than I was. I was nicer so people wouldn't be scared of me. I stayed calm, so I wouldn't seem too aggressive."

"But now, I realize that I did it because I feared what others thought," He hesitated again. "Maria, your father is a *very* powerful man but that doesn't mean that you need to make yourself small."

His words stuck with her long after their conversation ended. As she stared out the window, a rustling behind her caused Maria to turn to see her brother open his eyes. She crossed the bedroom floor.

Miguel stared at her with a sense of awe in his face. He opened his mouth.

"Ma...eeee..."

CHAPTER 25

"I can't believe we missed his first word," Paige spoke emotionally as they drove home on Sunday morning. Her eyes scanned traffic around them but she appeared uncomfortable. "He's growing up so fast."

"I cannot believe that his first word was Maria," Jorge said with laughter in his voice. "But his sister, she was very excited. Do not worry, *mi amor, mama,* it will be next."

She shrugged helplessly.

"You know, that is perhaps what he was trying to say," Jorge continued with enthusiasm. "Maybe Maria misunderstood and it was '*mama*' or 'mommy'?"

"It sounds like he was trying to say Maria but it was too much for him," Paige gently offered. "It's ok. I mean, I'm not upset that he said her name. It makes sense because she's always with him. I just wish I had been there."

Sensing the emotional maternal moment, Jorge decided to lighten things up.

"Well, you know," Jorge jumped in. "Maybe with the next baby, you will be there for his first words…"

"No!" Paige put her hand in the air. "No, I love my son but no, no more babies."

"But Paige, you still have some time before that change of life, you know, you could.."

"No!" Paige repeated and shook her head rapidly as Jorge grinned. "No, I don't want to do this again. I did it. I'm glad. But no, no more babies. No more pregnancies. I just can't."

Jorge replied with laughter and reached over to touch her hand.

"This is fine," He shared a smile with her. "I love my son too but I do not think I can handle two crying babies."

"You and me both."

"But I do love," Jorge spoke thoughtfully as they moved through traffic. "That Maria and Miguel are so close. This here, it makes me happy. I feel better knowing that whatever happens, they will always have one another."

Paige agreed with a gentle smile.

"Let us talk about something else," Jorge suggested. "We will soon be back to reality so let us enjoy our last moments of peace."

"Fair enough," Paige agreed as she sat her phone aside and tilted her head. "I have a question for you."

"And that is?"

"This weekend we were talking about the night we met in the suite," Paige began and turned slightly. "If I had been a man…"

"*Mi amor,*" Jorge immediately caught on. "If you were a man and broke into my hotel room and held a gun to my head, you would be dead right now. I would not care if it was a mistake or not."

"So, different rules for women?"

"Well, I would not say that, exactly," Jorge said and shook his head. "You know me, I do not give women many chances either. I have had a few women hold a gun to my head."

"Really?" Paige seemed shocked but after a moment began to nod. "I don't know why that surprises me."

"Maria's mother, she was one of them," Jorge quickly added. "But at the time, she was pregnant, so I let it go. Another time, I am not so sure."

"But you let me live?"

"You?" Jorge gave her a seductive grin and winked at her. "My hesitation, it was probably a bit to do with hormones, *mi amor.* Even that day, with a gun to my head, when I saw that *culo,* all I can think about is getting you naked."

"So it was my ass that saved me?" Paige began to laugh.

"Well, it was a little more than that," Jorge admitted sheepishly. "But yes, this is the first thing I see of you. But I look into your eyes and I think, I cannot kill this woman. I just know."

They shared a smile and drove in silence. It was as they arrived home that Jorge's phone began to beep. Turning the SUV off, he checked his message.

"*Mi amor,* this here," He said as he squinted over the iPhone. "This is why I want to retire."

"I can certainly understand," She replied while unfastening her seatbelt.

"Alec, he needs to speak with me," Jorge commented. "It's an emergency of some kind."

"Oh?" Paige raised an eyebrow. "That's concerning."

"The opposition, I assume," Jorge replied. "Lately, he has rattled their cages now that he wants to tax big polluting corporations more money. But then again, maybe it is another loose cannon in his party."

"It's pretty bad when you have to watch for enemies on both sides," Paige commented as she opened the SUV door. "Who knew Canadian politics was like this?"

"Ah! You Canadians," Jorge said with a grin. "Your naivety is both beautiful and unexpected at the same time."

She shrugged as she got out of the vehicle and he followed her lead. He opened the back and reached for the suitcases.

"I'm used to that in American politics or….well…"

"Anywhere but Canada?" Jorge met her as they made their way to the door. "*Mi amor,* even as you say the words, don't they feel sort of…"

"Ok, yeah, I get it," Paige agreed. "I guess they hide it well."

"You would not believe everything that is hidden in dark shadows," Jorge reminded her. "Your politicians, they are a magician with a cult leader's personality."

"So Charles Manson meets David Copperfield?"

"With a little more Charlie," Jorge teased as he reached for the door. "At least, when I have finished with Alec, that is my hope."

His phone beeped again as they walked through the doorway.

Sitting the suitcases down, Jorge reached for his phone.

"Diego," Jorge shook his head. "He has news from Mexico."

"Ahh....hopefully not another problem," Paige muttered as Maria rushed downstairs.

"I will tell him to come over and in the meantime, I will call Alec to see what this emergency is."

"What emergency?" Maria asked with wide eyes as she approached the two of them. "What happened?"

"Oh, nothing," Jorge shook his head and leaned forward to kiss his daughter. "It is just a government thing. They break a nail and think it's an emergency."

Maria laughed as Paige leaned in to hug her.

"So, my son, he talk this weekend?" Jorge asked. "If he's a true Hernandez, he probably will never stop now that he started."

Maria giggled. "He just talked that one time," She glanced excitedly toward Paige. "He was trying to say my name. It was *so* cute!"

"He loves you very much, *bonita,*" Jorge commented as he started to walk toward his office. "Tell Paige about it and I will catch up later. I gotta make a call."

Once behind the closed door, he took a deep breath and walked behind his desk.

Alec answered on the first ring.

"I just got home," Jorge said immediately. "What is the emergency?"

"The tax increase on corporations," Alec spoke in a shaking voice. "It's not going over well especially with big oil."

"Yeah, well fuck big oil," Jorge shot back. "My company, we are paying them too and we aren't big polluters like them."

"But the government always looks after them," Alec reminded him. "And since I'm not, they're digging their claws in."

"The problem here is that oil companies, they have run the show for far too long," Jorge reminded him. "They are the cartel of your country."

"They feel they're too valuable as an employer and to our economy so the rules don't or shouldn't apply to them."

"So they have a temper tantrum, who cares?"

"That's the problem," Alec paused for a moment. "I'm getting 'anonymous' death threats. I think it's from them."

"Of course it's from them," Jorge reminded him. "Who else? They aren't getting their way, so this here, is what they do."

"This is too much," Alec spoke honestly. "I can't live with a gun to my head."

"That is what they want," Jorge insisted. "You know this, right? They want to scare you. They want to pressure you into doing what they want or drop out. If you drop out, their opposition friends will move in and make nice with them."

"What am I supposed to do?" Alec countered.

"Expose them."

"But I don't have proof."

"In this time, you do not need proof," Jorge reminded him. "You just need to expose these threats in the media. Then you blackmail them behind closed doors. Say you got proof it was them and it would be a pretty nasty, public scandal if it was released."

Alec didn't seem convinced.

"Or you could handle business like I do," Jorge continued. "Not many people tend to argue with you when they get a parcel in the mail that has a…"

"I…I think we need to cut down on the violence," Alec cut him off. "There's been a lot lately."

"But *amigo,* you must admit that it has worked."

There was a pause.

"Can Paige find out if there's a hit on me?"

"Paige, she can find out anything," Jorge reminded him of his powerful wife. "She has the connections, for now, you need to stop running scared like a pussy. This here requires a powerful response. You must expose these threats to the media and be very clear on the fact that you're closing in on the culprit. I will also have Marco do some research on this matter."

"Ok," Alec didn't sound very reassured. "I have extra security."

"Yes, well, we must get the story out there that you are considering some *outside* security from *my* people. This here, it might send a message."

"Are you really considering that?"

"I may," Jorge thought for a moment. "Maybe Chase. I must see."

"I'm not sure if I can get it authorized but…"

"You're the fucking prime minister. If you do not have authority, then who the fuck does?"

Silence.

"You can do your part," Jorge continued. "And I will do mine."

Frustrated, he ended the conversation. Sometimes, he wondered if it would've been better to do the job himself. But then he remembered all the ridiculousness of politics and was happy on the sidelines.

A knock on his door interrupted his thoughts.

"*Sí?*"

"It's me," Diego called out.

"Come in."

There was apprehension in his *hermano* as he entered the room. It wasn't something Jorge expected, which gave him pause.

"Diego, you are scaring me," Jorge gestured toward the chairs. "What is it you want to tell me?"

His eyes were full of concern as he sat down and began to talk.

CHAPTER 26

"Everything, it is ok in Mexico?" Jorge asked as his eyes evaluating Diego's face. "You would tell me otherwise, *amigo?* Did someone threaten you?"

"No," Diego insisted, anxiously shuffling in his chair. "We took care of the loose ends. Enrique is safe and there are no others."

"He will be relieved to learn this news," Jorge nodded and took a deep breath. "So what are you *not* telling me, Diego? Is it the murderers that killed Jesús? Must we worry? Are there others?"

"Me and Marco are still looking into that," Diego replied carefully. "But it looks like no, there are no others."

"There must be others," Jorge noted that his friend appeared distracted. "Come on, I do not believe it was just the man we shot and his brother."

"It appears the group has disbanded," Diego explained with sadness in his eyes. "We got the two leaders. Without them, the others faded away."

"Are you certain?" Jorge attempted to understand the strange sense he was getting from his friend. "They will not…resurrect out of nowhere."

"They went back to the states," Diego gestured toward the window. "They're too busy tormenting immigrants down there."

"I am not sure I like this news more," Jorge spoke skeptically. "Are you certain they are no longer in Canada?"

"I have Marco doing more research but so far," Diego suddenly looked away. "I think it's fine."

"Then what is wrong, *amigo?*" Jorge pushed a little harder. "You are not acting like yourself. Did one of your boyfriends break up with you? Are you starting to lose your hair? Did one of your lime trees die? What is it?"

Diego grinned at the suggestion while his eyes widened but his response was lackluster at best.

"I haven't checked them today but my lime trees, they better be ok."

Jorge felt uncomfortable. He didn't like the awkwardness in the room. It was unlike his longtime friend to show hesitation. He was like a balloon that had lost its air. He lacked the usual fire. This wasn't the Diego he knew.

"Then tell me," Jorge insisted. "You come here today for a reason. I want to know, why are you acting so strangely?"

Diego hesitated before responding.

He took a few moments but finally spoke.

"When I was down there," Diego started. "I heard something but I don't know if it is true. It's probably wrong so I want to do some more research."

"You came here to tell me, did you not?"

"Yes, but now that I'm here," Diego appeared tense. "I'm gonna wait."

"Diego, can we stop playing this here game?" Jorge grew impatient and took a deep breath. "I want to know what it is that concerns you. I will consider that it might be false information and we will see but at least tell me."

"It's not good."

"Most news that I receive is not," Jorge reminded him. "Is someone trying to hurt Paige? Maria and Miguel? Me? Does someone want to kill me? Another cartel? Are there problems with one of our suppliers? Diego, my imagination, it is running out of control. Please tell me the truth."

"It's none of that," Diego assured him and paused for a moment. "I was talking to one of my contacts when I was down there and he told me that…."

Jorge gave him a look to encourage the words.

"You know what?" Diego suddenly sat back in his chair while shaking his head with relief in his eyes. "It can't be true. It's some stupid rumor."

"Diego," Jorge spoke abruptly. "I'm not fucking around here. Tell me what you know. None of these games."

"Ok," Diego grew serious again. "So this guy I know, we were talking. He mentioned Verónic."

Jorge cringed when hearing the name of Maria's mother. That woman had caused him so much misery, even in her death.

"What? Did this guy," Jorge started to guess. "he had an affair with her? Did they do coke together, what?"

"Yes," Diego spoke earnestly and took a long moment to continue. "Last week."

Jorge shook his head, confused.

"Diego, you obviously forget that my ex," Jorge spoke skeptically. "She is dead. Whoever this woman is, obviously has overtaken Verónic's identity. That is not so uncommon."

"That's what I thought too," Diego insisted and hesitated. "But he talked about how he thought she was dead, that you had killed her...he had a picture. I'm pretty sure it was her."

"This here," Jorge shook his head. "This is impossible. There was a funeral announcement..."

"But you didn't go to the funeral," Diego reminded him. "Remember, her parents didn't want you or Maria to go."

Jorge thought for a moment.

"But it was in the papers...online...."

"Her parents wanted you to think she was dead," Diego suggested. "So you would leave her alone."

A sudden roar of fury lit up his heart and ran through his body as Jorge jumped out of his seat, grabbed a nearby lamp and threw it across the room. The heavy object merely bounced against the wall and crashed to the ground, making a loud banging noise that sent a ripple through the house. Feeling unsatisfied, he started for an empty chair but before he could, the door flew open and Paige ran in while at the same time, Diego was attempting to block him from the chair.

"It could be wrong," Diego was speaking rapidly while Paige approached them with fear in her eyes. She briefly glanced toward the lamp. "It could be photoshopped. Maybe my eyes were wrong..."

"What the hell is going on here?" Paige cut in and reached for Jorge's arm, immediately calming him. "Why did you throw the lamp? Why are you so angry?"

Without answering, he turned his back to them and attempted to calm down. His chest felt heavy as if a brick weighed it down. Cold sweat immediately followed and he closed his eyes, if only for a moment while Diego hurriedly explained.

"I was in Mexico…"

"No!" Jorge cut in and put his hand up. "Close the door first before you tell. I do not want…"

"Ok, ok," Diego replied and could be heard rushing across the room, while Paige continued to comfort him.

"Jorge, you need to calm down," She spoke softly. "No matter what it is, we can resolve this."

"The door is shut," Diego could be heard returning and Jorge finally felt relaxed enough to turn around. "You look terrible, Jorge. Maybe…"

"Just, please, tell her," Jorge said as he returned to his chair. Reaching in his desk drawer, he found some CBD pills and popped one in his mouth.

Diego quickly went on to repeat the entire story to Paige who seemed to take the news with ease.

"So, there's no proof other than this picture he showed you?" Paige asked skeptically. "Pictures, they can be fixed."

"But why would he just happen to have a fixed picture on him?" Jorge asked and shrugged. "This does not make sense. How did her name even come up in the conversation?"

"I told him I was in Mexico working on something for you," Diego admitted but spoke to Paige, as if trying to avoid Jorge's wrath. "That's when he said, 'Hey, you know his ex? The lady who liked to party?' I assumed it was a story about back in the day…in fact, that's what I thought he meant at first until he showed me the picture with last week's date on it."

"The date was on the picture?" Paige asked.

"Yes," Diego nodded. "That's when I started to ask questions. Like, what the fuck is going on? She's dead."

"And he said…." Jorge asked, suddenly feeling calmness fill his body; the brick in his chest disappeared.

"He said that her parents, they're the ones who arranged this," Diego replied with wide eyes. "They knew you would kill her if they didn't. I guess they found her, got her into a hospital and paid off someone to tell you she was dead."

"Yeah, well that guy," Jorge jumped in angrily. "*He's* going to be dead when I find him."

"He already is," Diego replied, putting his hand up. "I tried to find him to learn more but found out he was killed on duty. Ironically, by another cartel."

Jorge took in this information and shared a look with Paige.

"First, we must find out if this is true," He insisted and thought for a moment. "This man, did he not realize that he was poking the lion when he tell you this?"

"He was drunk so I guess…."

"Bullshit!" Jorge replied sharply. "You don't really believe that, do you?"

"Of course not," Diego replied. "I told him he better not be fucking around."

"Then why did he bother? What is in it for him?"

"He wants money to lead you to her."

"I will give it to him if he can stand her in front of me," Jorge insisted and then glanced at his wife. "So I can kill her myself."

CHAPTER 27

"It is, how you say," Jorge suddenly felt as if his English was slipping away. He closed his eyes momentarily, attempting to avoid his wife's face. News of Maria's mother potentially being alive had rocked him to his core. His brain was a jumbled mess.

"Jorge, you need to calm down," Paige interrupted his thoughts before he could continue to speak, a gesture he silently welcomed. He opened his eyes and glanced around the office anxiously. "I've never seen you so infuriated by anything. I know you had a volatile relationship with this woman, but she's hardly more powerful than the enemies you've taken down in the past."

"But, Paige, you do not understand," Jorge said shaking his head, feeling as though he had finally collected his thoughts. Now that they were alone, he could show his vulnerability. "This here, it is not about Verónic. It is about my power in Mexico. There was a time when this could never happen. People knew not to cross me. But this time, this time was different and I must know why."

"What are you thinking?"

"I'm thinking that government officials helped her out," Jorge replied while shaking his head. "I must find out for sure because I do not want to learn there is a secret investigation going on. I do not have to worry about a SWAT team breaking down our door some morning at 5 a.m."

"I don't think that will be a problem," Paige insisted and thought for a moment. "To begin with, this happened in Mexico and it was after you were gone. I don't think they would suddenly turn against you now."

"But maybe the Canadian government," Jorge pointed toward the window as if to indicate the outside world. "Maybe they do not want me here. Maybe they contacted them in order…"

"Jorge," Paige cut him off and put her hand in the air. "You're going down a rabbit hole. First, we have to make sure that this is Verónic. Second, if she is alive, it wouldn't be such a shock that her parents paid off someone to say she was dead. After all, Mexico is known to be corrupt. Her father had some money, didn't he? That's why his daughter was such a party girl in the first place. She had the finances to do so, isn't that what you told me?"

"*Si,*" Jorge took a deep breath as he realized that she made a good point. "This is true."

"It seems pretty easy to believe they paid off people," Paige calmly continued. "If this were Maria, wouldn't you do the same thing? And even more importantly, if you were in Mexico, *couldn't* you easily have this arranged?"

"Her father, he was in government," Jorge nodded slowly. "This here, it is possible."

"What you need to do," Paige continued. "Is you need to contact someone you know in government. Someone powerful enough that they can find out the truth."

"The former *presidente*," Jorge said as he stared into space. "He was a close friend of mine while I was in Mexico."

"That's a good start."

"I would go to fundraisers as a businessman," Jorge said and watched her eyebrow raise in interest. "Of course, this confused people who thought I was a narco and suggested I was not. Why would such a powerful politician spend time talking to a narco in public?"

"I have a pretty good idea," Paige snickered.

"It worked, *mi amor,*" Jorge replied. "He got elected with my help. And also, we solved a few problems together through his presidency."

"It helps to have powerful friends."

"I will give him a call," Jorge said as he glanced at his phone. "Once we learn if she is alive, we can also learn where she is so I can kill her."

"Do you really want to do that?"

Her question surprised him.

"Jorge, I know you hate this woman," Paige continued. "But she is Maria's mother."

"I do not want her in Maria's life."

"You've said before that you couldn't kill her," Paige reminded him. "You specifically said you set her up with the right mix of drugs to die but you couldn't actually kill her."

Jorge leancd back and took a deep breath.

"This is me now," He finally said as he glanced at the desk and then back into his wife's eyes. "Now I see she made a fool of me."

"It wasn't her, it was her parents," Paige replied gently. "And we already took care of them."

Jorge's face lit up when he thought about their threats to take away Maria years earlier and Paige's assistance in their 'murder/suicide'.

"This here, it is true," Jorge nodded. "But she told this man her whole story. If this is the case, she is most likely telling everyone. Mexico must never forget who I am and how I became so powerful. If Verónic wanted to live, she should've kept a low profile, left Mexico and started a new life somewhere else. This here, she is waving red in front of the bull."

Paige didn't reply at first, appearing lost in thought.

"But how would your daughter feel if she ever found out?"

Jorge considered her words. "She already thinks she is dead. The beauty of people thinking you are already dead is no one misses you when you are killed."

"But let's say, she someday learns the truth," Paige suggested. "I think you should wait before you make a rash decision."

"For you, my love, I will consider it," Jorge nodded and glanced at his phone again. "Oh yes, I'm going to see Marco. I must talk to him about this…and this reminds me, Paige, I also need your help."

"Mine?" She titled her head. "I can see what I can find out about Verónic.."

"No no," Jorge shook his head and sat forward in his seat, leaning on the desk. "Today, before all hell broke loose, I talked to Alec."

"And?"

"You know the taxes he wants to put on corporations?"

"Yes, you mean the environmental tax?" Paige asked as she wrinkled her forehead. "I saw something about it on the news earlier today. He's getting a lot of backlash."

"Yes, that is why I need your help," Jorge replied. "It appears that he is getting death threats and we believe that big oil is behind it."

Paige raised her eyebrows and didn't say anything. He attempted to read her expression but she was good at hiding her emotions.

"They are angry over these taxes and believe they should be excluded," Jorge continued to speak. "Alec has said no and suddenly, he gets threats."

"It does seem rather suspicious," Paige said as she reached for her phone. "I'll make some calls and see what I can find out."

"And me, I will be at the office," Jorge said as he pushed his chair out. "Diego is with Marco now. I want to see what he can find about both Alec's threats and Verónic. I wonder if he has access to any information that will be helpful."

"Meanwhile, is Alec safe?" Paige asked the innocent question but caused a ripple of jealousy to shoot through his veins. He was, after all, her ex-lover. Perhaps it was many years ago but it still stung.

"I am thinking," Jorge ignored his feelings. "I may have to see if Chase can be part of his security team. I am not sure if I can trust the people he has with him."

"It won't be that easy to get him in."

"This here, he is looking into now," Jorge replied. "I would think he is entitled to have his own security."

"And would Chase be the best bet anyway?" Paige wondered. "He *is* learning to shoot a gun but still…"

"I know, *mi amor*, I know," Jorge replied as he stood up and walked around the desk. "But Chase, he is always looking. He is observant. Unlike the others, he knows what to look for and these security men, they only look for guns. Chase, he will look for something that is out of place."

"It won't be allowed," Paige slowly shook her head as she stood up. "Whoever looks after his security isn't going to let a nightclub manager on their team. It's not going to happen."

"The threats, they most likely mean nothing," Jorge said as he turned on his phone. "It is not the first time he has been threatened. I believe it is merely to send a message. They see him as weak and therefore, someone who will give in to their requests"

"You're probably right."

"Of course, *mi amor,* I am always right," He teased and she grinned.

"Should we all meet later to make sure we're on the same page?"

"Yes, that does sound like a good idea," Jorge said and took a deep breath. "We have many irons in the fire so it is important to touch base, to communicate and see where we are later today."

"Ok," Paige leaned forward and gave him a gentle kiss. She glanced at the lamp he threw against the wall, now laying on the floor with a crack in it. "Just promise me that you'll remain calm, regardless of what you find out. We've slain much bigger dragons than Verónic in the past. If anyone is vulnerable in this situation, it's her, not us. We can take care of her either way."

"I know, *mi amor,* but this woman," Jorge started and hesitated for a moment before continuing. "She has risen from the grave. There is something very unsettling about that to me."

"It's because you're used to being in control," Paige reminded him with a soft voice that caused his breath to increase, pleasurable sensations to flow through his body. "You like being in control. You thrive on it."

"I do," He replied as his breathing increased. His fingers reached out and traced down her back, leading to the curve of her hips. "It does give me great pleasure."

CHAPTER 28

"Ok, so this here will be a fast meeting," Jorge interrupted the chatter around the boardroom table. Since it was the weekend, they were alone in the office. "There has been some…upsetting news today and as you all know by now, I do not exactly plan to sit around and see where the chips fall."

"Is it true that Maria's mother, she is alive?" Jolene asked with a look of shock on her face. "How does that happen? I thought…I mean, I think, did you not kill her?"

"I did not kill her, Jolene," Jorge spoke abruptly to make certain that the group didn't start having doubts about their leader. "She was a drug addict and I learned she overdosed on fentanyl."

"But you did not see the body, no?" Jolene appeared confused, only causing Jorge's frustration to grow. "Then how did you know that…"

"Jolene," Diego snapped at his sister. "The *policia* told him plus it was listed…

"Ok, enough!" Jorge cut off Diego, recognizing it was time for him to take over again. "This here is enough. I did not kill Maria's mother. She was a drug addict and my understanding was that she died. I do not have to explain myself to any of you. No one here is as shocked as me that she is still alive."

"Verónic's family was very good at making it seem real," Paige immediately added. "We had every reason to believe it was true."

"What kind of psychopaths lies to their grandchild?" Jorge repeated the same words he said to Paige on the way to the meeting. "It is clear now that they were planning to fight to take Maria away from me, perhaps so that Verónic could have her back. At the time, I simply believed it was out of revenge for their daughter's death."

"But if you didn't do…" Jolene started but her words drifted off.

"It doesn't matter," Paige replied curtly. "They still blamed Jorge for her addiction."

"Even though she was a cokchead when I met her," Jorge spoke sharply. "Now, there will be no more question and answer period. We do not have time for this. There are too many things to discuss that are much more important. The past isn't one of them."

"Sir," Marco suddenly spoke up. "We are looking online but are unable to find anything about this lady. I am trying to think…did she have an email address, bank account, anything that might be active?"

"This is ok, Marco," Jorge replied and then addressed the group. "I have spoken to some powerful people in the Mexican government that advised me on this situation. We have an address."

"It might be a trap," Diego spoke up with a concerned look on his face. "What if you go there and God knows who is waiting for you."

"That has crossed my mind," Jorge replied with a shrug. "However, I do not plan to sit on my hands either. I think that we need to take care of this right away."

"So, what then?" Diego asked. "If Verónic suspects you're looking for her, she might take off again."

"I have some people watching the house," Jorge replied. "I need to evaluate the situation before I make a move. We still haven't seen her."

"Are you going to kill her?" Jolene asked.

"I haven't decided yet."

"Does Maria know?" Chase spoke up for the first time during the meeting.

"No," Jorge replied. "And I'm not sure whether to tell her."

"That would be so confusing for her," Jolene quietly said to no one in particular.

"I'd be confused too if my mother came back from the dead," Diego spoke bluntly.

"Anyway, this here," Jorge continued. "We can only wait to see. As I said, I am not certain what I will do over this matter. It is…complex. She knows a lot."

"So what about Athas?" Diego suddenly changed the subject. "Me and Marco were looking for something all afternoon and…"

"I got something," Paige interrupted. "I talked to my contact earlier today and it would seem that the threats are real."

No one replied so she continued.

"And…the money being offered is pretty outstanding," She continued with no expression on her face. "Someone wants him dead but they want to make it seem like an accident."

"That's scary!" Jolene's eyes grew in size. "Can they do? Does he not have security with him always?"

"He does but no one is without their vulnerabilities," Paige reminded her. "If anyone wants someone dead, no matter who, it can happen. It might be an extreme method but it's possible."

"But what can we do?" Jolene appeared concerned. "Can we do anything?"

"We need to expose the people," Paige replied with some hesitation. "Alec's having a press conference in the morning to talk about the threats he's receiving. He wants to send a message to the people behind them that he's not hiding in the corner. This is against his security's recommendations, of course, but there's power in saying something out loud."

"It will look bad if Big Oil is exposed as the fucking savages that they are," Jorge added. "I do not think they want that image in the media."

"Can we get prove it?"

"Sure," Jorge replied with a shrug. "If not, we can *make* the proof. I am not concerned with following rules."

"But who is it?" Jolene asked as she leaned on the table. "Can we not find the person making the threats?"

"It's a bunch of them, isn't it?" Diego spoke up. "Not just one guy?"

"It is more than one person, yes," Paige nodded. "These companies, although they're competitors, they do work together when it comes to fighting the government. They're used to getting their way and aren't happy when Athas doesn't fall in line as the others have."

"So, can we trust his security?" Chase appeared skeptical. "How do we know that Big Oil hasn't got them to look the other way?"

"We don't," Jorge replied. "It is unsettling."

"Sir, I have hacked some emails," Marco pointed toward his laptop. "But so far, I am finding nothing."

"They're too smart to put that kind of thing in emails," Paige said with a shrug and Marco quickly nodded. "I'm guessing when word got around about these taxes, they met in person to discuss it."

"So, what kind of proof could we possibly have that they're involved?" Chase asked.

"I'm not sure" Paige replied with some hesitation. "One plus is that so far, it hasn't been assigned. You must be high in the food chain to be trusted with such a task."

"These sources, they can't tell you who put the hit out?" Chase asked with interest.

Paige shook her head. "No, but the amount of money that's being offered, couldn't be just anyone."

"But this, it does not make sense," Jolene said with concern on her face. "Even if they were to kill him, there is no proof that the next person who take over, would not do the same thing."

"If they had secret information he was assassinated because of his decisions," Jorge reminded her. "It might be a whole other thing."

"So, what do we do now?" She asked. "What can we do here?"

"This is another wait and see situation," Jorge replied with frustration in his voice. "Unfortunately, it's at a standstill now. Once Athas makes his announcement in the morning, we must see where the cards fall. If the hit is still on, we take it from there, otherwise, it might make them back down."

"They aren't going to back down," Diego challenged.

"Well, then," Jorge considered. "We must make sure that they do."

"Makerson will be having a private interview with Alec tomorrow as well," Paige added. "In it, he will hint that he suspects who's sending the threats, so that might be helpful too. We'll see."

"We tighten the grip until they either back down or we strangle the fuckers," Jorge insisted. "Either way, this must be taken care of immediately."

"Why do we do this?" Jolene continued to ask questions. "He has his own security and what does he do for us?"

"Are you serious?" Jorge snapped at her. "He takes care of us, so we take care of him. That is how we work, Jolene, in case you had not noticed."

"I know but he has security…"

"I would feel better if one of us were there," Diego cut in.

"Not allowed," Paige replied. "Too much red tape."

"But Jorge has a way of cutting red tape," Diego reminded them.

"Not this time, my friend," Jorge said and shook his head. "The government, I do not have time for its stupidity. We will do things the easiest way possible."

No one replied.

"If that is it, we are done here," Jorge said as he pushed his chair out.

Before anyone could reply, he exchanged looks with Paige and the two headed for the door.

CHAPTER 29

"That was a waste of my time," Jorge announced as soon as they got in the SUV and headed for home. Glancing at Paige, he searched her wife's face for a sign of agreement but was met with a look of confusion. "No?"

"I...I don't understand," Paige replied with some hesitation. "It was like all our meetings. It's to get on the same page about everything."

"But I had nothing for them," Jorge replied as he started the SUV and backed out of his parking spot. "Everything is at a standstill. They expect me to always have a solution and this time, I do not."

"Your hands are tied with both situations," Paige reminded him as they pulled into traffic. "You can't jump in with both guns blazing. It's a delicate situation with Verónic because she's Maria's mother and with Alec...it's tricky. There are no simple solutions this time."

Jorge didn't reply at first but drove in silence. His thoughts were going in every direction. Ignoring a sudden tightness in his chest, he attempted to express his feelings to Paige.

"I do not want this anymore."

"You don't want what?" Paige asked.

"All of this," His hand rose in the air and he shrugged. "This life. I am tired of solving problems. I am tired of meetings and making decisions. Back there, I could tell that they were looking at me skeptically as if I am losing my power and you know what? I think they are right."

"I don't think anyone questions your power," Paige was quick to point out and shook her head. "I think these situations have sent us all in a tailspin. You're tired. Everything will make more sense tomorrow."

She was wrong. Jorge barely slept that night, spending most of his time staring at the ceiling, wondering what to do next. He felt as if his entire life was at a gridlock while the others waited for his guidance. In the past, Jorge would've thrived on such a level of anxiety but this time, he wanted to walk away from it all. He wanted someone else to solve these problems for a change.

As it turned out, things were about to get much more complicated.

The press conference took place the following morning and Jorge watched on his laptop. Alec Athas addressed the nation, speaking openly about the threats he received through his office and where the RCMP was with the investigation.

"The police are where they always are with any investigation," Jorge spoke flippantly into his coffee. "Nowhere."

"That's pretty much what he's saying," Paige replied as Maria came downstairs with the baby. "Only in a nicer way."

"Miguel continues to say my name!" She spoke proudly. "Sorry guys, he might get around to saying your names *someday.*"

"Yes, Maria, we do look forward to that," Jorge forced a cheerful voice.

"He loves me best," She giggled causing the baby to laugh.

"Maria, he…"

"Oh my God!" Maria suddenly pointed at the laptop, where Alec continued to speak. "He's getting death threats! Why do they want to do that, *Papa,* I don't understand?"

"Sometimes when people are in a position of power," Paige immediately started to explain. "They get threats from all sorts of crazy people."

"Wackos!" Jorge corrected her. "These here, are wackos that want to scare or intimidate him. But it will not work. That is why he is going public."

"Wow…" Maria hugged the baby closer causing him to attempt wiggling out of her arms.

"Maria, the baby," Jorge pointed toward her then reached out. "Here, give me Miguel and go have breakfast."

"I was going to feed him," Maria said.

"That's ok," Paige calmly replied. "We'll take care of Miguel. You go eat something."

Rising from the chair, she gently tapped Maria's arm, taking her out of a trance as she stared at the laptop. Meanwhile, Jorge was placing Miguel on his lap. A smile instantly touched his lips.

"This here is what I need today," Jorge said as he ran a hand over Miguel's back. "Baby smiles."

"They make me feel better," Maria commented. "He's always smiling. Maybe he has some evil plan or something."

"Maria, he's one," Paige said as she prepared his bottle. "I don't think he has many evil plans just yet."

"Ah! But he's a Hernandez," Jorge laughed and kissed Miguel's forehead. "So maybe so!"

Maria giggled and Jorge lifted the baby up to stand on his lap. Looking into his eyes, he watched as Miguel tilted his head. Opening his mouth, he spoke.

"*Pa.*"

Joy filled Jorge's heart and he was unable to speak. The world was suddenly a beautiful place again; if even for a moment.

"He said *pa!*" Maria spoke excitedly and clapped her hands. "Good job, Miguel!! Now you just have to say 'Ma' next."

The baby instead slid his fingers into his mouth.

Paige returned with the bottle and although she gave the impression she was excited for him, Jorge saw a hint of sadness in her eyes. It was conflicting to him as he felt love flow through his heart.

"Miguel!" He leaned forward and kissed him on the forehead. "You do not know how much I needed to hear that today."

"That's wonderful!" Paige replied as she reached for the baby. "Maybe after his bottle, he can say my name."

Maria giggled and Jorge winked at her.

"I'm going to take him upstairs to feed and give him a bath before Juliana starts," She commented as Miguel reached out and touched a strand of her blonde hair. It was only after she was out of earshot that Maria turned to him.

"I think she was a little sad he didn't say her name yet."

"I think you are right, Maria," Jorge agreed. "He will. Soon, he will."

By the time Makerson started the live stream interview with Athas about the threats, Jorge was alone again. He listened to everything said, noting that his words were carefully chosen to imply he knew or suspected the person who was threatening him but needed more proof.

Jorge's phone rang. Slightly irritated, he answered.

"He's dead."

It was Diego. Jorge glanced back at his laptop at Athas.

"Who?"

"The guy who told me about Verónic, he's dead."

"What?" Jorge shook his head. "How do you know?"

"My contact down in Mexico," Diego continued. "He called. They found him last night. He was shot."

"Oh fuck."

"Do you think she did it?"

"I do not think she would be that handy with a gun, no," Jorge thought for a moment. "But then again, up until yesterday, I also thought she was dead."

"I'm trying to get in touch with your guys watching her," Diego continued. "To see if she left last night."

"We gotta move fast, this cannot be left much longer."

The two ended the call and Jorge felt a heaviness in his chest. This was too much.

He turned to see Paige walking downstairs and head into the kitchen.

"Paige, we must talk."

"It's ok," She immediately put her hand up in the air. "I'm not upset he hasn't said my name yet. I know it's a matter of time. I get it."

It took Jorge a moment to understand what she was talking about, his thoughts elsewhere. This wasn't like him. He wasn't usually this scatterbrained. It was like he was in a fog.

"Oh yes, Paige, it will be ok," He immediately started to reassure her. "This here, it will be fine."

"It's disappointing but…." She stopped and pointed toward the laptop. "How's the interview going?"

"He seems, you know, careful about what he says," Jorge commented as Alec continued to speak. "Political talk, as usual."

"Hmm…."

"Paige, I received a call from Diego," He returned to his original thought. "The man who told him Verónic is alive, he is dead."

Jorge heard a huge gasp and it took him a moment to realize that it wasn't coming from Paige. Maria stood behind him.

CHAPTER 30

"What did you say?" Maria rushed across the room with a look of horror in her eyes and Jorge felt his heart drop. "My mother is alive! Have you been hiding this from me all along?"

"Maria, please," Paige attempted to step into the conversation but was quickly waved away.

"No! What did *you* say?" Her eyes were full of fury and Jorge felt his stomach do flips. He had never seen his daughter so upset. "Verónic is alive! How long have you known that my mother was alive? Were you ever going to tell me?"

"Maria, this here.."

"Where is she?" Maria cut him off before he could answer. "Do you have her hidden away somewhere? Was she there all along? Is that why we didn't go to her funeral?"

"Maria, that's not what he's saying," Paige attempted to comfort her by touching her back but was quickly shrugged away.

"Tell me!" Maria screamed.

Upstairs, the baby began to cry and Paige gave Jorge a hopeless look before rushing away. Miguel grew louder as Maria continued to rant.

"*Papa,* I know you've hidden a lot from me because you think I'm just a child but…"

"Ok, this here," Jorge began to speak over her. "This is going to stop now!"

Much to his surprise, Maria shrunk back but this time, her face was full of sorrow. Although he had regained control of the situation, it was a bleak victory when he saw the pain in her eyes. The last thing he wanted to do was to hurt his daughter.

"Maria, you must listen to me," Jorge lowered his voice slightly but was stern. "I have not hidden anything from you."

"But I just heard you," She started and her voice broke as tears formed in her eyes. "I heard you say. *Papa,* I am not a child! Please stop treating me like one."

"Maria, you are not quite 13 yet," Jorge reminded her. "To me, this here, it is still a child and regarding your mother, I did not tell you because I wanted to make sure it was true."

"So you didn't have her hidden away all this time?" Maria asked skeptically as she continued to shrink in front of his eyes. "I want to know the truth."

"This here, it is the truth," Jorge insisted and reached out to touch her shoulder. "Diego, he was in Mexico recently to investigate something else for me. While he was there, this is the news that he found out. *Bonita,* I thought she was dead also so I was as shocked as you are now."

Maria's defenses seemed to lower again. Suddenly appearing weak, Jorge reached for her hand.

"Let us go sit down in the living room and talk about this…calmly," Jorge suggested, feeling his heart rate begin to slow down. He didn't like this tight feeling in his chest. "I will tell you everything I know."

She nodded and took his hand, as they headed for the couch. Sitting down, before saying another word, Jorge reached out and kissed her on top of the head. He noted tears falling down her face so pulled her close and let her cry. Although empathy wasn't his strong point, he did realize how shocking it must've been to learn this news.

"Maria, I am truly sorry that this is how you learned the news," Jorge began as his daughter looked into his eyes. She wiped a tear away with her hand and nodded. "I was careful to not speak where you could hear but today, I guess I'm not myself. There are a lot of things on my mind including, of course, this situation."

"Are you worried about Alec too?" Maria referred to the man who had been around the house many times and to her, was a business associate of her father's. "He's a nice man, *Papa,* why would anyone want to kill him? And why is my mother still alive? I don't understand."

"I barely understand," Jorge confessed and noted a shared look of confusion. "Regarding your mother, I have contacted some government officials to confirm it is true. We have someone watching the home where she lives. At this time, I wanted to make sure before saying anything to you."

"But you think it is true, don't you?"

"Yes, Maria, it does seem that way," Jorge admitted. "I honestly didn't know what to do about it. I was not sure how to tell you or if I should go there to see Verónic with my own eyes first. This is a very unusual situation."

"But I don't understand how it can happen," Maria asked in a shy voice. "How can someone fake their death?"

"Anything is possible, *niñita,*" Jorge reminded her. "Which is both comforting and terrifying at the same time."

"So, where is she?" Maria asked. "Where are you watching her?"

"In Southern Mexico," Jorge replied. "I want to see her myself to make sure."

"Can you bring her here?"

Her question shocked Jorge.

"What?"

"Can you bring her here?" Maria repeated. "I want to talk to her."

"You do…"

"I want to ask her why she would pretend to be dead?"

Jorge knew the answer to this question but didn't reply.

"Was it the drugs?"

"I don't know Maria," Jorge said and thought for a moment. "But Verónic, she was never a *real* mother to you. You must remember this."

"I know," Maria nodded. "Paige is the one who's looked after me."

"This is true," Jorge nodded. "Paige loves you very much and would do anything for you. Verónic…"

"Pretended to be dead," Maria finished his sentence. "Because she didn't want to be in my life."

"Oh, Maria, no!" Jorge insisted. "This was never about you."

"Are you sure?"

"Maria, how could she not want you in her life?" Jorge quickly corrected her. "It was me that she wanted to think she was dead, it was not you."

Maria shared a look with him but didn't reply.

"Your mother," Jorge continued. "She was always a mixed-up woman. The only reason why she was in my life was because of you. You are the only good thing that woman ever did."

Maria was apathetic.

"I know this is a lot to take in," Jorge continued. "And again, I am sorry. This is why I didn't tell you sooner. I just found out. I wasn't hiding this from you. Maria, if I ever hide anything from you, it is for your protection. You know this."

Maria suddenly looked tired. Jorge related. It was already an exhausting day.

"So, now what?" She asked in a small voice.

"Maria, if you want me to bring her here…"

"I do," She insisted. "Or we can go there, to talk to her."

Jorge considered his options.

"No, Maria, I do not think we should go to Mexico now," Jorge said and shook his head. "There is too much going on. Maybe we can bring her here but I do not wish for her to stay."

"I want to look her in the eye."

Jorge felt this was a mistake but his hands were tied. Then again, maybe his daughter needed peace with the situation. Maybe he did too.

"Maria, you know, I will always do what I can for you," Jorge admitted as he pulled her close and kissed her on the top of the head. "You, Miguel and Paige, you are my world."

"I know, *Papa,* I know," Maria leaned in and gave him a warm hug. He felt his body relax as she let him go. "When will this happen?"

"Soon."

"Ok," Maria spoke in a voice that made her seem younger as she rose from the couch. "And Alec?"

"He will be ok," Jorge insisted. "We will make sure."

The truth was, he wasn't sure.

Glancing at his phone, he saw that Diego had tried to reach him. He was on his way to the house.

Jorge barely had time to get up and pour another cup of coffee, when the doorbell rang.

"We gotta talk," Diego flew in the door as soon as it opened. "I've been thinking..."

"Can we take this in there?" Jorge pointed toward his office. "It has been a crazy morning."

Diego appeared concerned but nodded. Once behind the closed door, Jorge told him about Maria's confrontation earlier that morning.

"Oh fuck!" Diego replied as the two men headed for the desk. Jorge sat behind and Diego in his usual seat. "Fuck, she knows?"

"It was me, I was being careless talking about Verónic in the open," Jorge confessed. "Lately, Diego, it is as if I am not myself."

"Maybe you're sick again."

"I am fine, Diego. Now, what is the breaking news you are here to tell me."

"Alec's interview," Diego said and pointed toward the closed laptop on Jorge's desk. "Did you hear it?"

"Only some, this is when Maria confronted me," Jorge replied. "Why, did it not go well?"

"A little too well," Diego's eyes bulged out. "He said he knew exactly who was making the threats and he was going to say names if it didn't stop."

"Oh fuck!" Jorge shook his head. "This here, it is too far."

"I know but he was agitated in the interview," Diego continued as he relaxed and crossed his legs. "What the fuck is going on? Is the world falling apart? People are rising from the dead and others are trying to become dead!"

"Ok, Diego, relax," Jorge replied and put his hand in the air. "I have already dealt with one drama queen today, I need to catch my breath before dealing with another one."

"He could be inviting the shooters to his door," Diego continued to speak excitedly. "We put him there, we gotta look after him."

"Diego, we will," Jorge assured him. "We will. This here, it will be fine."

"I don't know, *hermano,* I don't got a good feeling about this one," Diego admitted as he adjusted his tie and started fidgeting. "Not this time."

CHAPTER 31

"I do not like this, Paige," Jorge spoke candidly that night as they got into bed. Placing his phone on the nightstand, he felt no comfort as he lay down. "This day, if only I could go back and erase it. Start again."

"It wasn't all bad," Paige quickly reminded him. "Miguel said 'Pa'. I know that meant a lot to you."

"Of course, *mi amor,*" Jorge quickly replied as he snuggled up to his wife. "But this here, is what I want to experience more. These beautiful moments with my family. Not the rest. I feel like the old me, he would've had this solved in a minute. But now, I feel useless and soon, the others will see it too."

"I hardly think that the devil is about to morph into an angel," Paige was quick to remind him. "But I think it's that your priorities are not the same anymore. You're tired of the rat race."

"I'm tired of a lot of things, Paige," Jorge spoke honestly. "I'm tired of taking care of everything, of everyone….but this is a side of me that I cannot show anyone but you. The vultures they see a sign of weakness and they are ready for the kill."

"I think you need a break," She suggested. "We never have vacations because there's always too much going on. You need to pass more responsibility on to the others."

"I guess since Jesús has died," Jorge said and took a breath. "It has changed me. I see the world much differently now. I didn't want to become a different man but it has happened. Ever since…"

"I know," Paige replied and leaned in and kissed him. Neither said a word. It had been a horrific night but it could've been much more tragic, had their enemy been successful in his plan.

"Regarding Verónic," Paige said as her hand ran over his chest. "She never has to see the light of day again. Perhaps she'll run away and we can't find her. Maybe she'll have an unfortunate overdose. There's more than one way to skin a cat. We don't have to bring her here and really, does Maria need to see her?"

"I know, *mi amor,* I know," Jorge quickly agreed. "I keep thinking the same. This would've been so much easier if she hadn't heard me speak."

"Say you were wrong," Paige suggested. "That she's not alive. There was a mistaken identity. Someone who swiped her ID. It's not impossible."

"But if the truth comes out," Jorge argued. "My daughter, she will never believe me again."

"Sleep on it," Paige finally suggested. "You will see things differently in the morning."

Jorge couldn't relax. Long into the night, he was still awake. The darkness in his heart was overflowing and for the first time, he began to question a lifetime of horrific deeds. Had it been necessary? Much had been done to keep and regain power. In the end, what did power really bring to him? And why was he allowing it to slip away?

There was a heaviness in his chest for days. It cluttered his mind, his thoughts and stole the fire that usually engulfed his soul. It was as if he were only half the man he used to be but he struggled more with hiding this fact than he did attempt to prove it was wrong. How did he find his way back?

It was when the sun rose in the sky, as he stared at the ceiling that it happened. It was sudden, like a bolt of thunder running through the house when an army of men invaded his bedroom wearing black, protective gear. Jorge jumped out of bed with his hands in the air while down the hallway, he could hear Maria's blood-curdling screams.

"On the ground, Hernandez!" One of the men pointing a gun at him yelled. "Now! It's over!"

His heart pounded in fear. Jorge glanced at Paige who lazily rose from beneath the covers and glanced around. However, rather than being horrified, she instead rose from the bed calmly, as if nothing were amiss. Glancing toward Jorge, she shrugged.

"It's over, Jorge."

"Wha…" He suddenly couldn't breathe. "Paige…"

"On the ground, Hernandez!" The man closest to him yelled. "If I shoot you, no one's going to give a fuck!"

"Paige?" Jorge couldn't move but continued to stare at his wife. "What…I.."

"I've been working with them for months," Paige replied as she calmly reached for her robe. "years, actually."

"What?" Jorge was confused. "I do not understand."

"On the ground, Hernandez!" The man continued to yell as he moved closer.

"This, none of it is real," She continued. "I'm not an assassin. I never was. But you believed I was and that was my way in. I've gathered so much evidence against you since we met. You're going to die in prison."

"This here, this is a joke, right?" Jorge asked as his heart sunk through the floor. "Paige, you didn't pretend to love me…"

"I did," She coldly replied without even batting an eyelash. "Who could love a man as evil as you? Verónic is alive. I've known all along. She's taking Maria back with her."

"What!" Jorge shook his head as the man in the uniform got closer to him. "No!"

"And Miguel," Paige shook his head. "He's not even yours."

"What?" Jorge shook his head. "No! Paige…"

"You aren't listening Hernandez!" The man in the uniform got closer and shoved him on the ground, his boot coming down hard on Jorge's back but he couldn't feel a thing.

Nothing mattered anymore. He was dead inside.

"Jorge," He heard Paige's voice from above and it gave him a glimmer of hope. "Jorge…."

The weight of the boot holding him down made it impossible to move. "Jorge…"

He felt a hand on his back.

"Jorge…..are you ok?"

How could he be ok? He would never be ok again.

"Wake up!"

Suddenly alert, Jorge's eyes darted around the bedroom. Sunlight shone through the curtains as Paige watched him carefully. He turned around in his bed to see an empty room; no one had broken in the door. No one was holding a gun to his head. His wife was beside him with worry in her eyes and Jorge felt sweat running down his back.

"Are you ok?" She asked with alarm in her eyes. "You kept saying, 'No, Paige'. I had to shake you a few times to get you out of it. You scared me."

"Oh, Paige," Jorge took a deep breath and reached for a glass of water on the nearby table as his heart pounded. "You have no idea the dream I just had. It was worse than death, this I tell you."

"What happened?"

Jorge shook his head and drank the glass of water before he started to relax. Returning the empty glass to the nightstand, he leaned against his pillow and finally spoke.

"Paige, I wanted to die, it was such a terrible dream," Jorge spoke candidly. "Police, the SWAT team, whatever you call this in Canada, they broke down the door. There were guns pointed at us. You told me that you were working with them all along and that you had evidence against me. That Miguel, he was not my son. That Maria, she was going to live with Verónic."

"You had a nightmare," Paige said and moved closer to him. He automatically leaned his head against her. He began to relax. "That's not going to happen."

"Please just shoot me if it does."

"Jorge, you're very anxious lately," Paige reminded him. "That's what the dream is about. I don't think anyone is trying to double-cross you. Definitely not me."

"So, our marriage, it is real?" Jorge felt ridiculous confirming the obvious. "Not an elaborate scheme to gather evidence against me?"

Paige laughed. "Yes, I guess you figured me out."

"I know, *mi amore,* I am sorry," Jorge said and began to laugh with her. "It was so *real.* Do you think this here, it is a warning?"

"I think it's a warning that you need to relax," Paige spoke softly. "I'm worried about you. Why don't you let me take the reins for a change?"

"Paige...I..."

"No, seriously," Paige cut him off. "You're supposed to take a call with Alec today, let me take it. I was going to get up and feed and bath the baby. You do that. I think spending time with Miguel is what you need now. I'm going to deal with the rest."

"But...you..."

"No!" Paige cut him off. "Do you trust me?"

"Of course!"

"Then do as I say," Paige gave him a quick kiss. "Take a shower before the baby wakes up."

Following her instructions, Jorge rose from the bed and headed for the bathroom. While Paige checked her phone, he closed the door and climbed into the shower. The hot water that poured over him filled Jorge with unexpected relief, almost as if his nightmares, fears, and concerns were washing down the drain. He thought of nothing other than his son. He could trust Paige.

Finishing the shower, he quickly dried off and pulled on some comfortable clothing. Heading out of the bathroom, Paige was walking back into their bedroom wearing her robe and slippers.

"Miguel is waking up," She pointed toward the bedroom next door. "I already told Alec I would be dealing with him."

"And Verónic?"

"One thing at a time," Paige calmly replied. "Go see your son."

Heading for Miguel's room, Jorge automatically felt at peace when he looked into his son's eyes. It made him think of his brother.

CHAPTER 32

"Have a seat," Paige spoke softly as she pointed toward the chair she usually sat in while she walked behind Jorge's desk to take his chair, "I think I sorted out some things while other stuff popped up along the way."

"Yeah, things, they have a way of popping up along the way," Jorge watched Paige sit down and ease the chair forward. "This here is my every day."

"I see that," Paige replied as she sat up straight and glanced toward the desk. "I'll give you a quick rundown."

Reaching for a piece of paper, she picked it up.

"You have notes?"

"A lot of stuff happened this morning," Paige raised an eyebrow with a mischievous grin on her face. "I don't want to miss anything."

"Ok, beautiful lady," Jorge relaxed in his seat. "Solve all my problems."

"I don't think I solved all your problems, but I do have a handle on a few things."

Jorge nodded with interest.

"First, I talked to Alec," Paige began and took a deep breath. "This one is tricky. He has gone full Jorge Hernandez with this oil company situation."

"Ah!" Jorge nodded with a grin. "This here I like already."

"Well, you mightn't when I tell you what he did," Paige informed him and shook her head. "Since his announcement in the interview that he 'suspects' where the threats are coming from, big oil has pushed him even harder and he's pushed back."

"What they want now?"

"To drill in a national park."

"Are they fucking crazy?" Jorge asked. "The country, they will never agree with that. Environmental groups will be all over it. Everyone, they will be mad."

"They want Alec to suggest 'some work' is being done in the park and try to either cover it up or try to justify it."

"Of course they do," Jorge replied with light sarcasm. "A CEO might need another yacht this summer or maybe he needs the money to pay off an expensive assassin."

"I think that falls under business expenses," Paige spoke gently. "Like a 'consulting fee' or something like that."

"Is that right?"

"I've *consulted* for these kind of people," Paige reminded him. "I believe that's what they put on the books."

"So, Athas said no?"

"He not only said no," Paige replied with some hesitation. "Along with removing all subsidies, he's threatened to increase fines for oil spills especially if they are found negligent. Hefty fines."

"Wow," Jorge said with a grin. "Although, this here seems like a great idea on paper..."

"He's asking to get killed?"

"I have said that big oil, it is our Canadian cartel, did I not?" Jorge replied. "Unfortunately for them, I am also pretty experienced with cartels and unlike them, I do not worry about getting my hands dirty."

"The problem is that we still don't know where the threats are coming from," Paige reminded him. "I've checked with my contacts but they aren't saying much which means, no money has exchanged hands yet. What if we're assuming it's big oil and it's someone else?"

"Nah, I do not see who else..."

"Another country?"

"But what country?" Jorge shook his head. "We have a good relationship with most, do we not?"

"Yes, but we've ruffled a few feathers lately," Paige reminded him.

"Nah, I think that's a normal day in politics," Jorge shook his head. "This here, you will need to do some more looking."

"I feel like I'm hitting a dead end when I do," Paige admitted. "Marco, he's not having any luck either."

"Did you speak to him this morning?"

"I spoke to everyone," Paige said with a shrug.

"Everyone?" Jorge was surprised. "But it is only early..."

"I'm organized."

"I usually go to see people."

"But it's so much easier to call them."

"Paige, *mi amor*," Jorge hesitated. "This here is not a good idea. We should not be talking about any of this on the phone."

"I don't."

"Oh..."

"Trust me, Jorge, I'm careful," Paige insisted. "This isn't my first time on the merry-go-round."

Jorge grinned.

"So, I discreetly asked Marco about his latest projects and said I was touching base for you," Paige went on. "He said that unfortunately, his research has been unsuccessful so far."

"That's it?"

"Big oil won't be inboxing each other about these things," Paige continued. "But maybe they're just threats and they'll back out the last minute. Alec seems like an easy target, someone they might think they can scare."

"This would be my assumption too," Jorge replied. "This is why I'm surprised he's fighting back."

"Like I said earlier," Paige reminded him. "His inner Jorge Hernandez is coming out."

He laughed and nodded.

"You know me, Paige, I love to inspire others."

"So for now," She continued. "We're unfortunately stuck. I think Alec has also threatened to bring his ideas about subsidies and fines to the media and if he does that, it will blow up. We'll have to wait on this one."

"I guess, that is all we can do now," Jorge nodded.

"In the end, we can help," Paige continued. "But we can't do his job. This is up to him. We can jump in when we have something of substance."

"And your sources…"

"They will contact me as soon as something new comes up but it's tricky…I wouldn't want this assignment if I was still an assassin."

"Now can you wave your magic wand and get rid of Verónic?" Jorge decided to move on. "This would be wonderful."

"I think your wish came true because we can't find her."

"We can't find her?" Jorge was puzzled. "What about the men…"

"I had them go into the house and she's not there."

"But they were watching?"

"Apparently, not very well," Paige said. "There is a lady there but it's not her."

"So it was never her?" Jorge grew frustrated. "So, we do not know where she is? My sources lied?"

"No, they were right," Paige insisted. "She was living there at one time but when asked, her roommate? Whoever the woman is, she said that she let her stay for a while but she was 'too much' so kicked her out."

"Where is she now?"

"We don't know," Paige replied. "I have Marco on it but maybe you should touch base with your connections although, she clearly doesn't want to be found."

"So I can honestly tell Maria that we cannot find her mother?" Jorge chewed on the news. "This here, it might be good."

"We'll keep looking," Paige suggested. "See what you can find."

"Yes, well the last time I did this," Jorge spoke with aggravation in his voice. "I did not get much. The government, they only had her last known address."

"Jorge, do we need to find her?" Paige considered. "Can we leave her?"

"No, because I need to know she isn't talking," Jorge replied. "I do not need her causing problems for me. She is the one person who could. Maybe this here is what my dream was telling me last night."

"I would think she'd be easy to find if the price is right," Paige suggested. "If you're worried, when we find her, we'll threaten..."

"Nah, we need her gone," Jorge replied. "It's too risky. The fact that we found out about her at all, this suggests that we cannot trust her to keep a low profile."

"True."

"We will find her and I will kill her."

"But what about Maria?"

"Fuck!"

"Jorge, let her see her mother," Paige suggested. "For closure. Then do whatever you feel is right."

"What I feel is right?" Jorge sniffed. "She should join a pile of bodies in Mexico that no one can identify, that's what I think is right. The woman is poison to me and my daughter."

"Well, we know that can easily be arranged," Paige reminded him. "Your resources are more plentiful than hers."

Jorge nodded. He felt his power rising.

"When we find her," Paige continued. "Were you thinking Diego and Enrique get her?"

"I think we still need to make sure we can trust Enrique first."

"Apparently, Jolene trusts him," Paige commented. "In fact, she trusts him a lot..."

"What does this mean, *mi amor?*" Jorge asked.

"When I spoke to Chase earlier, he said he's been checking the cameras like he does every morning..."

"And?"

"He said, you might need to replace the couch in his office."

"What?" Jorge appeared slightly intrigued by this comment. "Do I..."

"He said they have grown quite close..."

"Well, Paige, we did think this would happen."

"Yes, but not necessarily in Chase's office."

"During work time?"

"I believe so."

"But other than his lack of willpower and disloyalty to his wife," Jorge felt his brain churning. "Do *we* have any other reason to trust or distrust him?"

"It looks like he's doing his job," Paige replied. "I think we need to give him an assignment like this one and see how he does. He's not in the position to speak up against you and he knows it."

Jorge nodded.

"By the way, did you know that Chase is seeing his LINE teacher?"

"The man?"

"Actually, it's a woman," Paige replied. "Interesting though how you assume it was a man."

"Paige, we already know I can be sexist, no need to remind me."

She grinned.

"Do not tell Maria, this here will break her heart."

"I'm not going to say a word," Paige replied. "But they do talk regularly. He said she already called him to say they should go for coffee to talk about her recent 'drama'."

"Well, my Maria, she does like drama."

"She wants to talk about her mom," Paige said. "But the good news is she didn't talk about it on the phone."

"It is important she learns these things now," Jorge pointed out. "There are many secrets that we need to keep within the family."

"I guess she's listening."

"As much as a teenager listens…"

"That reminds me," Paige continued. "She wants a boy/girl party for her birthday this summer."

"Wonderful," Jorge spoke sarcastically. "This here is all I need. A bunch of horny boys running around my house."

"Well, maybe we can arrange to keep it outside at the pool."

"My daughter, half-naked in a bathing suit at a boy/girl party?" Jorge grunted. "I do not think so!"

"Luckily, we don't have to figure out this problem yet."

"Is there anything else, Paige?" Jorge rubbed his forehead.

She shook her head.

"I gotta stop by the office," Jorge said as he stood up. "Perhaps, I will stop by the bar first and help Chase burn that couch."

CHAPTER 33

"What the hell is going on here?" Jorge shouted immediately after jumping out of his SUV. He walked toward a police officer who was talking to Chase in the *Princesa Maria* parking lot. Noting that his employee was in gym clothes and behind the wheel of an expensive car, Jorge quickly put the pieces together.

"Sir, this does *not* concern you," The older, white man spoke in a warning tone. "Please just step away."

Jorge ignored his command and boldly walked towards him and Chase.

"What's this about?"

"I dunno," Chase shrugged. "I was just getting to work and he stopped me."

"Sir, if I have to ask…"

"*Please tell me,*" Jorge turned and glared at the police officer. "Why are you harassing my employee? Did he do something wrong while driving? I do not understand. He needs to be inside *my* club to receive an order."

"And you are…"

"Jorge Hernandez."

The police officer automatically recoiled, his eyes scanning the two men. He handed Chase back his ID.

"Everything looks fine here," The officer replied as he continued to fall under Jorge's dark gaze. "Sorry for the inconvenience. Enjoy your day."

The officer quickly got in his car and drove off. Jorge stepped back as Chase got out of his car and the two men headed inside the club.

"This here, does it happen to you often?" Jorge asked as they walked inside and Chase quickly turned off the alarm. "It is because you're dressed like that, you know, right?"

"No joke," Chase glanced down at his clothes. "Some indigenous kid dressed like a bum, driving a nice car, sitting in a bar parking lot this early in the morning."

"Are you doing the walk of shame or what" Jorge grinned as the two men headed for the office.

"No, I was running late so I figured I'd just come here from the gym and go home later to change," Chase replied as he collapsed behind his desk and took a long sigh. "Then this cop comes out of nowhere. As you would say, the fucking police have to look like they're doing something productive."

"I am glad my wisdom is rubbing off on you," Jorge said and his eyes fell on the couch across the room. "Speaking of things rubbing up against one another.."

"Let's not," Chase said and put his hand up as if to block his view of the couch. "Paige told you about my discovery?"

"Yes, and I think maybe there must be some boundaries set," Jorge said with a grin. "But this here is between the three of you. Me? I got no horse in this race."

"I don't care what they do," Chase shook his head. "But don't do it in my office."

"Fair enough."

"I was speaking to Maria last night," Chase continued. "She wants to meet for coffee. When did she start drinking coffee?"

"*Amigo,* I do not think that sugar-based drink is really coffee, you know?" Jorge replied and watched Chase grin. "But this here is part of her plan to grow up too fast and I cannot handle it. Maria wants to talk to you because she overheard Paige and me talking about Verónic."

"She heard? Shit."

"*Chica,* she lost it," Jorge admitted and paused for a moment. "Maria, she wants to see her. If you can, when you have your 'coffee date', please try to find out why."

"Do you want me to discourage her?"

Jorge thought about it for a moment.

"No, this here, it might be closure for her," Jorge considered. "I feel that now that she has had Paige looking after her for a few years, she will see what a real mother is and hopefully, after that, we can get rid of Verónic for good."

Chase nodded.

"Wait, Clara…was she in?"

"She was in before me," Chase said. "I make sure she's in at six every morning."

"Perfecto."

"So, are you going to Mexico?"

"No, I plan to maybe have Diego and Enrique bring her here," Jorge replied and bit his bottom lip. "If I can trust him."

"I have no reason to distrust him," Chase replied. "He seems eager to do anything. He told me the other day that he can shoot a gun if needed."

"What did you say?"

"Nothing."

"And you," Jorge wondered about Chase. "Can you shoot a gun or is this…"

"I can," Chase spoke with some hesitation. "Jolene has been helping me."

"I can get you a gun," Jorge reminded him. "Or anything you need for protection."

Chase nodded.

"Then again, you've killed two people without a weapon," Jorge reminded him. "Perhaps, you will end up being the most dangerous of all of us."

"I'm not sure if I'm there yet."

"Chase, my friend, my senses tell me that you will be there soon," Jorge spoke honestly. "From the day we were first introduced, I knew there was something about you. I could see it in your eyes. You've always been far more powerful than you realize. Even now."

On that note, Jorge decided to leave Chase with that thought as he headed to the office. Feeling empowered again, he knew it was time to let others know that he hadn't lost his touch.

Scanning his card, he walked through the doors to see the blonde receptionist behind the desk. Giving a quick nod on his way by, he hadn't expected her to jump up and immediately rush in his direction.

"Mr. Hernandez!" She spoke excitedly. A candy scent filled his lungs as she stood a little too close to him. "I have been *dying* to meet you. I was such a fan of yours when you were running in the election and I…"

"Thank you," He cut her off while accidentally glancing down her blouse and quickly looking away. "Diego is he…"

"Would it be possible for us to meet sometime?" She moved closer to him, her hand eased down his back. "I'm thinking about getting into politics and…"

"Look, lady," Jorge started to move away. "This here is not appropriate office behavior."

The receptionist appeared stunned by his words and pulled her hand back.

"You and I, we will not be meeting…for any reason," He glanced over her body and denied his lustful thoughts. "I got a meeting."

With that, he walked down the hallway. Through the glass doors, he noted Diego was already having an intense conversation with Jolene.

"…situation and that's the last thing we need, Jolene," Diego snapped as he hovered over his defiant sister, who sat with her arms crossed over her chest. Nearby, an awkward Marco pretended to work, clearly avoiding their conversation. "This here it ain't one of your Spanish soap operas."

"What the hell is going on here?" Jorge asked and quickly realized that he was once again attempting to get a grip on the situation. "Why are you two fighting this time?"

Diego crossed his arms and his face scrunched up.

"Do you want to tell him, Jolene, or do I?"

"It is none of his business!"

"She's fucking Enrique!" Diego blew up, swinging his arms in the air. "Like this is all we need. Like we didn't have this problem when she was screwing Chase and look at the mess that turned out to be. Enough! Jolene! Go on a fucking dating app or do something normal."

"But Enrique, I like…"

"He's married, Jolene."

"Yeah, well that doesn't stop some," Jorge cut in, hoping to sway Diego's attention. "Your receptionist, she just came on to me when I walked through the door."

"Me too!" Diego's eyes widened in an exaggerated expression. "I could not believe it. She touched my bum!"

"Well, Diego," Jolene cut in. "She does not know you are gay."

"Does it matter, she touched my bum!" Diego complained. "I'm calling the temp agency and telling them to get someone else."

"She asked to meet with me to discuss politics," Jorge laughed as he headed for his chair. "Good thing Paige was not here."

Jolene cringed and Diego nodded.

"Good! Don't you ever cheat on Paige," He warned.

"Diego you do not have to release the hounds," Jorge said as he sat down. "I did not and will not cheat on Paige. This here I promise."

"And with Verónic, don't cheat with her either."

"Diego, I think it is pretty obvious that this will not happen. I hate the woman."

"Hate and love, they are close," Jolene reminded him. "There is passion."

"I do not have that kind of passion for Verónic," Jorge assured them.

"You did, don't you remember?" Diego reminded him, immediately causing Jorge to feel a heaviness in his chest. "You two used to be all over one another back in the day…"

"When I was high on cocaine?"

"Yeah, I guess," Diego said and sat down. "But still, you.."

"Diego, she is missing."

"Who?"

"Verónic, we must find her."

He turned his attention to Marco.

"And I'm gonna need your help." Jorge paused for a moment. "With a couple of things."

CHAPTER 34

"Well, this here," Jorge said as he gestured for the prime minister to enter his office. "This is a rare treat. If I had known you were coming, I would've rolled out the red carpet."

Alec Athas let out a tense laugh as he walked across the room and sat in his usual seat. Jorge closed the door and quickly made his way behind the desk.

"So…..what do I owe this pleasure?"

"I was in Toronto for a few days and I needed to talk to you in person," Athas replied as he placed his laptop bag on a nearby chair. "Sometimes, I just want to do something without scheduling it weeks in advance. I feel like my life, it's not my own."

"You are the prime minister of Canada," Jorge reminded him. "Are you not a servant of the people."

"The people, I can handle," Athas said as he relaxed in the chair. "It's these other assholes, I'm not so sure about."

"Ah, yes, big oil…."

"Was….is it, Clara you have come in…"

"Yes," Jorge replied. "We are fine."

"Do you ever find anything?"

"Not here, no," Jorge shook his head. "The people who come to this office know better than to spy on me."

Athas nodded. Jorge noted the dark circles under his eyes, while the grey was popping up around his ears. The new job had aged him in the brief few months as prime minister.

"You look tense," Jorge commented as he leaned back in his chair. "Tell me, are you still seeing the…what was it, a yoga teacher? Meditation? What did you call her again?"

Athas grinned and raised an eyebrow before he finally spoke.

"I like to keep these things for my personal time."

"You, *amigo,* look like you might need much more….*personal time…* don't you have political groupies wanting to fuck you?"

"I wish I had the luxury," Athas laughed. "Big oil is keeping me on my toes. And I have another problem."

"Oh yeah?" Jorge was intrigued. "Bigger than Big Oil?"

"It's connected," Athas said and shook his head. "And it's coming from my office."

"Again, *amigo,* how do you make so many enemies within your own party?" Jorge asked as he leaned ahead on his desk. "Are you sure about this one?"

"I've had some phones tapped, some listening devices planted….let's just say, I took a lesson out of your book on how to do things."

"I'm impressed," Jorge nodded, a devious grin slipped on his lips. "Is this here…legal? Are you allowed to spy on your employees?"

"Right now," Athas spoke sternly. "I don't give a fuck. I need to get to the bottom of this. I'm not sleeping at night and it's distracting me from things that need my attention."

"Ah, yes, but isn't that the point?" Jorge countered and titled his head. "Who needs you busy looking to the right, so they cut your throat from the left?"

Athas nodded and reached for his bag.

"And that's exactly what's happening."

"You must ask who has something to gain?"

"Remember way back when," Athas asked as he opened his bag and pulled out an iPad. "We were talking about how the opposition wanted to bring back 'family values' and criminalize pot again? Last year, remember a little group called Canadians for Conservative Values?"

"Oh fuck, not them again," Jorge shook his head and briefly closed his eyes. "And fucking Elizabeth Alan."

"Yes, *fucking* Elizabeth Alan," Athas repeated as he turned on his tablet. "She's back and is behind this shit. She wants me out because, in her eyes, we both fucked her over from being prime minister."

"As if she would ever win," Jorge made a face when he recalled his broken promise to endorse her after stepping down from politics the previous fall. "I promoted the person I felt had the best shot at winning and that was you. I was right. You won the leadership vote and then the election."

"But she thinks she could've won so she's working from the inside to bring me down," Alec touched the screen and turned it around for Jorge to see an audio clip. "Listen to this."

He hit play and Elizabeth Alan's voice could be heard.

Everyone knows this is all Jorge Hernandez. He might not be prime minister but he's still running things. He's a snake.

Jorge merely grinned and raised an eyebrow, sharing a look with Athas.

A male voice added to the conversation.

Unfortunately, until we get Athas out, he's always going to be backed by criminals.

Jorge took it in stride while Athas grew tenser.

Elizabeth Alan continued.

If he keeps pushing Big Oil's buttons, we won't need to do anything. They'll push him out. Then the party will be weakened. It was a miracle they survived last year. They can't survive another scandal.

Isn't that what we want? I have a meeting with Athas later today. I'm going to tell him he's up in the polls since he called out Big Oil. That will egg him on more and keep going with this….

Athas stopped the recording.

"This guy you're hearing," He pointed toward the iPad. "That's the guy who's been advising me. I thought I was on the right track but he encouraged me to push it further. He said that's what the people want, Big Oil to take responsibility."

"And the death threats?"

"He said, 'they're just threats, they don't mean anything' as if I was worried for nothing," Athas complained. "He said he's been in government longer than me and that elected officials are constantly getting them. It's part of being in the public eye.'"

"How old is this man?"

"Old as fuck, that's what...."

"So he's not trying to make a name for himself?"

"No, he's trying to be in control.."

With that, Athas tapped the recording to play again.

...I'm telling my contact that I can't talk any sense into him so now Big Oil is going to come down hard on Athas.

But we can't have him killed. I will have no part in that!

We don't have to. After he's pushed it too far, I'll advise him to step down for his safety. I've already heard that the threats are going to extend to his family.

But no one will be hurt?

No. I've made sure of that.

I still don't like this...

Elizabeth, you know I would never lie to you.

Jorge raised an eyebrow.

Look, Liz, he'll have no choice but to back down. This will make him look weak to the Canadian people and the opposition is already preparing to attack him on it. We can only win from here.

I still say Jorge Hernandez is the real problem here.

Oh yeah, you're going to take on the cartel king? That man is dangerous. Keep out of his crosshairs. Let me worry about this one.

I'm not scared of Jorge Hernandez.

Jorge started to laugh.

Liz, let me take care of this. You trust me, right?

There was a pause.

Of course.

Then let me handle this. When I'm done, Athas will back down, the opposition will strike and the threats will increase until he steps down from the party. We're going to get him out, one way or another.

Athas tapped the screen and sat the iPad aside.

"That man there," Jorge pointed toward the iPad. "He's fucking her."

"What?" Athas started to laugh and pointed toward the iPad. *"Her?"*

"Yes, *her,* I guarantee he's fucking her," Jorge said with confidence. "I can tell."

"You can tell?"

"His voice, *amigo,* how he talks to her," Jorge insisted. "Liz. Who the fuck calls her Liz? The way he makes those promises in a gentle voice. I know people, Athas, and those two, they are fucking or if not, they soon will be."

"Really?"

"Yes, I am sure of it, *amigo,*" Jorge said. "I'm gonna get Marco on it. I promise you this is happening and you know what? I'm fucking tired of this bullshit. You're going to call the top dogs at Big Oil and say you want to negotiate something reasonable but you don't tell lover boy," Jorge gestured toward the iPad. "And me, I'm taking care of this nonsense once and for all."

Athas nodded, his face brightened up.

"And I promise you this," Jorge continued. "No one…and I mean, *no one* in your party will fuck with you again when I'm done with these two."

CHAPTER 35

"Finally! I got something for you!" Marco exclaimed as Jorge walked into the boardroom a couple of days later. "I feel that lately, I only come to dead ends when researching."

"Marco," Jorge said as he walked across the room to join him at the table. "I never doubted you. People, they are getting better at covering their tracks."

"Not these two," Marco said as he pointed toward his laptop. "It certainly does seem you are right about Elizabeth Alan and this man because they do have a series of emails. I was also able to hack into her cell phone provider to find text messages."

"I knew it!" Jorge laughed and clapped his hands together. "I knew they were fucking!"

Marco grinned as he tapped a few buttons and turned the MacBook around.

"There are only a few emails," Marco insisted as Jorge moved his chair closer and squinted at the screen. "But the texts are plentiful and they are in regular contact, sir. I'm sending a document of everything I got. As you can see, they are talking about meeting for drinks, for coffee..... sometimes more."

"Oh! Let me see the 'sometimes more' texts," Jorge said with a huge grin on his face. "Any sexting?"

"I don't think they are at that age," Marco shook his head. "I do not think Ms. Alan is someone who is about to send pictures of her private parts to anyone."

"Well, as much as I don't want to see that, Marco," Jorge shook his head and leaned his elbow against the table. "It might come in handy. But here, it says they are planning a weekend getaway? I wonder where that could be."

"I am monitoring their messages to see where and when," Marco's expression grew serious. "I should have something for you soon. It appears that they are trying to find somewhere out of town to have their weekend together. My understanding is they are both married?"

Jorge nodded.

"I assumed that was why they are being so careful about when and where they meet and who sees…"

"Yup, the church lady gotta keep up appearances," Jorge said as he moved away from the screen. "Marco, tell me something, what do you think about people who have affairs?"

"Sir, it is none of my business," Marco spoke honestly. "I do not believe in it, no. I can understand it sometimes but I think that you can never heal a relationship from an affair."

Jorge nodded.

"Why do you ask, sir?"

"Marco, I have never been a saint," Jorge said as he glanced toward the clock and back at his employee. "But this here isn't something I've thought about doing since getting married. But I will admit, the other day, that receptionist at the desk, she comes on to me and I…for a second, I did think about it."

Marco raised an eyebrow but didn't say anything.

"I am not proud of this fact," Jorge quickly added. "And I had no intention of doing anything but it made me…wonder if people, they can ever change, you know? Maria's mother…I cheated on her a lot. I didn't even try to hide it, you know? I did not care."

"Well, sir, I do think we can change if we want to," Marco said as he closed his laptop. "I think it is normal for people to be tempted. We are human, after all, but that does not mean we must act, you know?"

Jorge nodded.

"So, I'm not an asshole husband?"

Marco laughed.

"No, sir, you are not."

Jorge didn't reply but shamefully glanced at the floor.

"And sir, the lady you are speaking of, she is no longer here," Marco continued. "Diego fired her."

"I thought we decided a long time ago that we weren't going to bother with a receptionist anyway," Jorge quickly looked up. "Why was she here? Who was she?"

"I think from a temp agency? HR hired her. I'm not sure why."

"Marco, I need you to look into her," Jorge commented. "I got a weird feeling. Maybe it's nothing but Diego said she hit on him too."

"Sir, she was quite *friendly* with a lot of men here," Marco titled his head. "I noticed a few times. Maybe to find out something?"

"Yeah, well, there's nothing like having a man in a vulnerable situation to make him talk without thinking," Jorge gestured toward the glass door. "She wasn't here long?"

"Maybe a week?" Marco thought.

"Yeah, I want you to look into her, Marco," Jorge confirmed. "And keep an eye on Elizabeth Alan and her boyfriend. Anything new on Verónic?"

Marco seemed to hesitate.

"Is that a yes?"

"Well, I did find something," Marco opened his laptop again and signed in. "But I am still investigating, sir. I don't know if it is her but I found someone with the same name recently opened a bank account. Are you certain she is still going by her real name?"

Jorge shook his head.

"See, this is the problem," Marco commented. "She may have a new identity or it could be someone else. Did the man who told Diego about her….would he know this?"

"Dead."

"Oh…this is not good, sir."

"I don't believe he mentioned a different name," Jorge replied. "Tell you the truth, Marco, I didn't even think of this…"

"It is a possibility if she is trying to hide from you," Marco suggested. "But this account opened in her name, I am monitoring it to see activity. If we can find a location, that might be a start."

"I got people everywhere, Marco. If she's out there, I will find her."

"This is good sir, I...

Diego suddenly barged in the door, halting their conversation.

"Great news!" He exclaimed as the door shut behind him. "I got a closing date on the house. We'll be neighbors soon!"

"Lucky me," Jorge spoke sarcastically causing Marco to laugh. "Finally, I can get those fucking lime trees out of my house!"

"They better still be alive," Diego said with a warning glance.

"Yes, Diego, they are all still alive," Jorge replied. "A few less leaves, courtesy of Miguel but still alive."

"So, I'm thinking," Diego spoke abruptly as if he hadn't heard Jorge's last comment, he sat down beside him. "I'm getting a safe room put in."

"That there, it is a good idea," Jorge nodded. "I got bulletproof windows in my house but I do not have a safe room."

"Get one and you know what, we could even have one built between the two houses."

"But we may not be there forever."

"Then we fill it in if the time comes."

"Let me think about it."

"I'm also considering getting a dog," Diego continued. "For protection."

"That's an interesting idea."

"One that will be trained to bite the ass off anyone who tries anything."

"I see but Diego," Jorge thought for a moment. "Do you really want a dog?"

"What I really want is a pet tiger and to throw enemies in the pen with him but you know," Diego said with a smug expression. "We gotta be realistic here."

Marco laughed and closed his laptop.

"And I will be super close if you need help with anything," Diego continued excitedly, "or a babysitter."

"But, Diego, who's going to babysit you?" Jorge teased.

"I tried to convince Chase to move in too," Diego spoke wide-eyed. "There's a basement apartment, he'd have a place to himself."

"But close enough to spy on him," Jorge pointed out. "Do you want this?"

"I'm over that," Diego insisted. "I just…I want my friend back."

"He never went away he just wasn't….you know…."

"I know…he's not gay," Diego said with a long sigh. "the biggest disappointment of my life."

"Well, we all have a few," Jorge reminded him. "This here, you will survive."

"Who knows what the future will bring?"

"I don't think it will bring…quite what you want," Jorge reminded him. "Speaking of Chase, he met with Maria recently for a 'coffee date'. My daughter, she is 12 turning 25…I don't know…"

The three men laughed as Jorge shook his head.

"I think it's cute that she has a crush on him," Diego offered.

"Does everyone have a crush on Chase?"

"Not me, sir," Marco said with a big smile. "He's too tall."

The three men laughed again.

"At any rate," Jorge continued. "He talked to her about Verónic and now Maria no longer wants to see her. This gives me great relief but I still need to find that woman. I cannot have her running around saying whatever to whoever. I must take care of this situation."

"We will find her sir."

"I know, Marco," Jorge nodded. "We will."

"I think Chase is good with Maria," Diego jumped in. "And who knows, maybe one day when she's older…"

"Diego, do not say it," Jorge cut in. "Chase, he is family but even when Maria is an adult woman….he is too old for her. This here, it would be too weird."

"She doesn't seem to think so," Diego reminded him.

"Well, she will," Jorge was insistent. "She will meet a boy…probably some little asshole that I hate, but she *will* meet a boy and forget this crush on Chase."

"Speaking of dating," Diego cut in. "What's the deal with Enrique and Jolene?"

"They are doing it on Chase's office couch."

"Oh God! I did not have to know that," Diego made a face. "How…"

"It was on camera," Jorge answered before he had time to finish. "Chase, he keeps tabs on the bar, even when he's not there to make sure no one gets in especially, after last time."

Diego nodded. Marco looked puzzled but didn't ask.

"Can we trust him?" Diego asked. "If a man isn't loyal to his family, why would he be loyal to us either?"

"That is a good question, Diego," Jorge replied. "A very good question."

CHAPTER 36

"And *Papa*, if someone comes up behind me and tries to grab me," Maria continued as she demonstrated a series of moves in the family living room. "I grab him like this and then I turn like this…."

Jorge was a little lost with the series of moves his daughter was showing him but it still filled him with pride. The same girl who appeared tiny and frail to him now demonstrated power in a way that gave him some comfort. He wanted his children to be able to protect themselves when he was no longer around to look after them. He especially feared for his daughter.

"…then I do this," Maria continued before standing still again. "Because the key is to find their most vulnerable areas and attack. And also, the instructor says that if you have to, you can stick your fingers in their eyes. I think that sounds gross but he said, 'if you're in a situation where you fear for your safety, you'll have no problem doing it Maria.' He's probably right."

Jorge couldn't help but laugh at her wide-eyed innocence in light of the comment.

"Oh, Maria, I am so proud of you," Jorge offered as he stretched out his arms and watched his daughter shyly approach and hug him. "All this here, it makes me feel better. I want you to always feel safe and as you know, there are a lot of crazy people in the world."

"*Papa,* maybe I need to learn how to use a gun," Maria suggested as their hug ended. "You know, just in case…"

"Maria, you are too young," Jorge insisted. "I would, however, like to find some pepper spray or something of that nature to protect yourself, if ever needed."

"Paige says hairspray," Maria suggested as she sat beside him on the couch. "She said it wouldn't seem weird if a girl my age had a small can of hairspray in her purse to…obviously, fix her hair but then if some maniac tries to attack me, I spray it in their eyes so they are powerless."

"But Maria," Jorge automatically saw the problem with this plan. "This is not everyone. If a girl at school says mean things, you cannot spray her in the face."

Maria's eyes widened and she smiled, suggesting the idea hadn't crossed her mind.

"Maria!"

"No, of course, *Papa,* I won't do that."

"I'm serious, *chica,* I do not want a call from the school because you attack another kid," He warned as he turned toward her. "In fact, if we could make it through one school year without any calls at all, I would be very happy."

"I never mean for that to happen," Maria replied. "I'm usually defending myself, *Papa.*"

"Perhaps we should give peace a chance this year," Jorge suggested. "Just for once."

"Look who's talking!" Jorge heard the familiar voice and turned to see Diego walking into the living room, followed by Paige. "Maybe you need to give your father the same lecture."

Maria giggled and Paige grinned as both she and Diego sat down.

"Hey no, do not worry about me," Jorge said and winked at his daughter. "You know that I am, at heart, a peace-loving man."

"Oh yeah, you're up there with Mother Theresa," Diego quipped, causing Maria to laugh harder.

"How was your class today?" Paige changed the topic.

"It was awesome!" Maria replied excitedly. "I was showing *Papa* the moves I'm learning. I'm like a superhero now if anyone tries to do anything.

The instructor said that it doesn't matter that I'm small either, I can still be powerful."

"That's true, Maria," Paige nodded.

"And do not forget that *bonita*," Jorge jumped in. "This here is important. People who think they are weak, *are* weak."

"I know," Maria nodded and started to slide off the couch. "I gotta go text Chase and tell him about today."

And just like that, she was on her feet and halfway up the stairs, leaving the others behind.

"I'm so glad she's learning self-defense," Paige commented with a smile. "It's a scary world out there especially for a woman."

"You are so right, *mi amor,* there are no knights in shining armor out there to look out for her."

"Except Chase," Diego said and began to nod with his usual, dramatic expression. "I think the odds are good he will always look out for her, that we all will if she needs us."

"I know, Diego, but we must consider that we may not always be here," Jorge replied. "As much as I do not like to think of my death, it is going to happen one day. We will all die."

"So this is an uplifting conversation," Diego quipped. "What is wrong with you lately? This is not the Jorge Hernandez that I know, the one who says he will 'never die.'"

"Unfortunately, he had a reality check several months ago," Jorge said as he glanced at his wife who nodded. "Losing Jesús, it was not easy and it showed me what is to come, a 'preview' I guess you could say."

"We can't think like that," Diego shook his head. "That's when we get in trouble."

"It's kind of like what you told Maria," Paige reminded him. "If we think we are weak, we will be weak."

"I do not think we are weak," Jorge corrected her. "I am just realistic about life, that is all. We must be ready for what could happen at any time. It may not even be a dangerous situation, it could be health problems, a plane could fall out of the sky and hit us…we do not know."

"Wait, you're not having health issues again, are you?" Paige appeared concerned. "Please tell me if you are."

"No, I mean, you know, I don't feel as good as I did when I was 20," Jorge said with a shrug. "But I have a lot of stuff on the go plus a crying baby at night, I think this here is normal."

Paige opened her mouth to say something but stopped. She instead exchanged looks with Diego.

"Yeah, well you better tell us if you aren't well," He quickly jumped in. "You don't hide things from us."

"Of course not, Diego," Jorge shook his head. "You worry too much. Both of you, it is fine. My point is that we must be prepared *just in case*. I want my daughter to be strong, confident and able to look after herself. Many others, do not bring up their children this way and they get out in the world and can't handle anything. They are crying *bebes*"

"Speaking of crying babies," Diego changed the subject as he sat back in his chair and crossed his legs. "You should've seen that receptionist when I fired her the other day. You wouldn't believe the groveling she did to keep her job. She even offered…to do stuff….stuff that I don't want from her if you know what I mean."

"Perhaps you should've tried to see," Jorge teased. "Maybe you like? It could open up a new world for you."

Diego rolled his eyes as Paige grinned and Jorge laughed hysterically at his joke.

"Yeah, well, that's not going to happen," Diego rebutted. "Plus, that's exactly what she wanted. Marco found out that she's been from company to company, attempting lawsuits against big shots, saying that they sexually harassed her. Some paid her off to shut up. I guess she thought you would be next."

"This here did not work with me," Jorge spoke proudly and smiled at his wife. "I would not do that."

"She tried though," Diego reminded him and Jorge shot him a dirty look. "Did you tell Paige?"

"Tell me what? The receptionist hit on you?"

"Yeah, but it was nothing, *mi amor*," Jorge replied casually, wishing Diego hadn't said anything. "She was suggesting we get together to talk about her interest in politics….you know…"

"Politics! Right!" Diego said as his eyes bulged out and he waved his arms in the air. "That's what 'Madame fat tits' wanted, to pick your brain on the political situation in the middle east."

"Madame *fat tits*?" Paige asked curiously. "You called her that?"

"Behind her back," Diego assured her. "It was because she…well, had an exaggerated figure for being so small….and well she was French and…. she liked to show it all off."

Paige merely nodded and looked toward Jorge who was glaring at Diego.

"Must we talk about this anymore?" Jorge complained "I did not do anything wrong. The lady, she asked me to join her some time to talk politics, she was a bit too much to touch and I tell her that it was not appropriate to act in such a way at work."

"This is true, he did," Diego agreed. "And in fairness, she was like that with a lot of the men at the office. That's why we fired her."

"I hope she does not know about that nickname or we might be sued," Jorge reminded Diego.

"No, just me…Marco….you know…"

Paige looked humored.

"Is that why you are here, Diego?" Jorge asked, still mildly annoyed. "To tell me about her being fired and crying?"

"Just that and the updates," Diego replied. "Marco thinks he got something on Verónic. She was staying with a relative in southern Mexico. But, we got people checking it out and she's no longer there."

"Checking it out?" Paige asked curiously.

"They went into her home and ripped it apart," Diego replied. "Nothing and the relative, she said Verónic stole some money and took off in the middle of the night."

Jorge shook his head and sighed loudly.

"But good news," Diego continued. "We might have a time and place to catch Elizabeth Alan and her boyfriend together."

Jorge's ears perked up.

"I hope your weekend is cleared."

Jorge grinned and raised an eyebrow.

CHAPTER 37

"If you told me that this happened in Mexico," Chase started, pausing for a moment to make sure his phone was off. "I'd say, 'sure' I hear there's a lot of corruption down there, but…"

"But not here, am I right?" Jorge cut in as he drove away from Toronto and toward cottage country as the sun began to lower in the sky. "Do you really believe this does not happen in Canada?"

"We're not as corrupt as Mexico," Diego piped up from the back seat. He sat up straight, wearing a suit as if the three men were on their way to a business meeting. "But we got our problems here."

"Hey, this corruption, it goes both ways," Jorge was quick to point out as they drove along with traffic. "Don't think those politicians aren't living the high life on cartel money. They never had a problem taking it."

"But that isn't here, right?" Chase asked as he turned his head from the passenger seat. "I mean, you don't give Athas money, other than when he was running?"

"Nah," Jorge shook his head. "We got other ways of working with him and today, this here is one of them."

Chase nodded while in the backseat, Diego jumped in.

"I can't believe Elizabeth Alan is back!" He shook his head. "I thought she slunk away with her tail between her legs after the leadership nomination last year."

"Yeah, weren't you supposed to nominate her or something?" Chase asked with a grin on his face. "Then kind of fucked her over at the last minute?"

"Yes, it was a surprise she was not expecting," Jorge replied. "But for me, I do not worry about such things. After all, this is politics. I knew that she had no hope in hell getting in and if she didn't, that the opposition, they would have criminalized pot again and then, where would that put me?"

"And if she had got in," Chase added, "She might've done the same thing."

"Yes, you cannot trust these people who talk too much of their religion," Jorge reminded him. "It is like the people who post pictures on their social media of their happy family and then they divorce a month later. If someone is pushing a point home too hard, this is a warning sign."

Chase nodded in silence.

"She's a fucking hypocrite too," Diego quickly pointed out. "Church on Sunday after cheating on her husband on Saturday night."

"Well, the good news," Jorge spoke with excitement in his voice. "She will not be doing that *this* Sunday morning."

The three men laughed.

"Those angel wings, they don't come easy," Diego added with a sinister grin on his face. "As she might soon find out."

"So, I get why we're killing him," Chase spoke calmly, his voice full of naïvety. "He's driving a knife in Alec's back but her…"

"They were *both* trying to bring him down from the inside," Jorge shook his head. "Except, she did not think the death threats were serious. He played them down. He doesn't want his church-going girlfriend to know the truth. He is desperate to get Athas out in any way possible. There is nothing I hate more than a double agent, which is what he was doing."

"Like Michael…"

This came from Diego and referenced his former boyfriend.

"That there, was different," Jorge reminded him. "To a point anyway. He was double-crossing the police department he was working for and later, we find out he was doing the same to us."

"I can't believe…"

"Diego, let it go," Jorge advised. "This here, it is history. Let it go. We resolved it like we resolve all our problems, including this one today."

"But why would he act like he's on Alec's side," Chase asked as if they hadn't changed topics. "Why does he want him out so bad?"

"Because he got his own candidate that he wanted to get in…"

"Oh…."

"Exactly," Jorge pieced it together for the youngest of their group. "If he could get Athas out, he can get his side piece in and I am guessing, control her as he saw fit. He could not do this with Athas. Alec, as everyone knows, works for me. Our agendas are completely different."

"So, why are we killing her?" Chase asked. "Why not just scare the shit out of her?"

"Because she is constantly getting in my crosshairs," Jorge replied and sniffed. "I gave her chances and yet, she does not seem to understand. And the recording I was listening to, the one Athas made? She said she wasn't scared of me, so I'm going to show her she underestimated Jorge Hernandez."

"But if you just threatened her?" Chase asked curiously. "I mean, I'm not suggesting you're wrong. I just want to understand."

"Because my friend, small problems can quickly add up to big problems," Jorge said as he glanced toward a sign. "What starts as a nuisance can gain in power. It is like the puppy that takes little bites at you. It may seem cute and harmless when he's young but when he is three times the size and bites you in the ass, it is a whole other story, *si?*"

"Do you think she is only going to get worse?"

"I think she *is* worse," Jorge replied. "As much as she is being used by Mr. Politician, she is also using him. This here, it goes both ways. They are both playing a game but just because she comes in a lipstick-wearing package, this does not mean she is not as dangerous. Men, they have a way of underestimating women."

"Says the chauvinist," Diego spoke eagerly.

"I am not a chauvinist, Diego," Jorge insisted. "Making a few chauvinistic remarks from time to time does not necessarily make me a chauvinist. But I do believe that men, we underestimate women. I see it all the time when I was growing up, especially in my years in Mexico but even now, in this day and age, I see it here in Canada. It is unfortunate."

Diego looked skeptical.

"Isn't that what we're looking for?" Chase pointed at a sign as they passed. "This place is very...secluded."

"This here, it works well for us," Jorge reminded him. "Even more so for them. After all they cannot have anyone see them together."

"I think we turn off the road ahead," Diego said as he squinted over a piece of paper in his hand.

"Diego, your glasses!" Jorge teased him. "Where are your glasses?"

"Don't worry about me," Diego gave him a dirty look.

"But your old man eyes!"

"You're older than me," Diego reminded him.

"Yeah, but my eyes, they still work," Jorge remarked as he pulled off the road and parked. After the lights went out of his SUV, their surroundings were pitch black.

"Now, we walk for a few minutes, so they do not hear us coming," Jorge said as he reached for his gun. "This here, it will be fast and easy. We can even go for ice cream on the way home, it's gonna be *that* fast."

The three men got out of the SUV and started to walk. Jorge noted that Diego was the odd one out, wearing an expensive suit in a secluded area, while he and Chase kept it simple: jeans and a jacket. However, the most telling sign that they were out of place was the gloves they wore. It was a hot night in June.

The cottage was easy to find. Small, one single light and expensive cars in the driveway were the only indications that someone was there. The three men exchanged looks and walked up the driveway. Jorge reached for the doorknob and turned it.

"Unlocked?" He whispered. "You would be surprised how many people do this. Especially with all the criminals out there."

Chase grinned while Diego nodded with an exaggerated smile on his face. They all reached for their guns.

Going inside, they saw nothing. The small, living room was simple with a couch and table. Two wine glasses sat beside a bottle. Rustling sounds came from the next room, soft moans as a squeaky mattress signaled what the couple was doing at that moment.

Jorge cringed a bit and walked ahead of the others and right into the room. Naked, Elizabeth Alan was on top of the politician, grinding into him forcefully, completely unaware that they weren't alone. He opened his mouth to say something but before he could, a shot rang out and the same woman who was moaning in pleasure now fell over, blood splattered everywhere: The sheets, the ceiling, and all over Alec's colleague.

Turning to his right, Jorge saw Chase holding a gun. His face was pensive, his eyes detached, he continued to point the gun toward the bed. Jorge hid his shock and started to speak.

"Well, that there, that takes care of one problem," Jorge spoke calmly, ignoring the wide-eyed look Diego was giving a very calm Chase. "That lady, she may have gone to church every Sunday but she's still going to hell with the rest of us."

"I...I..." The man seemed to regain his composure and unsuccessfully attempted to push the corpse away from him.

"And you too, I am sure you are going to hell," Jorge cut off the politician. "Threatening to kill Athas? Not a good look for you....but then again, neither is this here..."

Jorge used his gun to point toward some of the many places her blood was splattered.

"But I do find it interesting," Jorge spoke to Diego and Chase. "That no matter what color you are, your blood, it always looks the same. No matter how rich or poor or religious you are.....your blood, it is always red. And here, it shows we are not that different after all."

The man managed to push Elizabeth Alan's body aside and pulled back into the bed as if he could back away and avoid his impending death.

"Hey!" Diego yelled. "Stay still motherfucker, no more moving around."

"Yes, we do not like sudden movements," Jorge confirmed. "It makes us nervous and when we get nervous," He tilted his head toward Chase. "Sometimes, we shoot and think later."

"Bringing the government down from the inside?" Chase spoke up, something that surprised Jorge. "What the fuck?"

"Yes, Athas does not like traitors," Jorge added. "And quite frankly, he was tired of you fucking with him. And *I* am tired of your fucking with him. See, without loyalty, you got nothing. And you, you are not a loyal man and..."

A shot rang out and suddenly, the same man who had worked against Athas for months, lay slumped over with blood pouring from his head.

Stunned, Jorge turned toward Chase as he lowered his gun. He slowly turned toward his comrades with a subdued look in his eyes.

It was a new day.

CHAPTER 38

"It is a new day," Jorge remarked to his wife over the breakfast table on Monday morning, "in so many ways."

"I can see that," She replied and glanced toward his laptop as they watched a news report.

"Elizabeth Alan, who led Canadians for Conservative Values was found…"

"It's interesting how they leave out so many details," Paige continued as she reached for her coffee. "Didn't you say they were in bed together at the time?"

"Yes, *mi amor,* they were a bit…preoccupied when we arrived," Jorge replied as he glanced at the reporter on the screen. "But ah, Chase, he soon ended that."

"I still can't believe he…"

"I know, *mi amor,* I know," Jorge muttered as he watched the footage as it repeated: pictures of the cabin where the bodies were found, professional photos of Elizabeth Alan and another of her lover, as he walked beside Athas the previous fall, shortly after the election. "The devil and his legacy will continue even when I one day step aside."

"Do you think you will?" Paige asked skeptically.

"I must," Jorge answered with a note of nostalgia in his voice. "The kids, it is best that I take them away from this. I do not want the same life for them but also, I do not want to end this organization."

"I don't know if that's possible," Paige commented as Jorge turned toward her. "I wish the same as you but do you think neither of the children will want to become involved in the business?"

"I would hope not," Jorge replied. "My wish is that they both go to university, find love and success and live happily ever after. I do not want them looking over their shoulders, especially if I am not here to protect them."

"Jorge, I..."

"I know, *mi amor*, I know," He leaned forward and took her hand in his. "But we have to be realistic. We must prepare and be ready for anything. If the children are separated from the business, living their own lives, they will be safe. That is what I want for them."

Paige nodded with sadness in her eyes.

"Chase, he will look after things," Jorge continued and leaned back in his chair, glancing toward the screen for a moment, he slowly closed his laptop. "I see now that the boy, he has become a man. He is fearless. There is something in his eyes that was never there before. He will keep Maria safe because she will listen to whatever he tells her. We see this now."

"And Miguel?"

"He is just too young to know what is going on," Jorge reminded her. "If we start to move away from this life now, by the time he is old enough to understand who we are, we will be something else."

Paige didn't reply.

Jorge merely grinned and leaned forward, kissing her on the forehead.

"Trust me, this here, it will be fine," Jorge insisted. "The company will continue. It will be my legacy. The children will also be my legacy. I have made my mark in the world. This is good. I feel I can slowly step away from this world we created."

"I don't know if it will be that easy...."

"Of course I can, *mi amor*, I can do anything."

"But do you really want to?" Paige asked as she shook her head. "That's what troubles me."

"I do," Jorge assured her. "It is time."

"And Verónic," Paige continued to speak in a low voice. "Maybe we should let it go…"

"No," Jorge insisted and shook his head, "absolutely not. I will not have that woman roaming around, telling stories about me. I need to end her and I need to make it look like an accident."

Paige nodded as her eyes scanned the floor.

Glancing at the clock, he noted the time.

"I must go," Jorge rose from his chair, reaching for his coffee, finishing it in one gulp. "I am meeting Chase and Diego."

Thirty minutes later, Jorge arrived at the club to find Diego's car in his own spot. Parking beside him, he headed inside to be met by his longtime friend's booming voice.

"…element of surprise and there's something to be said for that."

"Diego!" Jorge spoke loudly as he closed the door and glanced at the bar. "You are parked in my spot!"

"I don't see your name on it," Diego smugly replied as he turned in his stool. "Who the hell says you own it?"

"Because I own this club," Jorge playfully reminded him as he approached the bar. Chase stood behind it with a grin on his face while Diego appeared unconcerned as he sipped on his coffee. "So what's going on?"

"I see they found the bodies," Diego said with a raised eyebrow. "I still can't believe *this guy!*"

Jorge watched as Diego swung his stool around and pointed toward Chase.

"Never did I think I would see the day…"

"Yes, Diego, you said this, what?" Jorge cut him off as he sat beside him. "A million times on our way home the other night? It was a surprise but it is good."

Jorge nodded toward Chase who had something different in his eyes. It was bold confidence, a look of strength that went beyond his exterior self.

"I never thought I could do it," Chase was quick to reply then seemed to retract back. "I mean, at one time, I didn't even want to touch a gun let alone…"

"Time, it changes things," Jorge replied. "I have seen this in my life. Where you are heading down this path, I see myself heading back the other way."

"What the fuck you talking about?" Diego turned swiftly in his seat. "You becoming a man of God now or something?"

"I would not say that Diego, no," Jorge said as he watched Chase pour him a coffee and place it on the bar. "But as I said before, I see me moving away from all of this....you know, to a degree."

"I know but I thought it was some weird phase you were going through," Diego spoke abruptly, his eyes bolted wide open. "You trying to tell me you aren't a gangster anymore? That you're going to retire or something?"

"I do not know what the exact wording is," Jorge replied self-consciously. "But I do feel that I need to move away from this lifestyle, yes."

"Why?" Diego appeared confused. "I don't get it."

"Diego, I have children and I do not want the same life for them as I have now," Jorge commented and noticed that Chase was nodding as he put the carton of cream on the counter. "I want to slow down."

"Old age," Diego nodded.

"I am *not* old," Jorge quickly corrected him. "I just wish to stay alive to see my children grow. When that man broke into my house last year, he could've killed my family. This here, it crosses my mind every day."

"I know," Diego finally pulled in the reigns. "I get that but still..."

"It may not stop them," Chase reminded him. "It mightn't be that simple."

"I know but I have to try," Jorge admitted. "Jesús dying, it was pretty close to home. I want to be around to see my Maria grow into a beautiful young woman, who is smart and makes a life for herself. I want to see Miguel become a man. I do everything for my children and Paige. And this here, it is also for them."

Chase nodded while Diego looked depressed.

"Do not get me wrong," Jorge insisted. "I will still be in contact and advise but I want to be home with my family."

"You already spend most of your days at home," Diego quickly reminded him. "You're never in the fucking office..."

"Ah see, then you won't miss me," Jorge replied with humor in his voice. "You know me, I do not wish to be locked in an office. It is suffocating."

"So when does this all take place?" Chase asked.

"Soon…I am thinking at the end of the summer. "Maria will be back in school. I can stay home with Miguel and Paige. Touch base with all of you and work on some projects with Athas, but for the most part, I think it is time I slow down."

There was an awkward silence.

"You don't think that will happen, do you?" Diego spoke up. "Hey, I'm sure you want it to happen but let's face it, things don't slow down with you."

"But this time, they must," Jorge insisted. "Diego, I have you and Chase, he has stepped up many times in the last few weeks alone. Jolene, she is there and Enrique…well, I guess we are still learning about him."

"Jolene is keeping him…preoccupied," Diego rolled his eyes.

"This isn't a bad thing," Jorge insisted. "The thing about Jolene is that she is helpful when you need her."

"But a nuisance when you don't," Diego added. "I know, I get it. It's better she's not bored."

"This affair, it's getting pretty careless though," Chase commented as he leaned against the bar. "They're barely hiding the fact that it's going on now. I saw them the other day at the coffee shop, holding hands. It's been my experience that affairs, they rarely stay a secret."

Jorge merely shrugged.

"My sister, she is careless," Diego reminded them.

"This is why I like to keep her preoccupied with other things if I do not need her for something," Jorge added. "And speaking of Enrique, his work?"

"No problems there," Chase shook his head. "I think we can trust him."

"Marco was looking into him and he's clean…" Diego added.

"Ok, this is good," Jorge nodded. "Because as soon as I find Verónic, he is going to help bring her back here. This is our test."

"And if he passes?"

"He's one of us," Jorge replied.

"And if he fails?" Chase countered.

Jorge didn't reply. He just took another drink of his coffee.

CHAPTER 39

"They're running on empty," Athas confirmed over the phone while Jorge sat back and listened. "At first, they were looking at the spouses but both had an alibi during the time of the murders."

"Of course, the police, they will look at the most obvious suspects because it's easy," Jorge confirmed with a smirk on his face. "They are lazy and believe me, this is a hornet's nest they don't want to shake."

"I think that's the general feeling about this case with Elizabeth Alan and…"

"The police, they will wait until another news story diverts people's attention," Jorge insisted as he moved his chair forward. "Then they will push the file aside and take a nap."

"You really don't have any faith in the authorities do you?"

"Do *you?*" Jorge countered.

"Interestingly," Athas replied with some hesitation. "I used to."

"Well, *amigo,* it is a bittersweet reality check for you," Jorge said with a certain amount of affection in his voice. "But I imagine many things are since you became prime minister of Canada."

"It's been disheartening," Athas admitted. "But my duty is to the people and to give them confidence even when I doubt the system."

"This here, it has been my reality for many years," Jorge reminded him. "But, of course, from the other side of things. All we can do is what we can in an imperfect world."

"But I want to make it better."

"Athas, you already have."

Their conversation ended shortly after, leaving Jorge with his thoughts. Where he had once assumed the prime minister would be weak, Athas was strong. His strength came from admitting when he needed help and accepting it. Recognizing his role in the situation, Jorge felt satisfied.

Rising from his chair, a quick sharp jolt in his chest caused him to sit back down. Closing his eyes momentarily, he felt the pain go away and automatically looked at a nearby picture of his family. What would they ever do without him? He knew Paige was powerful and certainly capable of taking on anyone or anything but the children made her vulnerable. He closed his eyes again and leaned back in the chair. Being aware of each breath, Jorge felt himself calming down, his body began to relax. The pain went away.

Sir, you will never die. You are much too powerful. Others die. You triumph.

Jorge's eyes flew open as his head twisted back and forth rapidly, quickly taking in the entire room. He was alone.

Electricity shot through his body. It was Jesús who just spoke to him. Had it been a dream?

It felt very real.

Slowly standing up, he momentarily felt weak as his emotions reached the surface. Jesús had been more than a comrade, he was his brother and a friend. He had always been there for Jorge and saved his life on more than one occasion. And now, he was trying to save him again.

It took a moment to calm. His breathing suddenly relaxed while a shock ran through his veins, the lion deep inside his heart began to roar. He knew what he had to do. It was time.

Reaching for his phone, he turned it back on before leaving the office.

In the kitchen, he found Maria sitting with a cup of coffee as she looked at her iPad. He grinned.

"*Bonita,* you are just like your father," He spoke loudly, causing her to jump as she turned to see him enter the room. "A cup of coffee, checking the headlines…"

Glancing at her screen, he saw that her headlines were more about celebrity gossip than real news but it still pleased him.

"Well, *Papa,* it is important I stay informed," She spoke like a little lady as she sat up straighter and reached for her coffee. "As you know."

"Yes, my dear, I do," Jorge said as he leaned in and kissed her on the forehead. "Where is Paige?"

"With Miguel," Maria replied as she glanced toward the stairs. "He's getting another tooth and he's cranky as *fuck!*"

"Maria, the language, please…"

"But that's how you speak."

"Maria," Jorge paused for a moment. "You are better than me. Do not swear like that. It is….unpleasant."

She merely shrugged and took a sip of her coffee.

"I thought Miguel was going to say 'mama' today but he said my name instead," She raised an eyebrow. "I wish he would finally say it. I think it's making Paige sad."

"Maria, perhaps you should try to teach him," Jorge lowered his voice. "You're his big sister, he will always listen to you."

"I somehow doubt that," She shrugged and crossed her legs. "It's like Diego says, Miguel is pig-headed like his father."

"Pig-head?" Jorge was confused. "I do not understand."

"He means stubborn."

"Fair enough," Jorge nodded glancing at his phone. "I must go, Maria. Kiss everyone for me."

"I will."

In the SUV, Jorge called Marco.

"Good morning, sir."

"Marco, cómo estás?"

"I am good, sir," Marco spoke with his usual enthusiasm. "It is a beautiful day."

"Yes, I see this here," Jorge replied as he glanced out the window at the cloudy skies. "I do love a beautiful day."

"My day has started well," He continued. "I am making much progress."

"I will be in to see you a little later," Jorge replied, knowing that he had news for him. "I must meet with someone first but after that, I will swing by the office."

"Very good, sir."

He ended the call.

Maybe Jesús had been right. Maybe he was still the powerful man he had always been.

Arriving at the small café near the *Toronto AM* office, Jorge found a parking spot and went inside. After grabbing a coffee, he found Makerson at the back of the room, away from other patrons.

"Good morning," He automatically addressed Jorge with a tired smile.

"Good morning," Jorge replied as he sat across from him with a coffee in hand. "You look fucking exhausted."

"The life of an editor,"

"This is true," Jorge replied. "So, tell me, what are you hearing in the world of news?"

"Police are getting a lot of pressure to find the killers in this murder with Elizabeth Alan and her...friend."

"Of course," Jorge nodded. "He is, after all, one of the clowns that worked for Athas, it is important, no?"

"So important that they're putting all their resources in it," Makerson pushed aside his phone. Jorge noted it was turned off. "And not other cases."

"Such as?"

"There were some murders in the North end a few days ago," Makerson muttered. "Kind of swept under the rug."

"So they are not as important?"

"Apparently not."

"This sounds like the news you should have in your paper."

"The problem is no one wants to talk."

"Then how do you know?"

"Word on the street."

"Maybe the best approach would be to inquire about the deaths...."

"Already tried it," Makerson shook his head. "I was told to back the fuck off."

"I see."

"I was hoping that you could speak with the prime minister," Makerson suggested. "After all, it would be in his best interest to approach this…"

"Yes," Jorge nodded in agreement. "Perhaps he is worried that others are not getting fair treatment but it may also shake their trees a little too hard."

"Not if they can find an explanation that will satisfy the public," Makerson reminded him. "In the end, isn't that their only goal?"

"This is true," Jorge thought for a moment. "Perhaps they will find some proof that suggests it was random."

"I hear the cottage door was not locked."

"So it wasn't as if someone had to break in…"

"Maybe, you know, they find someone there they did not expect…"

"Shot before thinking."

"Then panicked and left."

"They could be a million miles away by now."

"Fuck Makerson, we could be police," Jorge said with a grin.

"I'll pass."

"You and me both."

"So can you put a bug in his ear."

"Consider it done."

"And I got dibs on the story."

"It is all yours."

Twenty minutes later, Jorge was at the office and speaking with Marco in the conference room.

"Sir, I am so sorry," Marco appeared upset when he sat down. "I had a lead on Verónic but then, she disappeared again."

"Where did you find it?"

"I see, I think it is her card being used near the Puebla airport."

"Do you think she was flying somewhere?"

"That is the thing, sir," He replied with frustration in his voice. "It did seem that way but then she disappeared again. She did not get on a plane, that I can see."

"But she would not use her real ID," Jorge assured him. "And if she paid cash…"

"I must hack into the airport cameras and see what I can find."

"Can you do that?"

"I can do anything, sir."

Jorge liked that answer.

"So, the question is, where would she go?"

"That, sir, I do not know."

"My guess is she is trying to escape me," Jorge replied. "She knows I have too many people in Mexico so she is trying to escape the country."

"We will find her."

"Marco, we must," Jorge insisted. "She is like a grenade that is about to explode. I do not care if she does but I don't want debris falling on my family, especially Maria."

"I understand, sir."

CHAPTER 40

"Diego, I look for you at the office and here you are," Jorge waved his arms around the empty club as he walked in. Diego was sitting on a stool and turned around to give a bored shrug while Chase watched him behind the bar with a grin on his face. "What? You don't go to the office anymore?"

"You said I would be taking over for you," Diego quipped. "So, I thought I would follow in your footsteps."

"As I told my Maria this morning," Jorge said as he sat beside him. "Do as I say, not as I do."

"That advice usually doesn't work," Chase reminded him as he turned around and automatically poured him a coffee. "With either kids or Diego."

"Same thing," Jorge teased and ignored Diego's dirty look. "So where's Enrique?"

"I got him running errands," Chase said as he placed Jorge's coffee on the counter and reached under the bar for the cream. "He just left so I thought I would take a break."

"Still doing good?"

"He's doing great," Chase replied. "I got him pretty well trained and honestly, he's probably doing better than me."

"Yeah, but does he…" Jorge stopped and whirled his hand in the air. "Was Clara in?"

"Yup."

"Then I must ask," Jorge continued as he stirred his coffee. "Does he shoot to kill or what? Cause you, *amigo,* you do."

"Yes, you've become a killing machine," Diego said with a quick eyebrow flash, something that Chase appeared to ignore. "Didn't I say that the other day? This time last year, we could barely get you to even pick up a gun, let alone kill. So, is there anything else you've changed your mind on lately?"

"Don't get excited, Diego," Jorge joked as he reached for his coffee. "I do not think that expands to all areas of his life…"

Chase laughed.

"Hey, he said he'd never pick up a gun," Diego reminded them both. "And he's more than done that so, hey….the point is that you never know."

Jorge took a drink of coffee and shook his head.

"If I ever decide I like men, Diego," Chase gently replied. "You'll be the first one to know."

"I appreciate that," Diego replied and gave Jorge a look. "I will be at the front of that lineup."

"If it happens," Jorge reminded him.

"It probably won't happen," Chase insisted.

"Anyway, we are getting off topic here," Jorge decided it was time to get back on track. "My point is that you've come a long way, my friend. You have stepped up when I needed it."

"You know and it wasn't even that," Chase spoke honestly. "It felt natural. Like, this is what I'm supposed to do and it's like…it's like I changed."

Both Jorge and Diego looked intrigued.

"I'm not the same person I used to be," Chase continued. "From helping Paige in Ottawa to that chick at the gym. I've changed. I don't have the words to explain."

"You felt more powerful?" Jorge suggested.

"Dangerous?" Diego offered.

"Kind of, I don't know," Chase shook his head. "Just different, you know? Like when I used to date those crazy S&M chicks? My tastes in women have completely changed. Weird things like that."

"This here, it makes sense," Jorge said with a shrug. "You feel more confident and this old way, it no longer appeals to you."

"So, what," Diego inquired. "You like the prissy, girl next door types now."

"Maybe he's saying is he likes, you know….normal women now?" Jorge asked.

"I guess if there's such a thing as normal," Chase replied. "I would rather date someone who is maybe a little more….sweet, maybe naïve."

"So, you want to date the old Chase, is that what you are saying?" Jorge teased and glanced at Diego who laughed out loud.

"Not quite like me," Chase clarified but smirked. "Someone with a sweet disposition who would not see my dark side."

"See this here, it does not work," Jorge insisted. "Because you will always be hiding part of your life if that is the case. Not that I suggest that you tell anyone what you do for me but…I guess it's an exception to have that opportunity."

"Yeah, like Paige," Diego offered. "She is like you except she's nothing like you."

"That does not make sense."

"She's dangerous," Diego spoke dramatically. "But not….whatever you are…"

Jorge shrugged and rolled his eyes.

"Anyway, we are getting off topic again," Jorge continued. "I am just saying that it is impressive how you stepped up."

"I worry about the police…"

"No need," Jorge replied. "They got nothing."

"As usual," Diego sniffed.

"I was talking to someone, they tried the most obvious suspects and now, they got nothing."

"We were careful."

"It is taken care of," Jorge said. "I have something in the works to divert their attention and after a few days, they'll eventually be told to drop it because they aren't getting anywhere. It costs too much money to run these kind of investigation and if the public isn't pressuring them, why bother?"

"What about the spouses of the people killed?" Diego wondered. "Aren't they asking questions?"

"If your spouse was fucking someone else when they died," Jorge reminded him. "Would you really care?"

Diego shrugged.

"Yeah, especially if you're trying to clear your own name," Chase added, "that's a bit distracting."

"But you are pretty good with a gun," Jorge jumped subjects again. "Is that from Paige teaching you?"

"Yes, and Jolene," Chase replied. "A lot of it is confidence."

"You definitely got that," Diego said.

"It don't matter," Jorge countered. "Guns, they are the easy way. Any idiot can pick up a gun and shoot but to kill someone with skill, now that is a whole other thing. That girl in the shower and buddy who broke in here, now that you did with your bare hands. Not everyone can do this, you know?"

"I agree," Diego jumped in. "Me? I like baseball bats."

"I hadn't noticed," Chase quipped and Jorge began to laugh. "I remember the first time I saw you hit that guy in the back of the legs with a baseball bat, I almost..."

"Yeah, yeah but you know what," Diego cut him off. "It gets the fucking job done and when you hit someone with a baseball bat, they know you aren't fucking around. They feel your anger, they *know* your fury. Plus it's cathartic."

"Words of wisdom from Diego," Jorge teased his friend.

"I got lots of them," He retorted.

"Yeah, the gun thing does seem too easy," Chase said just as the door opened.

All three men turned to see Enrique enter the room carrying a box in one hand, his phone in the other.

"Enrique, long time no see," Jorge called out. "Chase says you are doing well."

"I hope so," Enrique responded as he closed the door and walked towards them. "It is a nice bar. I do appreciate the opportunity."

"I appreciate your help."

"I feel that I should do much more for you," Enrique spoke with some doubt in his voice as he sat the box of lemons on the bar. "With all you've done for me."

"Oh, you are doing exactly what I need right now," Jorge insisted and noted the smirk on Chase's lips. "Do not worry, I will tell you if I need more. I suspect that in the future, I will have to get your help when I finally find my ex, Verónic."

"Yes, whatever you need," Enrique nodded. "I can help."

"You haven't found her yet?" Diego asked. "I thought you were getting closer."

"She is covering her tracks well," Jorge replied while shaking his head. "Because she knows that I am looking for her. Last check, she was around Puebla."

"Maria seems to have mixed feelings on the subject," Chase said.

"Yes, I wish she hadn't overheard me," Jorge shook his head. "I should have watched myself when speaking but when it comes to Verónic, I get so angry."

"She never brought out the best in you."

"And she never will," Jorge said. "That is why we must find her. I must make sure she does not talk."

"Do you want to bring her here?" Enrique asked.

"Not really," Jorge said. "My daughter, she originally wanted to speak with her but has since changed her mind. I hope that she can forget that woman ever existed."

"It's her mother," Diego reminded him. "So it's not likely."

"Paige, she is her real mother," Jorge reminded them. "This is the woman who looks after my Maria, more than Verónic ever did."

"And she knows that," Chase reminded him. "She loves Paige."

"Who *doesn't* love Paige!" Diego exclaimed.

"No one as much as you, Diego," Jorge teased. "But yes, Chase, Maria knows who is there for her. I am happy about this. Paige is a better role model for my daughter. I want my Maria to be strong and independent and this is what she gets from Paige."

"If I may," Enrique interjected. "I might be able to help. I know people in Puebla. If it helps, I can check to see…"

"Yes, please do!" Jorge said while nodding. "I will take any help I can get. Who you got down there? Anyone who knows where all the rats hide?"

"These people, Mr. Hernandez," Enrique replied. "They *are* the rats."

CHAPTER 41

"Prime Minister Athas has suggested that crime needs equal representation and not focusing more on the social elites, something his critics say…."

"Well, Makerson had a leg up on that story," Paige commented the following morning as she leaned toward Jorge, glancing at the iPad. With a grin on her face, she reached for her coffee. "So, is that true? Were the local police focusing all their attention on Elizabeth Alan and her boyfriend and ignoring other murders?"

"Yes, that is what I was told," Jorge confirmed as he continued to watch Makerson doing a live event on social media, breaking a story that other papers hadn't yet sunk their teeth into. "But this here is not a surprise. Me, I have always said the police were useless fucks."

"Well, we know how you feel about the police," Paige grinned as Jorge turned to wink at her. "But the real story here is that if you aren't *somebody* that crimes against you don't matter."

"Yes, I guess that is what this means," Jorge confirmed as he glanced at the laptop again as Makerson continued to talk about other highlights of the morning. "So, if you're a poor immigrant lady who has her purse stolen on the bad side of town, you probably won't get the same attention as the rich bitch who had her credit card swiped at the mall."

"That's unfortunate."

"That, *mi amor,* is a reality," Jorge replied as Makerson finished up his morning news highlights and Jorge turned his iPad off. "Money talks. This is a lesson we learn at an early age. That is why many of my people in Mexico kill each other to get to the top of the food chain. It is the same in Canada but here, you got your politicians to do your dirty work."

"Are you suggesting that politicians aren't corrupt in Mexico?"

"They are but they work for the cartel," Jorge reminded her. "Here, they work for anyone with a big enough wallet."

"You know me," Paige took a deep breath and paused. "I'm not for the police, however, the idea of some old lady having her purse snatched and essentially being ignored is particularly upsetting."

"She will not be completely ignored, *mi amor,*" Jorge replied as he began to push his chair back. "They will, you know, do some paperwork and ask her some questions before they shrug and say, 'Yeah, well, there ain't much we can do' and send her home."

Paige merely shook her head.

"The point here," Jorge continued as he stood up. "is that the public is now focused on the injustice. So it would be more scandalous if the police, they *did* spend too much time investigating the Elizabeth Alan murder. They've just been shamed in front of a nation."

A smooth grin ran across Paige's face as she leaned in and kissed him.

"Where are you going?" Paige asked as she stood up.

"I thought I would go see if Enrique found out anything about Verónic and then I have to…"

"What's the rush?" She asked as her hand reached out to touch his arm. "Do you have to go right now?"

"Well, no…"

"Didn't you notice how quiet the house is?"

Jorge waited for a moment.

"Where are the children?"

"When you were in your office earlier," Paige moved closer to him. "Juliana took the kids out for a day adventure. They're going to…"

Before she even had the words out, Jorge moved in and kissed her. Although gentle at first, he quickly grew more passionate, as he pulled her close. His hand slid under her tank top and over her soft skin, so smooth and welcoming as were her lips that pressed hard against his, causing him to tighten his grip on her body. He felt his desire quickly churning as he stopped to look in her eyes.

"Upstairs?"

"Anywhere."

"Let us err on the side of caution," Jorge glanced toward the door. He felt his phone beeping in his pocket but ignored it. "Let us go upstairs."

The couple was barely in their bedroom when his phone began to ring.

"Oh, *mi amor,* this here is going to be turned off," Jorge reached in his pocket, frustrated with the timing, he glanced at the number. "It can wait. It is just…"

Paige cut him off when she suddenly started to kiss him while her fingertips ran down the front of his shirt and toward his pants. Jorge abruptly tossed his phone on the nearby dresser and edged them closer to their bed. Moving hurriedly, he felt his pants falling to the floor as her hand reached inside his boxers causing him to gasp just as his phone rang again. Jorge ended their kiss.

"Oh for fuck sakes!" He moved away from her and walked out of his pants. "Who the fuck is calling?"

"I thought you were turning it off."

"I was but….fuck, can't anyone handle anything without me?"

"What is it?"

"It is something that I can deal with…." Jorge glanced over his messages and tapped on the phone. "It is something that can fucking wait."

He once again tossed the phone on the dresser and headed back toward his wife.

"We can be fast," She whispered.

"This here will work but soon," Jorge paused for a moment to give her a quick kiss. "We are going away so I can do this properly….with no kids, no interruptions…"

"That sounds like a dream," She replied as he leaned in, his lips taking hers gently at first but quickly regaining the same intensity he had before the phone interrupted them.

Jorge tried not to think about work as he slid his hand over the smooth material of her yoga pants, caressing as she worked to remove his shirt and tie until he was only wearing socks and underwear. Not that either of them cared. These days it was doing well to even get half undressed let alone completely naked to have sex.

Stepping back again, his breath grew heavier. He felt intense arousal as she quickly undressed and he removed his underwear.

"So, this here, no panties or thongs…." Jorge asked as she led him to their bed. "Is this a new thing?"

"Every time you see me in yoga pants," She sat on the edge and pulled her body toward the center of the bed. "Just remember, I'm not wearing any underwear."

"This here is distracting to me," He spoke breathlessly as he climbed on top of her. "That material, the pants, they are very tight."

"I know."

"Oh, *mi amor,*" His mouth met hers and he wrapped his arms around her. In a swift move, he switched positions, pulling her on top of him then moving them both into a sitting position. "The material, it looks so soft, does that not make you…"

Paige answered by abruptly kissing him and he wasted no time moving inside of her. As she moved quickly, Jorge didn't hear the phone ringing across the room but only focused on the pleasure that flowed through his body. His hands grasped on her hips and squeezed them. He followed her lead as she rocked against his body. Her moans grew louder as she increased her pace and he felt her hard nipples tapping on his chest as she rode him. Her grip on his penis grew stronger as she rocked faster and faster, her moans becoming more intense, louder until she finally collapsed against him.

Pulling her hips down one more time, Jorge gasped as pleasure rang through his body, his heart pounded wildly and he felt more alive than he had in weeks. He never wanted to leave the room again.

Unfortunately, reality came back to them within moments as the phone rang again. However, rather than growing angry, Jorge merely let out a sigh as the two of them rose from the bed. Paige went into the bathroom.

"Throw me a towel," Jorge called out and caught one mid-air before Paige smiled sheepishly and closed the door.

He wrapped the fluffy grey towel around him and found his phone.

Enrique's got big problems. We gotta try to help him.

WTF, Diego?

Come to the bar. We're here.

Jorge glanced through his messages. One was from Makerson. Another from Marco.

Sir, I have discovered something that may be of interest to you.

This was from Marco. It was unlike him to call unless it was important.

The shit is hitting the fan. You're not going to believe this.

That was from Makerson.

Just then, Paige wandered out of the bathroom wearing a robe. She glanced at the phone.

"I hope that was important."

"I do not know, Paige," Jorge spoke honestly as he watched her open her closet door. "Everyone, they think I can be in 10 places at once."

"You can't?" She teased.

"Not yet, unfortunately," Jorge shook his head and after a moment's thought, tapped the phone.

We'll all meet at the bar.

Jorge watched her select a summery dress. He noticed she didn't put on panties as she dressed. "I think you should come with me."

CHAPTER 42

"But does anything ever *really* change?" Jorge observed shortly after the group gathered in Chase's office. On one side of him was Paige, wearing a thin dress which was constantly diverting his attention while on the other side sat Diego, his dark eyes narrowing in as if he were about to spit fire. Chase quietly took his spot behind the desk. "Since coming to Canada, I am dealing with the same people as I did in Mexico except, you know, a milder, usually *whiter* version."

"People here ain't nothing like Mexico," Diego was quick to argue. "People here don't got a gun in your face every time you turn around."

"Hey, if you mind your own fucking business, this here isn't a problem," Jorge reminded him and Diego appeared to relent with a shrug. "Me, I see the similarities. This thing here with the police, it is just another example. Believe me, we got corrupt police like in Mexico and you had in Colombia. Every country, it got its crocked fucks that try to run things."

"You speak so elegantly," Diego replied with heavy sarcasm. "I can't believe you didn't stick with politics."

Chase snickered while Paige merely grinned and touched Jorge's leg. His thoughts were automatically off track.

"Anyway," Jorge said with a sudden urgency. "Are we doing this meeting or what? I got things to do today."

"Enrique is waiting to let Marco and Makerson in," Chase raised an eyebrow. "Is Jolene coming too?"

"Nah," Diego said and made a face. "We need to keep her in her own spot right now. She's one of the problems."

"Is she not always?" Jorge muttered.

"Hey," A voice came from the doorway and everyone turned to see Makerson walking through with some hesitation. Although he was occasionally joined them for a meeting, it was rare and his meekness proved this fact. "Sit anywhere?"

Paige smiled, nodded and pointed toward a chair beside her.

"So we just waiting on Marco?"

"I'm here!" He could hear a voice calling out as the red-faced Filipino rushed into the room. "I bike as fast as I could."

"Marco, there are such things as air-conditioned cars," Jorge reminded him.

"Nah, sir, in this traffic, I would never arrive that fast."

"A bus?"

Marco made a face and shook his head.

"Whatever, he's here," Diego cut in as the door closed and Enrique joined them, sitting on the other side of Makerson. "Let's get this show on the road. I need to get back to the office. I got a company to run."

Jorge grinned and didn't reply. He heard a slight noise coming from the back of Paige's throat and turned just as she jumped in.

"Ok, so, Jorge filled me on the way here," She spoke elegantly. "At least, with the information he had. Enrique, let's start with you, what's going on?"

The handsome Mexican appeared bashful and shook his head.

"No, nothing, this is nothing."

"It's something," Diego insisted.

"Not work-related, no," Enrique insisted. "We do not have to talk about now…"

"Tell us," Jorge insisted. "We deal with problems here. What you got?"

"His wife found out about Jolene," Diego quickly answered for the bashful Mexican. "He got home from the bar this morning and she was gone…with the kids…"

"Find them," Jorge said as if it were the most logical thing.

"She'll be most angry the first 24 hours," Paige insisted. "Tell her it was a mistake, get her back and be more….discreet."

Jorge was surprised by his wife's answer and gave her a look.

"Hey, you're the expert on a lot of things but I know how women think," Paige reminded him. "Chances are good, she doesn't want to leave. What she wants is for things to be back to where they were."

"No, but I cannot," Enrique shook his head sorrowfully. "She has returned to Mexico."

The room fell silent.

"It's still fixable," Paige insisted but Enrique was shaking his head.

"But this thing, with Jolene, I do not think I can end it," He spoke passionately while Jorge was already showing signs of frustration.

"This here soap opera," Jorge cut him off. "We don't got time for right now. You contact her, apologize, say it is over and get her back. That way, you have your children here, *si?*"

"But Jolene, her and I, we are in love and…"

This time, Diego rolled his eyes.

"You're right, Jorge, we can deal with this later," He insisted.

"What is your real issue here? Your kids, right?" Jorge leaned forward in his chair and looked in Enrique's face. He nodded. "You got rights. That does not change."

"Well," Chase cut in. "He has rights but good luck seeing the kids once they're gone. It's not that easy, trust me. And mine are in the same country."

"But if you go to that redneck town, you can, right?" Jorge asked and Chase shrugged and nodded. "He will do the same. Trust me, this here, we can work out."

"Enrique," Paige cut in. "We *are* sorry to hear this news and we'll help you but for now, we must move on."

Jorge felt desire fill him as he looked at Paige. There was something about her powerful stance that was causing him to become even more distracted, uninterested in the meeting. Visions of their encounter before leaving the house flashed through his mind.

"I do have something else," Enrique spoke quietly. "It's not much but I check with my sources and they say Verónic, she was in Puebla but is no more."

"Where the fuck did she go?" Jorge felt his blood boil as Paige gently touched his leg again, causing desire to shoot through his loins.

"She did take a plane," Marco cut in. "Sir, I…I don't know how to tell you this but…it looks like she came to Canada. Her plane didn't fly into Toronto but.."

"What the *fuck*?" Jorge fumed and turned toward Marco while Paige attempted to calm him. "Is she here *now*? What do you know?"

"Sir, I do not want to say for sure," Marco started again with hesitation. "But I believe, she may have arrived yesterday."

The room fell silent.

"You got to be *fucking* kidding me," Jorge snapped and noted the alarm in Marco's face and automatically put his hand up to indicate he had been too harsh. "Please tell me this here, it might be a mistake."

"No, sir, I think she's going under another name," Marco turned his iPad and hit some buttons. "The reason I say this is because I was watching the airport cameras."

"You hacked in?" Chase asked with surprise in his voice.

"Oh yes, they are very easy to hack," Marco replied and nodded.

"For you, maybe," Chase muttered.

Marco grinned with pride in his eyes.

"This lady here," He moved the iPad toward Jorge to show someone with their back to the camera. "Would this be her?"

Jorge squinted his eyes as he looked.

"Do you need my glasses?" Diego needled him.

"You worry about your own eyes," Jorge shot back and leaned in. Immediately, he felt his heart race as his face tightened. "I am going to find her and rip her *fucking heart* out with my own hands!"

"I think that's a yes, Marco," Paige muttered as she inspected the photo then turning her attention back to Jorge. "And you, you need to relax. It's the back of her head, you might be wrong."

"You said she used another name," Jorge ignored Paige's pleas. "The name?"

"She used…." Marco sat back down as if distancing himself from Jorge. "She used your daughter's name, sir. Maria Hernandez."

Jorge felt the blood rush to his face, his heart pounded erratically and just then, Paige gently touched his arm. He began to calm. Across from

him, Chase had a worried expression on his face while the entire room
had an echo.

"He's gonna have another mini heart attack if he keeps this up," Diego
was complaining. "Or a real one this time."

"Jorge you need to calm down," Paige sternly warned.

He didn't reply but seethed in anger.

"We need to stay focused here," Paige reminded them all as she lovingly
touched Jorge's leg. "She's in our world now and once we get her, she's no
match for us."

"We'll take care of this," Chase said to Jorge. "You know we will."

"Good," Paige nodded and turned her attention back to Jorge. The two
made eye contact and he immediately felt a sense of peace follow while his
eyes drifted down her body. He felt his desires, combined with his anger,
causing a heightened sense of arousal. He licked his lips. "Now, we need
to find Verónic. We need to make sure Maria is not vulnerable until we
do. She must have someone with her at all times."

"Where is she now?" Chase asked.

"With Juliana," Paige replied and turned her phone back on. "I'm
going to make sure they head home shortly."

"I'll go meet them," Chase volunteered and stood up. "Just to be safe."

"I would appreciate…" Jorge started but felt the words get caught in
his throat.

"That would be perfect," Paige nodded and began to tap on her phone.
"I'm telling her this right now. Don't worry though, Juliana is no shrinking
violet."

"Maria, she won't go anywhere with that lunatic," Diego jumped in as
if to reassure Jorge. "And you don't tell Maria to do anything she doesn't
want to do."

"Oh, Tom," Paige turned toward Makerson. "There was something
about shit hitting the fan you wanted to tell us about?"

"It seems pretty minor now," He replied. "But this whole story about
Athas publicly shaming the police seems to have broken things wide open.
Suddenly, cops are coming forward with stories that collaborate with what
he said. It's making a lot of people at the top very nervous."

"Well, that will keep them on their toes, won't it?" Paige asked with a smirk on her face. "I suspect this will make them a lot more...manageable, wouldn't you say?"

"There is talk of an internal investigation," Makerson replied with more confidence. "I plan to break that story open by tomorrow."

"This is the distraction we need right now," Paige nodded. "So the whole story about Elizabeth Alan..."

"That's all but forgotten in this fucking mess," Makerson shook his head. "The police had nothing anyway. They're stating that it was a random robbery gone....very wrong."

"And yet," Diego laughed. "Nothing was taken."

"Maybe they went in and there wasn't anything of value," Chase said as he walked toward the door.

"Ok, well, it seems like everything is being sorted out," Paige spoke confidently as the rest started to stand. "We'll touch base later today."

Everyone started toward the door and Paige turned toward Jorge.

"And we have to take care of something right now..."

CHAPTER 43

"Oh God," Jorge whimpered as he thrust into his wife. The couple had discovered the private bathroom stall in a nearby office building only minutes after leaving their meeting. It was perfect.

His hands grasped her ass, naked underneath the skirt. He felt desire building as he lifted her and she quickly wrapped her legs around him. Squeezing hard, Jorge gasped as he continued to push deep inside her as his heart pounded rapidly, this time in pure pleasure and not unbridled anger.

"Harder!" She whimpered as she arched slightly, her face displaying signs of pleasure. "I'm almost…Oh, God! Yes! Oh, God."

Her last words came out in a cry as she gasped and Jorge came inside her. Pleasure rang through his body. He felt weak as if he could collapse on the floor. She loosened her grasp around his waist. Soft in his arms, they slowly moved apart as Jorge reached out, his arm leaning against the wall as Paige ran water in the sink. Eventually, he felt like he could move.

"Oh Paige, my God," Jorge started but his throat was dry and he cleared it. "I do not….I cannot say what happened between us but we gotta…this here, we got to keep doing."

"Having sex in public places or me not wearing underwear?" Paige asked smoothly, her dress pulled back down, her breasts once again covered with the material, she was completely composed while he hadn't even pulled up his pants yet.

"All of the above," He replied before reaching for the paper towel dispenser. "This here, it was fucking amazing."

"I think you already had a lot of passion running through your veins," She reminded him. "Even before we left the office. The talk of Verónic.."

"That there is a different kind of passion," He reminded her. "Not this kind. I want to kill her."

"And you will," She reminded him. "But first we must find her. And we will."

Jorge didn't reply, as he pulled up his pants and fixed his suit. He went to the sink and washed his hands. Looking into the mirror, he saw the concern in his wife's face reflecting from behind him.

"Paige, this here, it will be ok," He assured her. "I will be fine. Do not worry."

"Of course I'm worried," She reminded him. "I know how angry she makes you."

"And the fact that she used Maria's.."

"I know," Paige nodded and moved closer to him, she reached out and touched his arm. "I do."

The couple left the washroom without being noticed.

Once in the SUV, Jorge was on his phone with Chase.

"You catch up with them yet?"

"No, but within the next 20 minutes or so," Chase insisted on the other end of the line, his voice echoing through the vehicle. "Don't worry, she'll be fine."

"Thank you," Jorge spoke sincerely and glanced at Paige. "I do not want her anywhere near my Maria."

"She won't be," Chase assured him.

They ended the call as they sat in traffic.

"We got this," Paige reminded him.

"But you do not understand," Jorge spoke with vulnerability in his voice. "This woman, she knows my weaknesses. She knows getting to Maria would kill me."

"She's not going to hurt her daughter," Paige reminded him but Jorge wasn't convinced.

They drove the rest of the way home in silence.

The quiet house now made him uncomfortable, unlike hours earlier when they were originally enjoying their time without the children. Jorge's phone rang. It was Diego.

"*Hola.*"

"We got the thing with Enrique sorted out."

Preoccupied with his problems, it took Jorge a moment to remember what Diego was referring to.

"Oh...yes?"

"His wife," Diego continued. "She ain't coming back. She wants to stay in Mexico but she has agreed to let him see the children. However, she wants nothing more to do with him."

"Well, that could change..."

"Nah, I think both parties are happy with that," He continued. "She moved in with her parents."

"Ok....so if that is good..."

"It's fucking full moon if you hadn't realized," Diego cut him off. "That's why everything is going to shit like this. It's a full moon."

"Diego, in some people's world, there is always a full moon."

Paige let out a short laugh from the other side of the room.

"My husband, the poet," She sang out.

Jorge laughed in spite of himself.

"Well, you got one today and if anyone has a full moon in their world every day," Diego starkly replied. "It's gotta be you."

"This here, I must agree with," Jorge replied. "I am still waiting on Chase."

"You got this," Diego reminded him. "There is nothing to worry about. I know Verónic and I know she drives you fucking crazy but she's manageable. We've dealt with much worse and we've won. She's no different."

"I want to..."

"Let's not get into that over the phone," Diego reminded him. "You're upset. We know..."

"I will be in touch."

They ended their call. He glanced at Paige.

"They really listened to you today."

"The meeting?" She asked as she walked toward him with a coffee in each hand. "That surprises you?"

"Not at all," Jorge replied as he reached for his coffee and nodded in thanks. "I just never seen you so…"

"Assertive?" Paige paused. "I know you want to step back. I just need you to know, for *them* to know, that I'm there for you. That I'm willing to take over in any way I can. But I'm not the only one. Chase, he's come a long way."

"Very long way," Jorge agreed and took a drink of his coffee.

"I remember when I first met him," Paige reminded Jorge as she led him to the couch. "He was a great leader, reliable but hesitant to step in with both feet."

"That is nothing, *mi amor,*" Jorge insisted as they sat down. "Before you met him, I knew him some time. He was even more reluctant. Our first meeting was in the same suite where you and I met. He was with Diego who felt it was time he knew more about the business. This man, he was so naïve. But yet, there was something in his eyes. He was a loyal man and that loyalty was not something I could overlook. I knew in time, he would change. I knew in time, he would grow into one of us."

"He was quite young."

"*Si,*" Jorge agreed. "He was only in his early 20s when Jolene took him on. He could be trusted to do what he was told and not ask questions. He just wanted to work. He wanted a chance. He wanted a job. He wanted to get out of his redneck town."

Paige laughed.

"And I do say, I do not blame him," Jorge said with a smirk. "He had a bad break with his family. Very disloyal to him. And this, it was something I knew personally. I knew that feeling. I knew that he was seeking a family. A *real* family. His ex-wife, she had moved on and even then, I could see she was doing exactly what Enrique's wife is doing now."

Paige gave a sad smile.

"First, he will talk to his kids all the time," Jorge insisted and tilted his head. "Then, less and less until he barely talks to them at all."

"That's so sad…"

"But this is reality," Jorge insisted. "In Enrique's case, maybe it is best his family is not with him."

"Do you think he'll leave too?" Paige wondered.

"No," Jorge shook his head. "Jolene, she did exactly what I thought she would. She has him....what you say? Hook, line, and sinker? This is powerful. Family is powerful too but he is a man who needs this.... reassurance? I see that in him. We can work with someone who is in this deep so fast because that means he will also get in as deep with us."

"I think we can trust him."

"I am still watching him, you know," Jorge assured her. "But yes, he seems ok. He will make his mark. You will see."

His phone rang. It was Chase.

"*Amigo?*"

"I got her," Chase replied.

Immediately filled with relief, Jorge let out a sigh and nodded to Paige who smiled.

"She's ok," Chase insisted. "But doesn't understand why I came to meet them. I didn't know what to tell her."

"Tell her nothing," Jorge replied. "I will take care of this. Just say that her *Papa*, he was worried."

"Will do," Chase replied. "I got both kids in my car. Juliana will follow behind."

"*Perfecto.*"

"We'll be there soon."

They ended the call.

He turned to Paige.

"Now, I must figure out what I am going to tell my daughter."

"The truth," Paige replied. "Minus the fact that you want to kill her mother."

Jorge raised an eyebrow.

CHAPTER 44

"…and Chase says that a lot of people are extremely successful at it," Maria rambled on excitedly. "You can learn anything now with the internet and the right computer. So, *Papa,* he said there might be certain software I'd need, he's not sure. I'm going to look into it and…"

"Ok, Maria, please," Jorge put his hand up in the air while beside him, Paige nodded in understanding. "This here, it will have to wait. We must talk about something else now. It is kind of important."

"But, *Papa,* I…"

"Maria," Paige started but had her attention averted when Miguel began to cry upstairs. Standing up, she paused and continued. "Maybe you should do some research then come back to your father. See what you can learn online, check out reviews, maybe try a free option before you jump in with both feet."

"Yes, Maria," Jorge agreed as Paige headed toward the stairs. "This here would be a good idea. It is not that I am not interested but I want you to make sure that this is what you want. I must remind you that you have already gone from acting to singing…"

"I know," Maria nodded as she slowly sat across from Jorge. "I know but this time is different."

Jorge stared at her.

"Why are you looking at me that way?"

"Maria, this here, it is how I always look," Jorge spoke slightly more gruffly. "Listen to what Paige has said. Research this and make sure. It might sound exciting to DJ but perhaps, you need to read the good and bad before you decide."

"It would keep me busy and out of your hair this summer."

"Maria, you are not in my hair," Jorge attempted to tackle her argument. "Again, can we please put this aside for now. I have something more serious to talk to you about."

"Am I in danger?"

"What? I..."

"You had Chase come pick me up again," Maria reminded him as she ran her fingers over her phone. "You always do that when you're worried."

Jorge took a deep breath.

"Maria, it has come to my attention," Jorge began and looked into his daughter's big, brown eyes and hesitated.

"It has come to your attention..."

"Maria, I do not know how to say this but I think your mother is in Canada."

Maria looked ill but didn't reply.

"I am looking into it," Jorge paused for a moment. "I want to be certain you are safe."

"Do you think my mother would hurt me?" Maria looked flustered.

"I do not know," Jorge answered honestly. "I like to think not but I would still rather be careful because your mother, she is not ok."

Jorge pointed toward his head. What he didn't want to tell her was that Verónic might have an ax to grind and he wanted to make certain she didn't hurt his daughter as a way to get to him.

"I know."

"So, it is just for now," Jorge continued. "Until we can find her, I want someone to always be with you."

"Are you sure she's here?"

"Yes, I am almost certain."

"But in Toronto? Canada is a big country."

"This here, I do not know," Jorge admitted, "but we must keep our minds open to that possibility.

"So, what? I can't leave the house."

"We will see," Jorge considered it for a moment. "I would like to keep a close eye on you for a few days."

"Ok," Maria commented and Jorge couldn't help but note that her original enthusiasm was completely drained.

Fucking Verónic.

"It may not be long. I will see what I can learn today."

"Ok."

"Are you sure this is ok?"

"I'm fine," Maria assured him. "I'm used to this craziness in our family."

With that, his daughter rose from the chair and gave him a quick kiss before heading upstairs. Jorge was left to wonder and to wait.

It wasn't until Diego arrived later that day that there was confirmation that Verónic was in the Toronto area. She had taken a bus from her original destination.

"The question is where exactly," Diego continued as the two men entered the office and Jorge closed the door. "And is she here to see you or Maria?"

"But she does not know where I live."

"No," Diego admitted as he headed for his usual seat while Jorge went behind the desk. "But that don't make me feel better for some reason."

"But why?" Jorge wondered out loud. "Why would she want to see Maria now? After all this time."

"She's her mother, it's not unheard of," Diego reminded him. "Just don't freak the fuck out yet. Maybe she wants to meet with Maria, have a conversation….it doesn't mean she wants to stay in Canada."

"Canada?" Jorge let out a laugh. "You think I'm going to let her live at all? You got high hopes."

"So you're going to kill your daughter's mother?"

Jorge looked away and thought about it but didn't reply.

"Look, relax and see what she wants," Diego reminded him. "She's gonna find you."

"How?"

"I dunno," Diego said with a shrug. "Maybe you gotta find her first. Maybe that's what she's counting on."

Jorge didn't reply.

"By the way," Diego switched gears. "Did you know there was a media shitstorm about the police not doing their job."

"Yes, we talked about it earlier in the meeting."

"Nah nah," Diego shook his head. "I mean more now. Some big shot that used to work with the police *and* they let go is coming forward with all these accusations. Said when he spoke up he got fired."

"So, our little story about Elizabeth Alan is long gone."

"Down the fucking stream and out of sight."

"Which is where we want it," Jorge agreed. "The police, they do something right for a change. Finally, some good news today."

"I got more good news! My house," Diego lit up as he pointed toward the window. "It's almost ready to move in. They're starting the safe room tomorrow. You should do the same."

"I'm thinking about it," Jorge confessed and glanced around. "Can these guys keep their mouths shut?"

"They gotta," Diego nodded. "Unless they want me to call immigration." Jorge nodded.

"The heat, it gets a little too hot at times," Diego reminded him. "And I don't want to catch on fire."

"None of us do, Diego," Jorge replied anxiously.

"You need to start mediating with Paige."

"What?" Jorge was caught off guard.

"You're fucking tense," Diego pointed at him. "You look like your fucking head is about to explode."

"My crazy ex is lurking around," Jorge snapped. "Do you not think I have a right?"

"But still, you gotta let it go," Diego insisted. "There's always a crazy person lurking....this here, it ain't new."

"But this crazy person..." Jorge started and paused without continuing.

"I know," Diego nodded and put his hand up defensively. "I'm not saying it's a good thing. You need to calm the fuck down or you'll get sick."

"Diego, I am fine."

"But her name comes up and you go batshit crazy. I'm just looking out for you.."

"I know and I appreciate it," Jorge replied and sighed. "I do but this here, it's complicated. Verónic and my life with her, it was complicated."

"She always got to you."

"Not in a good way," Jorge insisted. "I cannot stand the idea that she is in the same city as me. How does she keep hidden?"

"It won't be much longer," Diego said and shook his head. "We'll get her."

Jorge didn't reply but watched as Diego jumped out of his seat.

"You gotta go?"

"I got a date."

"I'm not even going to ask."

"Best you don't," Diego grinned. "Someone new, I found on a dating app."

"You really do put the 'whore' in hormones, don't you, Diego?" Jorge teased.

"I put the 'whore' in a lot of things," He spoke dramatically as he swung both arms over his head. "But hey, keep me posted."

Jorge sat at his desk and glanced toward the window. The sun shone through and touched his desk. It was as he stared at the bright light that an idea came to him. A grin formed on his lips.

CHAPTER 45

"It will work."

"I think you have to be careful," Paige calmly warned as Jorge sat on the edge of their bed. "I know you want to find her but is this how you want to do it?"

"It is a guaranteed way to get her," Jorge insisted as he joined Paige underneath the covers. "If she thinks there is something in it for her, that bitch will make sure we find her and find her fast."

"Then she finds out you aren't going to let her see Maria…"

"It will be too late," Jorge replied and looked into his wife's eyes and twisted his hands in opposite directions as if to indicate snapping a neck. "Then we will take care of her. No more Verónic."

"I think it would be better to sound her out," Paige suggested. "Let me talk to her."

"No," Jorge shook his head. "No, this here, I will take care of. She has no reason to talk to you or Maria."

Paige didn't appear convinced but he understood. She didn't know Verónic or what she was capable of but he did. He wouldn't let her inflict poison on his family.

He made sure the proper people got the message that would draw her out of the slums and bring her to him. Knowing that she would never meet him in private, he suggested a public place. However, first he had to deal with her relatives and they were skeptical of him, like him of Verónic. They were non-committal but Jorge knew his ex. She would fall for the bait.

The following morning he felt brighter, more relaxed. Jorge was finally in control again and that realization was enough to give him an extra boost first thing in the morning. He felt alive in a way that he hadn't in weeks. Perhaps it was merely a phase that put him out of synch but he felt his animalistic nature return full force as he sat at the table while Paige rinsed an apple under the tap.

Beside him, Maria was despondent. Although he was surprised she was up so early, he was happy to see her at the table. The fact that she was playing with her food and not eating was a concern.

Glancing down at his iPad, Jorge realized he had attempted to read the same news story three times and still wasn't able to focus, his eyes shifting back to Paige as she reached into the cupboard.

"You're staring at Paige's bum again. It's gross."

His daughter's sudden remarked accompanied by such a nasty tone completely threw him off guard.

"Maria!"

"You were! I saw it. You do it all the time," Maria said with an angry look on her face while Paige could be heard laughing as she located a bottle of honey. "It's gross."

"Maria, I was just looking in her direction," Jorge lied. "I was thinking."

"I know what you were thinking of.."

"Maria! Enough!" Jorge snapped. "This here, it is too early for this attitude."

"You don't have to be so mean," Maria said with a sigh. "I'm just telling you the truth."

Jorge ignored this remark.

"Did you find my...Verónic yet.."

Jorge shook his head and reached for his coffee.

"I don't understand why she's here," Maria spoke with a stiff upper lip but her eyes said otherwise. "Why now? Why did she pretend to be dead? Who *does* that?"

"Maria, I do not know," Jorge lied, knowing exactly why she had faked her death. "People sometimes, they do terrible things to one another."

Paige returned to the table with a sympathetic smile on her face as she sat down her coffee and bowl of cut-up fruit. She gestured for Maria to take a piece, which she did.

"Jorge?"

He shook his head.

"It's good for you," Maria reminded him.

"I'm not hungry."

"Maria," Paige started as she sat down. "We can never understand why people do the things they do and we would go crazy if we tried."

"Why does life have to be so complicated?" Maria asked.

"Because, Maria," Jorge attempted to answer. "Us people, we are complicated."

His phone beeped and he saw that Athas was attempting to contact him.

"I must go take a call in my office," He glanced at his daughter who watched him with interest. "We will talk later, ok Maria?"

She nodded and he glanced at Paige before heading into his office, relieved to get away from this particular conversation.

Within minutes, he was talking to the Canadian prime minister.

"*Hola,*" Jorge said as soon as Athas answered.

"Good morning," He replied. "It slid under the wire like you said."

"Forgotten, as are most things," Jorge replied with a grin. "You started a shitstorm with the police."

"It had to be done."

"No argument here."

"It worked though," Athas continued. "For the first time since I started this job, everyone is falling in line. I don't have anyone in my own party trying to fuck me over."

"That you know of," Jorge corrected him. "But I believe we sent a strong message. You work with some intelligent people. I would assume they can connect dots."

"I'm trying to make it more appealing to work *with* rather than *against* me," Athas continued. "I have some big ideas for the future."

"I have some big ideas myself."

"We can work on them this fall."

"Yes, the season where you politicians hibernate is about to come up," Jorge teased. "But this fall, we will start with a bang."

"I suspect as much but we will be in contact," Athas insisted. "Once I've been in a year, it's time to make big changes happen."

The two men ended the conversation and Jorge felt excited. He had so many ideas for the country. He could finally carry out the many things he wanted to do all along. The beauty of being behind the scenes was that it allowed him to work out a plan in peace without dealing with the bullshit.

Checking his iPhone, he noted that Diego had sent him multiple messages. Jorge called him.

"Good morning, Diego."

"Morning!"

"How was your hot date?"

"It was pretty hot….I.."

"Let's not go into details," Jorge said and shook his head. "What you got for me this morning?"

There was some hesitation.

"When I was out last night," Diego replied. "I'm not sure but I could've sworn I saw Verónic out of the corner of my eye. Now, maybe it's because you were…"

"What? Where?" Jorge was suddenly very alert. "Where were you?"

"Downtown."

"That doesn't narrow it down."

"It doesn't matter," Diego was quick to take over the conversation. "I'm not saying it was her but….It kind of looked like Verónic. Whoever it was, she looked at me. Verónic knows me…"

"Where?"

"Just walking down the street," Diego replied. "We were going for a drink after dinner and…"

"And you saw her?"

"I *think* I saw her."

Jorge felt his blood boil but took a deep breath. He couldn't let her get to him this way.

"Ok, so she might be staying somewhere around there?"

"Does she know anyone in Toronto?"

"No."

"No relatives? Friends?"

"Me, I do not exactly know who she associates with now but no...not that I am aware of."

"And hey, it might not have been her," Diego reminded him. "We were talking about her earlier so maybe it was my imagination, you know? It can be quite active."

"Was she alone?"

"Yes."

"And you didn't notice where she was going?"

"We were in a crowd, it was busy so no," Diego paused for a moment. "I think there was a bus stop nearby so maybe that's where she was going."

"Was she carrying anything? A bag?"

"No."

Jorge thought for a moment.

"Cameras?" Jorge thought out loud. "If you have a location and time, perhaps we can get to the cameras."

"You know Marco," Diego reminded him without getting into details.
"*Perfecto.*"

"But don't lose your shit yet," Diego insisted. "We don't know it was her for sure. Let's just see and take it from there."

"I won't."

"One more thing," Diego hesitated. "It wasn't that far from the club."

"I am heading there shortly," Jorge rose from his chair. "Let us hope the rat gets into my trap."

CHAPTER 46

"Is this necessary?" Jolene piped up loudly as the three men stared at the laptop on the boardroom table. "Even if she is here, what can you do? There is nothing."

"I think we know what I can do," Jorge quickly corrected her but she merely shrugged. "Why are *you* here, Jolene?"

"I am meeting Enrique here because he is to sign a paper and I say I can help him with it."

"What? He can't sign a paper himself?" Diego snapped. "Do you not have work at the warehouse?"

"I am tired of being at the warehouse," Jolene whined. "I never see anyone there."

"That might be a good thing," Diego pointed out. "You *see* Enrique and you broke up his family."

"That is not fair!" She shot back. "You do not understand, Diego, he…"

"Ok, enough!" Jorge put his hand up in the air while glancing away from the computer for a moment. "Can we have our little arguments elsewhere?"

"I am just saying," Jolene continued. "I say that I will help Enrique with the forms, to read and understand, you know?"

"The blind leading the blind?" Diego pointed out. "That seems really helpful."

"My English, it is not great," Jolene admitted. "But these forms, I also filled out in the past so I understand."

"Payroll, Jolene, they would've helped him," Diego reminded her.

"Anyway," Jolene snapped. "I also want more things to do. Jorge, give me some real work. Just because I'm a woman does not mean..."

"Ok," Jorge cut her off and pointed toward the laptop. "Find my fucking psycho ex and kill her."

"Ok," Jolene nodded as if it were no big deal. "What does she look like?"

"I don't exactly have a lot of pictures of her around," Jorge admitted. "Marco, he saw one picture and Diego knows. He thought he saw her last night."

"Where?"

"Downtown."

"This here, it does not narrow it down," Jolene pointed out.

"Ok, thanks *guys,*" Diego shot back. "I get it! I noticed what I think was her out of the corner of my eyes and didn't see where she went. I was trying to be casual. I didn't want it to look too obvious."

"Anyway," Jorge pointed toward the laptop. "I am not seeing her."

"But why is she here, I do not understand," Jolene asked. "Me, if I thought Jorge Hernandez wanted to kill me, I would not be here."

"That's what you would think," Diego said as he shrugged and sat down in a nearby chair. "So she wants something."

"To see her daughter," Jolene spoke with some apprehension. "That is why."

"I think it's revenge..."

"Nah.." Jolene shook her head. "I promise it is to see her daughter."

"That's not going to happen."

"It might make her go away."

"After she tells Maria what?" Jorge countered. "That I tried to kill her. That I killed her parents?"

"You are afraid of what she say?" Jolene asked and nodded. "I do not think this is her goal. She wants to see her daughter."

"Even if she were in these videos, sir," Marco shook his head. "This doesn't mean she is still in the area. She could be anywhere."

"She was using a fake ID with Maria's name," Diego reminded him. "Maybe she is staying at a hotel under the same name?"

"Marco?"

"I am on it sir," Marco began to type furiously. "It may take some time…"

"That is fine," Jorge said as he moved away as everyone's comments flowed through his head. "I must find a better picture of her."

"Would Maria have one?" Marco asked as he continued to stare at the screen, his finger tapping on the keyboard.

"Yeah," Jorge reluctantly sent a text to his daughter.

"Because sir, I am only going by the one you show me," Marco reminded him. "It was grainy and hard to see. Even an old picture would be helpful."

Jorge nodded and took a deep breath.

"Yes, because maybe she come to the warehouse," Jolene shrugged. "Who knows? I want to see."

"She's not going to go to the warehouse," Diego rolled his eyes. "If anywhere, it would be here, the office."

"Or the club," Jorge added.

"If she knows about the club," Diego reminded him. "Maybe she hopes to find you there."

"At least Maria is not in school," Jolene reminded him. "She cannot find her there."

"Security is too high at Maria's school," Jorge insisted. "It better be for the fucking money I pay."

"Is she dangerous?" Jolene asked with some hesitation. "Or is it you just do not wish her around?"

"Jolene, let it go," Diego snapped. "Does it matter?"

"I just say a question!"

"You can't *say* a question, Jolene, you *ask!*"

"Ok, enough, you two!" Jorge cut in. "This here is enough. I do not know if she is dangerous but I do not trust her around Maria. I do not want her near my family. Everything in me is saying to keep her away. My instincts, they are never wrong."

"But it is a little close to home," Diego gently reminded him. "There's a lot of bad blood between you two. That could be coloring your judgment."

"If she had stayed in Mexico, it would be one thing," Jorge reminded him. "But she made the trip here and there is a reason."

"I think he is right," Jolene jumped in. "I would not trust."

Jorge's phone beeped. It was Maria with a series of pictures of Verónic. "I got them."

"Forward them to us all," Marco instructed.

Everyone reached for their phones.

"She is pretty," Jolene was the first to speak up. "I see Maria, she looks like her."

Jorge didn't reply.

"I doubt time has been that good to her," Diego piped up, "after the drugs. There's no way she still looks this good."

"It is not if she looks good," Jorge reminded them. "We are not trying to put her in a beauty pageant. We are trying to find her."

"She looks familiar sir," Marco said as he leaned back in his chair and stared at his phone. "I have seen her somewhere before."

"Really?" Jorge felt his heart race. "Here?"

Marco shook his head. "I do not know sir, I just know that this face is familiar to me. This picture is much better than the one you show me before."

"On there," Jorge pointed toward the camera footage they had reviewed.

"I don't think so, sir," Marco replied. "but somewhere, recently."

"Here? Maybe she was around this building?" Diego asked.

"No, I don't think so...." Marco replied. "I feel it was somewhere else. She is familiar to me."

Jorge didn't reply.

"I have not seen," Jolene added in a husky voice.

"Me neither," Diego added. "Other than maybe last night, if that was her."

"Just because we do not see her here," Marco pointed toward the computer. "It does not mean you didn't see her. We can only rely on the angles of the camera and not all images are very good."

"I wonder if she's been around the bar," Jorge said. "Chase hasn't replied to me yet."

"What about Enrique?" Jolene asked "He works nights. Maybe he see…"

"Is he here yet?" Jorge asked.

"No."

"It is too bad for Maria," Jolene said with a sigh. "What does she think of her mother being in town?"

"She is confused," Jorge answered. "I do not like that it is upsetting her. She thought her mother was dead and now, suddenly, she is alive and here. My Maria, she has seen too much for such a young age. I regret this."

"It can't be helped," Diego reminded him. "Plus, it's better than if she was too sheltered."

Jorge shrugged.

"This is true," Jolene suggested. "I know you do not like, Jorge but she should be aware. That way, she is safer."

"How's the self-defense going?" Diego asked with interest.

"Good, it is very good," Jorge replied. "This here is important to me. I want my little girl to be able to always protect herself. It is a scary world."

"She's got us," Diego reminded him and he noted everyone was nodding. "that's a guarantee."

"But Diego, we will not be here forever," Jorge repeated his same comment from many times before. "And we cannot be with her all the time."

"It is good, she knows this," Jolene remarked. "I agree. It can be scary for a woman."

"Sir, it was at the McDonald's," Marco suddenly spoke up. "this lady. I saw her at the McDonald's near the office a few days ago. I had my kids there."

"Are you sure?"

"Yes!" Marco replied. "I remember, she spilled her coffee and looked quite embarrassed, sir."

"Isn't there a hotel across the street from that McDonald's?"

"There is!" Marco lit up. "I will look to see what I can find."

"Just because she is there, it does not mean…" Jolene started

"Jolene, that's all we got," Diego reminded her. "It's a start."

Jorge didn't reply but was lost in thought.

"Sir, I am checking their guest list, I will see if I can get in their cameras...."

"Isn't that place kinda pricey," Diego threw in as he glanced over Marco's shoulder, "can she afford it."

Jorge didn't answer.

"Maybe she is not alone," Jolene reminded them. "We do not know."

"Oh, she's alone all right," Diego assured her. "I can't see it any other way."

"Just see."

Silence.

"Jorge, what are you thinking?" Jolene asked.

He didn't answer.

"Jolene, leave him alone," Diego snapped and the two exchanged glares.

"No, nothing here in her or Maria's name," Marco sounded disappointed. "I will look at cameras though and check places nearby."

Jorge felt his attention drawn to the door. He turned slowly to see Enrique entered the room.

"Mr. Hernandez, I received your text," He spoke quickly. "I do not know who this woman is but I have seen her. She has been at the club."

CHAPTER 47

"That guy, he looks like a boy I bullied in high school," Jorge pointed toward the screen on Chase's laptop while Diego looked over his shoulder. Beside him, Marco began to laugh. "I swear to God, it looks just like him!"

"Maybe he's with…." Diego's eyes bugged out.

"Nah," Jorge laughed and glanced toward his wife on the other side of the desk. "He's dead."

"I think there's a line where it's no longer considered bullying," Diego quickly pointed out, standing a little taller. "I think when.."

"No no!" Jorge quickly cut him off. "I did not kill him. He died in a car accident."

Chase raised an eyebrow as he leaned back in his chair. His eyes quickly shifted toward Enrique as he joined them in the office.

"Sir," Marco started to laugh hysterically. "This shouldn't be funny but I cannot stop laughing."

Enrique looked puzzled as he sat beside Paige.

"No no! The funny part is that he and his father both died in a car crash that year," Jorge continued with a shrug. "And I say, that family, they should not be on the road. Not thinking…."

Marco laughed harder with tears running down his face.

"Oh sir, I know it is wrong to laugh," He stopped and wiped his eyes.

Jorge grinned and glanced at his wife.

"I don't understand," Enrique said as he shook his head.

"My husband has a cruel sense of humor," Paige quietly replied. "That's all you need to know."

"Paige, you know me, I cannot help it."

She grinned and shook her head as he winked at her.

"OK, sir, we must continue to look," Marco said as he leaned forward to stare at the laptop.

"Enrique, come join us," Jorge gestured at the empty chair beside Marco. "It was you who saw her."

"I think it was her," Enrique replied as he stood up and walked around the desk. "This lady, she was Mexican, that is what caught my attention. I am not used to seeing that so much here in Canada."

"About what time?"

"Oh sir, I cannot say," Enrique sat beside Marco. "It was later in the night but I…"

"Oh, stop!" Jorge pointed toward the screen. "There, that looks like her."

"I will zoom in, sir."

Paige rose from her chair to walk around the desk and Chase pulled his chair closer.

"That looks like her," Diego echoed his thoughts. "Holy fuck, how many times has she been here?"

"I think at least twice," Enrique replied as he nodded. "That was the lady I was thinking of."

"It looks like she's alone," Chase commented. "Do you remember seeing her with anyone Enrique?"

"Nah," He shook his head. "Not that I see anyway."

"She must've talked to someone at least one of the nights."

"Not really," Enrique replied. "Not that I see. I see her mostly at the bar, looking at her phone."

"Probably using the free wi-fi," Jorge commented. "Hey, Marco, can you trace who used our wi-fi or…"

"Sir, we can but there are so many on any given night," Marco replied and thought for a moment. "Yes, I think it would be like…as they say, a needle in a haystack? That is the expression?"

"Yes," Paige replied. "But it mightn't be required. If she's been here a few times, we can probably find her in here tonight."

"And if we do, we can easily pull her aside," Chase replied.

"Lock the bitch in the office until you get here," Diego added.

"We have to be careful if there's a lot of people around," Paige reminded them. "We don't need a scene."

"She would cause one too," Jorge added.

"When she is here," Enrique added. "She stays for a long time. I do not think we would have to capture her. Maybe just let you know so you can come here and talk to her."

"That sounds easy enough," Paige said. "Isn't that what you were suggesting to some of her relatives, Jorge?"

"Yes, but no one answered me," He added. "There is a good possibility that they want to distance themselves from Verónic."

"Well, knowing her ex is a former cartel guy who kills like it's in fashion," Diego quickly jumped in. "I can't say I blame them from wanting to distance themselves."

"Yes, Diego, that would be the only reason," Jorge quipped and turned his attention to Enrique. "Now, this here, you're telling me you've seen her a few nights in a row?"

"Yes," Enrique nodded.

"Always alone, she don't talk to anyone and leaves alone?"

"I never see her leave but I have no reason to think so."

"So she's working alone," Jorge said. "Is she hoping to find me here? I wonder if she has asked staff anything?"

"I can find out," Enrique said. "They will be in later. I will see if anyone was asking questions about you."

Jorge nodded.

"So tonight, we should all be here," Diego pointed toward the VIP section. "We'll have a get together."

"I'm going to stay home with the kids," Paige said with some hesitation. "I would feel better if I was there. The only reason I'm here now is because Jolene wanted to see Miguel. She said she'd watch things while I was gone."

"Juliana, she would be fine too," Jorge reminded her.

"I...I would just feel better there," Paige shook her head and Jorge nodded.

"I understand."

"We should have Jolene," Diego pointed out. "If Verónic is here, she mightn't be as skeptical of another woman."

Jorge shrugged as he stared at the screenshot of his ex sitting at the bar.

"This here, it does not make sense to me," He finally spoke. "What does she want? Why is she coming here?"

"She's trying to rattle your cage," Diego spoke boldly. "Remember how she would say things just to piss you off?"

"That there, is a lot of women," Jorge reminded him. "It is fine. We will catch her tonight and this, it will be over."

"That woman has always been trouble," Diego insisted as he walked around the desk and sat on a chair. "It's time to cut the chains."

"I plan to cut more than chains," Jorge bitterly replied. "My daughter does not need this madwoman in her life."

"Well, let's calm down," Paige replied as she walked back around the desk to sit beside Diego. "If she wants to talk to Maria, maybe we can make arrangements but only if she leaves immediately after."

"You do not know this woman," Jorge rebutted. "She is not suddenly a compassionate mother who misses her daughter. She must go and go for good."

"He's right," Diego agreed. "She ain't no saint."

"Anyway," Jorge cut in. "We will spend time here tonight and wait for her to arrive. When she does, I will be speaking to her alone. I do not want to drag this out any longer."

"Ok," Jorge stood up and saw the others do the same with some hesitation. "We will meet back in the VIP room at…."

"I usually see her after 9," Enrique let them know.

"Ok, so then 8:30?"

The group started to leave.

"I think you should talk to her," Paige repeated her earlier comments as the two made their way to the SUV. "See what she wants. There must be a reason why she traveled all this way."

"Torturing me would be enough for this woman," Jorge insisted. "She has an ax to grind. It does not matter what all of you say. After everything I've done to her, I know that is the real reason she wishes to find me."

Paige didn't reply as they got into their vehicle.

"I just…"

"Paige, no," Jorge put his hand in the air. "Please do not make excuses for her. She is poison. That is who she is."

Paige opens her mouth as if to say something but quickly closed it.

"Do not worry, Paige," Jorge continued. "This will be sorted out tonight. I can fucking guarantee it."

CHAPTER 48

"My life was very different back then," Chase reminded everyone sitting around the table. "I was a different person."

"I know I saw the videos," Jorge teased him and Diego automatically started to laugh while Marco appeared confused.

"You were in the movies?" Marco innocently asked.

Chase turned red and shook his head.

"Ah, it was nothing," Jorge automatically jumped in and shook his head, "just a little soft porn."

"Really?" Marco's eyes widened. "You were in *that kind* of movie?"

"It was only a couple," Chase reminded them. "And it was a long time ago. I was just a kid."

"You're still a kid," Jorge remarked as he reached for his beer and glanced around the VIP room. Outside, the music could be heard as people started to gather in the bar, "At least beside me."

"Age is all in how you think," Diego suggested as he sipped on a cocktail.

"Tell that to my body some days," Jorge replied with a sigh. "When you're young, you think you will never die. That there are no consequences but then you learn, this is not true. It is a hard lesson."

"But you didn't have kids to think about back then either," Diego reminded him. "It was a different time."

"No, no kids and no wife," Jorge agreed with a nod. "And I thought that would always be the case. It was the last thing I wanted when I was young but once Maria came along, it changed everything. I start to shift how I saw the world and what I wanted for her."

"Children, they do change everything, sir," Marco nodded as he glanced at his laptop while reaching for his bottle of water. "You never know how much till you have them."

"Suddenly, your life, it matters," Jorge insisted, "if not to you, to someone else. That little *bebe*, it relies on you and you must be responsible."

"That little baby turns thirteen this year," Chase said as he leaned back in his chair. "She reminded me today. I guess there's a boy/girl party?"

"Oh, Jesus!" Jorge shook his head. "We will *see* about that one."

"I feel sorry for the boy who tries to date Jorge Hernandez's daughter," Diego began to laugh almost spilling his drink. "No pressure there."

"I demand respect for me and my family," Jorge said as he glanced at the laptop again. "Especially from the little fuckers that date my daughter and even that, it may not be as soon as she thinks. She is too young."

"You can't keep her a kid forever," Diego reminded him.

Jorge didn't reply.

"I think boys are different," Chase piped up. "You don't have to worry about the same stuff as girls. But then again, there's other stuff…"

"It is no better or worse, it is different," Jorge remarked. "Just as we are all different. This is how we learn. But the lessons, they aren't always easy."

"Tell me about it," Diego shook his head, his eyes bulging. "I think the lessons get harder as you get older, not easier."

"This here, it is true," Jorge nodded. "You learn who you can trust and who has loyalty. I always say, if you know these two things, then you know who's your family. You may disagree on many things but it is those you can trust on a dark day that you keep in your life."

"Amen to that," Marco nodded.

"And me, I got all you," Jorge gestured around the table, "and sometimes, Jolene."

Everyone laughed.

"This here makes me a lucky man," Jorge spoke honestly as he glanced at all the faces. "I am grateful and I recognize this loyalty. And from me, you have the same."

There was a moment of silent acknowledgment that flowed through the room as each shared a look of understanding.

"Now," Jorge continued. "We must catch Verónic. It is time to get her out of my life once and for all."

Hours passed and the four men continued to talk, constantly checking on the floor with Enrique but with no success. As it grew late, Jorge felt his original confidence begin to fade as frustration crept in. The realization that Verónic mightn't show up infuriated him.

"Sir, if you wish, you can go home and we can let you know if she.."

"No," Jorge shook his head. "No no, I want to stay here. She better show up."

"Do you think she knows you're here?" Diego wondered.

"How would she?" Jorge countered. "And I refuse to play this game of cat and mouse. If she wants to talk to me, she better fucking talk to me."

"She might show up yet," Chase predicted.

Marco appeared anxious while Diego shared Jorge's frustration.

Jorge thought for a moment.

"I should call Paige."

"Do you think…"

"I do not think she knows where I live," Jorge said with some hesitation. "But if she goes near, Paige, she will not be so welcoming."

Grabbing his phone, Jorge called Paige. The phone rang several times but there was no answer.

Everyone shared a look and finally, Diego attempted to explain.

"She probably is busy with the baby…"

"Or maybe fell asleep?" Marco asked.

Jorge felt his heart begin to race. He sent her a text and waited.

Time passed.

There was no reply.

He tried to call again.

No answer.

"This is not her," Jorge insisted. "She always answers."

Diego tried.

"Call Maria…" Chase suggested.

"Good idea," Jorge said, attempting to calm himself.

To his relief, his daughter answered right away.

"Maria! Is everything ok there?"

"*Si, Papa,* I am in the tub," She said with a giggle in her voice.

"Maria, this is very serious," Jorge hesitated. "I keep calling Paige's phone and there is no answer. I am concerned that she is ok."

"I think so?" Maria said with some hesitation. "But I haven't seen her in a while. I was in my room dancing then I decided to take a relaxing bath…"

"When did you talk to her last?"

"Hours ago."

"Ok, Maria, you must listen to me carefully," Jorge spoke as calmly as possible. "You must get out of the tub now and do not hang up."

"Ok," Maria sounded hesitant. "Is everything ok?"

"Juliana isn't answering either," Diego offered at the end of the table.

"Maria, it will be ok," Jorge reassured her. "You are a Hernandez, so you are brave. Please, go lock the bathroom door."

"It is locked," Maria replied as water could be heard splashing.

"Do not leave that room."

"Ok."

"And stay on the phone."

"Ok."

"Tell me if you hear anything at all…"

"*Papa* is Paige ok," Maria started to cry. "I want to go find her. What if something is wrong with her and Miguel…"

"Maria! No!' Jorge spoke frantically. "You must stay where you are."

"*Papa,* I know self-defense, I am…"

"No, Maria!" Jorge insisted. "You cannot leave that room and you must stay on the phone. I'm on my way home."

Jorge gestured toward the laptop while everyone in the room appeared alarmed.

"I'm coming with you," Chase insisted.

"You must stay here."

"Take him," Diego shook his head and moved the phone from his ear. "Jolene, she's on her way. You got her, me and Enrique. If Verónic shows up, we'll get her."

Jorge nodded as he flew out the door with Chase in tow. Both men jumped in his SUV.

"Maria, are you still there," Jorge spoke abruptly. "I'm putting you on speaker. Chase is here with me."

She was crying.

"Maria, it will be ok."

"*Papa,* I'm scared."

"Maria," Chase spoke up as the SUV shot on the road. "We will be there soon. Just keep still and listen. Tell us if you hear anything. I'm going to keep calling Paige and Juliana."

"There's nothing," She sniffed. "Oh no, what if someone broke in…"

"Maria, please, you must relax," Jorge spoke calmly despite his own fears. "You can think more clearly that way."

Glancing to the passenger side, Jorge saw the concern in Chase's eyes and a glance into the review mirror, he recognized the same in his own.

Once he finally made it to the highway, Jorge shot through traffic like a bat out of hell. Nothing could've stopped him at that point. There was no cop, no one person who would've stood between him and his family. The thought that Verónic might be behind this only added fuel to the fire already simmering in his veins.

As he focused on his driving and prepared himself for whatever he might find, Chase continued to talk to Maria in a soothing tone while trying to call Paige on his phone.

It seemed to take forever before Jorge made it to their street. Pulling in the driveway, he slammed on the breaks and both men raced toward the house. Unlocking the door with gun in hand, Jorge pushed it opened to find an alarmed Paige sitting on the couch.

"Oh, *mi amor!*" Jorge rushed to her side. "Why you not answering your phone?"

"What are you talking about?" Paige appeared frazzled. "I…."

She turned around and checked the empty spot beside her.

"It's here somewhere. What happened?"

"You," Jorge said as he took a relaxed breath and watched Chase running upstairs. "You were not answering the phone and I was worried. I called Maria who couldn't hear you so…I tell her to lock the bathroom door and hide."

"Oh my God!" Paige appeared shocked. "No, everything is fine. I'm sorry. Miguel was sick earlier and by the time I cleaned it up and….washed him up, changed his sheets…"

"The phone must be upstairs," Jorge said and glanced toward the door. "And Juliana, she was not answering."

"She had a migraine," Paige shook her head. "She's probably sleeping."

Jorge nodded as his phone rang. It was Diego.

"It is ok," He automatically said when he answered. "She didn't hear the phone."

"Oh thank God!" Diego exclaimed with emotion in his voice and then after a short pause. "Look, we got her."

"Verónic?"

"Yes."

"I'm on my way."

CHAPTER 49

Time had not been good to Verónic. She was once a beautiful young woman with sharp, snappy eyes and lush lips but now, her face looked older, haggard and full of bitterness. In fact, it was the bitterness that he recognized the most when he walked in the VIP room; along with fear.

"Wha…what do you want from me?" She spoke nervously as he closed the door. Chase was with him.

"Verónic," Jorge spoke sharply as his heart rate increased, causing his blood to begin to simmer. "Time, it has not been good to you. You have lost weight. You are now almost as small as Maria."

"I want to see her…" Her voice faded as she spoke, her eyes softened. "Please."

Jorge shook his head.

"That right, you have lost a long time ago," Jorge spoke with strength in his voice as if he suddenly realized the power he had in this situation. "Verónic, the drugs? The neglect? You have done so much to make yourself not worthy of my Maria. She does not need you."

"I'm her mother!" She said with tears in her eyes. "I have a right."

"You, you have no right," Jorge shook his head and glanced at Chase who immediately crossed his arms over his chest. "Maria, she has a mother now; my wife. She is more of a mother to my daughter than you ever would be."

"Please…"

"This here conversation, it is over," Jorge insisted and shook his head. "There is no way I will allow you to see Maria."

"I came all this way…" Her voice began to fade again. "I want to see my daughter one last time. That is all I ask."

Jorge didn't reply.

"Please, you have taken everything from me," She said with a shaking voice as tears ran down her face. "My parents, my home…I have nothing."

"Oh, but that is where you are mistaken," Jorge reminded her and stepped forward. "I have not taken your life. I could have…many, *many* times and yet, I allowed you to live. So I must ask you, why you are here? Why would you take such a risk when you could have escaped? Started a new life somewhere else, with your parent's money. I do not understand."

"I tried," She cried out as her sobs grew stronger. "*Por favor,* Jorge, I know you hate me but I just ask to see Maria one more time. Please…"

She started to walk toward him and Jorge automatically reached for his gun. Beside him, Chase stepped forward with fury in his eyes.

"I will do anything."

Jorge didn't respond.

"Anything."

There was a flash of something in her eyes that reminded him of when they met. The passion between them had been erotica filled with anger, both drunk with fury and pain, the dysfunction seemed to grow deeper with every encounter. It was as if she pulled him further into her dark web, a heaviness filled his chest even thinking about it. She was poison to him.

"There is nothing I want from you," Jorge shook his head. "The only reason why you are even still alive is because you are Maria's mother. Do not make me doubt that decision."

"Then please," Verónic said in a soft voice and begging eyes. "Please, allow me to see my daughter one more time. Then I will go away forever. I want to say good-bye."

Jorge didn't respond.

"That is all I want," Her voice was flat, weak. "I do not want to cause any harm. I have traveled this far to see my *bébe*. I want to talk to her. To see her. To hug her. To tell her I love her. To say good-bye. How can you take this away from me?"

Jorge exchanged looks with Chase who showed no emotion.

"Verónic," Jorge said with a pause and glanced at the floor before his eyes met with hers. "This here is not possible. You will never see your daughter again."

He hadn't expected it. The sobs were so powerful that Verónic's entire body shook as she collapsed to the floor. Her cries came like waves and grew louder, a lifetime of hurt filled the room as she showed a vulnerable side that he hadn't thought existed. He felt it in his soul.

Glancing at Chase, he relented.

"Verónic," Jorge paused for a moment. "I can see. Perhaps Maria will agree to meet with you one last time but….."

She raised her head with hope in her eyes.

"I cannot promise anything," Jorge swiftly added. "But that is all. It *will be* the last time."

She seemed to process his words and finally nod.

"Whatever….you can do…" She sobbed.

Jorge hesitated for a moment, unsure if this was the best decision.

"I will do whatever you want," She repeated and cleared her throat. "I do understand."

Jorge nodded and texted Paige. He needed reassurance that this was the best decision.

Are you sure about this?

No.

What made you change your mind?

When I say no, she was heartbroken. I did not expect this. It was unsettling.

We have to be careful.

I know but I do not think she can cause us harm.

It can't be at the house.

No, I agree.

I can ask Maria how she feels. It's late though.

We must do this tonight.

"Can you watch her?" Jorge muttered to Chase who nodded as Verónic slowly rose from the floor as tears continued to stream down her face. "I will be back."

Everything felt surreal when he walked out of the VIP room and into the bar. The music sounded unusually loud while the room, oddly silent.

Almost all the guests had left as the night grew late. At the bar, he found Jolene, Diego, and Enrique. They watched him as he approached.

"Do we....need to pull the van around the back?" Diego asked with wide eyes and appeared surprised when Jorge shook his head.

"Really?" Diego appeared puzzled.

"She wants to meet with Maria."

"You cannot do," Jolene automatically jumped in. "This is not a good idea."

"But she…"

"No! This woman, I think she is dangerous. I see it in her eyes."

"I think we can handle her."

Jolene appeared unsure.

"She got no weapons," Diego muttered. "And she weighs what? 90 lbs? I don't think she can hurt us."

"What if the police…"

"I checked her....thoroughly," Diego assured her. "She's clean."

"She does seem…harmless," Enrique added. "Maybe she is ok?"

"I thought I knew what to do but now," Jorge shook his head. "I do not."

"If Maria wants to see…." Jolene started but her voice trailed off as if she was unsure too.

"I think you're all crazy," Diego confirmed. "When did you get soft?"

"Diego, sometimes, these things are complicated," Jorge said.

"And sometimes, they're not," Diego corrected him. "This one is not. Kill her."

"But then what?" Jorge shrugged. "Maria, she knows she is alive. I tell her that her mother is dead…*again*. Try to explain why? My daughter, she is aware of things now. She will put it together."

His phone beeped. Jorge took a few seconds to check it and a few more to process what it said.

"She say no?" Jolene asked.

"She wants to see her," Jorge said with some reluctance in his voice.

"The fact that you aren't sure how you feel," Diego jumped in again. "This is a sign. Don't. Just tell Verónic no and then tell Maria…"

"That I shot her mother?"

Diego didn't reply.

"I can go if you want?" Jolene jumped in. "I can look after Miguel and Paige can bring her."

"If you don't mind?"

"No, I never mind seeing my godson!" Jolene spoke passionately. "He always makes me happy."

"Thank you," Jorge spoke sincerely and Jolene nodded as she stood up from the barstool.

"She can still change her mind," Jolene reminded him. "And if she do…"

"We will act accordingly."

"You're making a mistake," Diego insisted.

"Perhaps but as you said," Jorge reminded him. "She was checked and is ok. What can she do?"

He returned to the VIP room to find Chase alone.

"Where is she?"

"Bathroom," Chase nodded in the direction.

"She wants to see her mother. Am I making the right choice, Chase?"

He paused for a moment.

"I really don't know."

CHAPTER 50

We all have a legacy. It's often something that words can't quite capture. It's the look in your eye when something makes you smile or the helping hand you give when someone's in need. It's the bond you have with your family and the reflection you see in their eyes when they turn to see you walk in the room. But most of all, it's the essence of your entire being. That fire that comes through your spirit that no one could ever forget.

Jorge Hernandez knew all about legacy. Since the death of Jesús Garcia López, it was something he thought about every day. It was in those rare, quiet moments that it charged through his mind like a racehorse flying down the tracks while other days, he would stare at his son and feel a sense of inner peace, an assurance that it would all work out. He would be as powerful in his death as he had been alive.

It all happened so fast.

One minute, Maria was hesitantly entering the room, nervously staring at Verónic who put her arms out to welcome her daughter. Jorge stood back beside Paige who appeared uncertain, while beside her were Diego, Chase, and Enrique. All three men were expressionless but there was something in Chase's eye that suggested he didn't trust Verónic. Jorge should've seen it as a sign. His connection with Maria had always been strong, so protective. He should've trusted it. He should've respected it.

His heart dropped when it happened. He wanted to die. It would be forever etched in his brain; that moment when Verónic grabbed Maria, forcefully pulling her away from the others with one arm while holding a gun to their daughter's head.

"*Papa!!*" Maria called out as tears filled her eyes and poured down her face. Her body began to shake in fear.

"Verónic, please!" Jorge felt his heart pounding frantically while all around him, everyone was pulling out a gun and pointing it in her direction. "Do….do not do this…"

It was nearly impossible to keep the panic out of his voice but he knew it was necessary. He had to stay calm. He had to think clearly.

"No! Do not tell me what to do!" Verónic's voice shook as she stepped back, forcing Maria to do the same. "You will kill me. I know you will kill me after I see Maria one last time. I was stupid to think otherwise."

"Verónic, I…"

"No, you took everything I loved, you ruined my life," Her voice began to shake as tears filled her eyes. "I hate you! I want to make you suffer."

"No, Verónic…" Jorge attempted to keep calm but it was getting more difficult as the pressure built in the room.

"Verónic," Paige spoke up. "This is between you and Jorge. This has nothing to do with Maria. She's only a child. She's *your* child. You can't hurt her."

Tears poured from Verónic's eyes while Maria appeared frozen as she stared at her father.

"If you hurt her," Paige calmly continued. "Then you ruined *your own* life because no matter what, you'll always be the woman who murdered her daughter."

Verónic let out a loud cry but her grip continued to tighten on Maria.

"You can get over drug addiction," Paige continued to speak in her smooth tone. "You can leave here today and do anything you want with your life, go anywhere you want. But if you kill Maria, if you even leave a mark on her, there are four guns pointed at you. And I don't have to tell you what people from the cartel do to their enemies. It's a long, torturous death and you will suffer for every second of it."

"But if you let Maria go….." Paige continued. "You can walk out of here."

"I don't believe that," She shook her head. "I know Jorge. The minute he walked into this room, I knew he was going to kill me."

"If he wanted to kill you," Paige calmly replied, "he would've already."

She didn't respond but appeared to be processing the words. She suddenly turned toward Jorge.

"I hate you!"

"You can hate me," Jorge answered and stepped forward. "You perhaps have every right to hate me but you do not hate Maria."

"How did you get the gun?" Diego suddenly called out. "I checked you!"

"Maria had it in her purse."

A guilty look passed over the young girl's face as their eyes met and the two exchanged a look.

Jorge stepped forward again.

"Maria, where did you get the gun?" Jorge attempted to piece it together.

"I found it in Paige's dresser."

He heard it. A small sound escaped his wife's lips. He knew what that meant.

Nodding, he lowered himself to his knees and put his hands up in the air.

"This day, I knew it would eventually come," Jorge started to speak with confidence as reassurance flowed through his body. "I did not know who would be on the other end of the gun. I did not know if it would be the police or an enemy. All I knew is that this day, it would come. It is me you want, Verónic. It is me you hate. You say I ruined your life. Then you must take mine."

Maria looked as if she was going to be sick. She gasped for breath and her face grew pale. He attempted to send her a reassuring look but was unable to capture her attention.

"I just ask," Jorge continued with emotion in his voice. "That you do not make your daughter see her father being killed. Let her turn away. Let this nightmare end here."

Maria became hysterical. Tears were dripping from her face and suddenly her legs gave out and she started to fall forward.

That's when everything happened.

A shot rang out and for a moment, Jorge closed his eyes and couldn't breathe. Was it him? Had he not felt it? Was it Maria? If it was his daughter, how could he ever open his eyes again? He felt grief wash over him, fear so intense that he didn't think he could survive. Either way, his life would end. There was no way his heart could take a break so powerful, it would shatter him in a way that no bullet ever could.

It was when he felt her arms around him that he finally opened his eyes again.

"Papa!" Maria cried as she pulled him into a powerful hug while his own body went weak. Her sobs were loud and he glanced down, expecting to see a pool of blood around him but instead, his heart skipped a beat when he realized that there was none. He was safe. His daughter was safe. As he continued to hug his sobbing child, he noticed a commotion as the others rushed toward Verónic. She was on the floor.

His eyes met with Diego's and he gave a nod.

Paige was by his side.

"We should leave the room," She muttered.

Knowing the bar was empty, staff had left for the night, Jorge nodded as he slowly stood up, helping his daughter do the same. Maria continued to clasp on to him as they left the VIP room, her eyes closed and he feared what this would do to her. She had seen too much already in her young life but this was by far the most horrific thing. He didn't want her to lose the dreamy, child-like hope that was so strong in her.

"Maria," He leaned in and held her shaking body. "It is going to be ok. You know we will always protect you."

She nodded but continued to squeeze her eyes shut.

"Maria," Paige reached out and touched her hair. "It's ok to be scared. We were all terrified but your father is right, we will always protect you. Your mother, she...had problems and..."

Suddenly, Maria's brown eyes popped open and fire ran through them.

"She is *not* my mother!" She snapped. "I hate her! I hope she's dead."

Her moment of power was followed by more tears as she rushed to Paige who hugged her tightly.

"Who..." Jorge started to ask.

"Me," Paige replied. "I waited for my chance. When Maria started to fall forward, I had my opportunity."

"I want to learn how to do that!" Maria suddenly let her go as her teeth continued to chatter and Jorge instinctively pulled her close. "I want to learn how to shoot a gun. My self-defense, it can't stop someone with a gun."

"Maria, a gun, it is not always the solution…." Jorge calmly reminded her. "Today you had a gun…."

"I'm sorry," She looked back at Paige. "I was scared and I knew you had one in your room…."

"Maria, we will talk to you about this later," Jorge insisted. "This is not the time."

He could hear movement in the VIP room. Chase suddenly walked out of the door and looked toward Maria.

"Chase," Jorge called out. "Do you have a blanket, a jacket, something for Maria? She is in shock. Maybe some water?"

"Yes," Chase immediately approached them and reached out to hug Maria.

She began to cry again as soon as she was in his arms and Jorge had to look away. The power of the emotional night was hitting him harder than he would've expected.

"It's going to be ok," Chase assured her. "Let's go to my office. I have a blanket for you."

After they left the room, Jorge hugged his wife and felt all his emotions come to the surface.

"Oh, Paige…I cannot think." He muttered.

"I know," She stopped and turned toward him. "I wasn't sure what we were going to do until Maria said where she got the gun. Jorge, there weren't any bullets in that gun. I just had to wait for my chance."

"I cannot believe I misjudged this…"

"She was Maria's mother," Paige reminded him as she slowly shook her head. "How *could* she do this?"

"I have seen some terrible things in my life," Jorge replied as he reached for her hand and they walked toward the bar. "But none were like tonight. If she had…"

"No, don't go there," Paige said sternly. "Have a seat and I'll get you a drink."

Jorge obediently followed her orders. His body felt heavy.

"It was a reasonable decision," Paige reminded him as she reached for the bottle of tequila and poured some into a shot glass. "I think she just panicked."

Jorge grabbed the glass and knocked back the drink. It burned all the way down his throat, which was exactly what he needed.

"But this here," Jorge spoke calmly as he reflected. "It means something. It is time for me to retire."

"What?" Diego could be heard as he walked toward the bar. "Not this again!"

"But tonight, Diego, my judgment," Jorge started to explain.

"Your judgment was just fine," Diego insisted. "That there, was a fucking fluke."

"As it turns out," Paige muttered. "Your first instinct was the right one."

"Yes, well, I will always listen to my first instinct now," Jorge spoke confidently and took a deep breath. "That is my lesson here. We always know what to do but we do not always listen."

"Enrique's bringing the truck around back and we'll get rid of the problem very soon," Diego muttered, glancing toward the office. "Then we'll clean up…"

"Whatever you got to do," Jorge replied. "That is what I say."

Maria walked out of the office with a blanket wrapped around her and a bottle of water in hand. Chase followed and gave Jorge a reassuring look. He always knew how to deal with Maria. She was much calmer than she had been earlier. She now looked exhausted.

"How are you doing," Diego asked as she walked by, stopping to hug him. "And what's with you carrying a gun?"

"I know," Maria spoke shyly. "But a woman has to protect herself."

Jorge smiled.

"But Maria," He immediately spoke up. "This here was a terrible night for you. I worry that it is too much….I wish…I wish I had said no when she asked to see you."

"It's ok," She shrugged. "I said I would see her."

"This is a lesson for you, Maria," Paige spoke from behind the bar. "Guns, knives, it all can be turned against you too."

"You gotta be one step ahead of your enemy," Diego cut in. "And sometimes, two."

"Is that why you said she could shoot you?" Maria asked her father. "Was that part of a plan?"

Jorge thought about how to answer that question. He didn't want to scare her but he wouldn't lie.

"No," Jorge replied. "Maria, you are my daughter. I would gladly give my life for you or your brother….Paige…and not give it a second thought. You are my family. That is more important to me than anything, including my own life. I would do anything for you."

Tears welled up in Maria's eyes as she stepped forward and hugged him. Her embrace was full of warmth this time, rather than the desperate fear of earlier, a loving gesture that caused the entire room to fall silent. When Jorge looked up he saw tears in more than one set of eyes and he felt them in his own.

"We, here," Jorge said as Maria moved away and wiped her face. "We are family."

His eyes scanned all the faces in the room.

"You are *all* my legacy. Nothing and no one is more important than what we have in this room tonight and I am proud of that. Family, loyalty, it is stronger than anything and that is why I always insist on it. And nothing…*nothing* will ever take that away."

No one replied but stood in a powerful silence as the sun began to peek through the window. It was a new day.

Have you checked out the rest of the Hernandez series yet? Go to www.
mimaonfire.com to learn more!
Thank you for reading! Gracias y besos!

Printed in the United States
By Bookmasters